THE LADY SOLDIER

Spain, 1812. Jem Riseley is the perfect soldier in Wellington's army: brave and daring — but also a gentle-born lady! Her deceit is tested when she meets the handsome Captain Tony Dorrell, who knew her as Jemima. When the pair are trapped behind French lines, Jem has to battle the enemy as well as her desire for Tony . . . From the fighting in Spain to London's drawing-rooms, Jem will preserve her secret. However, the reappearance of an old adversary causes Jem to confront her past in order to save her own, and England's, future.

Jennifer Lindsay is the pseudonym for the two authors who co-wrote *The Lady Soldier*.

Kate Allan is the Features Editor of *Solander*, the magazine of the Historical Novel Society. A History graduate, she lives in Hertfordshire.

Born and raised in America, Michelle Styles now resides in Northumberland. In addition to writing and reading, she is a keen gardener and beekeeper.

Visit the authors' joint website at
http://www.jenniferlindsay.com

JENNIFER LINDSAY

◆

THE LADY
SOLDIER

Complete and Unabridged

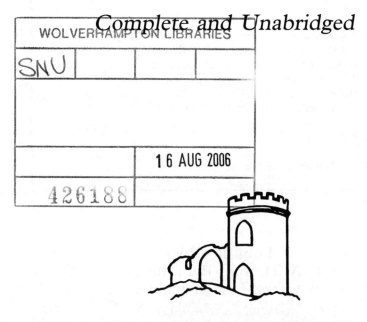

ULVERSCROFT
Leicester

First published in Great Britain in 2005 by
Robert Hale Limited
London

First Large Print Edition
published 2006
by arrangement with
Robert Hale Limited
London

British Library CIP Data

Lindsay, Jennifer
  The lady soldier.—Large print ed.—
  Ulverscroft large print series: romance
  1. Women soldiers—Fiction 2. Great Britain—
  History—George III, *1760 – 1820* —Fiction
  3. Love stories 4. Large type books
  I. Title
  823.9'2 [F]

  ISBN 1–84617–289–6

Published by
F. A. Thorpe (Publishing)
Anstey, Leicestershire

Set by Words & Graphics Ltd.
Anstey, Leicestershire
Printed and bound in Great Britain by
T. J. International Ltd., Padstow, Cornwall

This book is printed on acid-free paper

Prologue

28 December 1808, Cullen Park,
Warwickshire, England

She must keep every muscle in her shaking arm steady, her line of aim absolutely straight. She had to ignore the fat black crow sitting on the bare elm tree squawking at her through the dawn that she couldn't do it.

She could.

Jemima Cullen pulled back the trigger and fired, stumbled back but kept her footing, heard the roar and the kick and then nothing. She opened her eyes. The brown bottle stood on the tree stump intact, just as it had the other six times she fired. Jemima gritted her teeth and prepared the pistol for another. She would hit the bottle and win the wager. Her honour and a pair of ivory silk dancing slippers depended on it.

'Charlie, what on earth are you doing out of bed so early?'

Jemima's heart sank to the tops of her boots. No one was supposed to be up yet and find her practising — and in her brother's cast off trousers.

'It's not Charles, my lord. It's his sister Jemima,' she called back and told herself to breathe evenly, something that she had found surprisingly difficult to do in the presence of her brother's tall friend.

'Good morning, Miss Cullen.'

Jemima glanced over her shoulder. Last night in his lieutenant's uniform, she thought Viscount Fordingley had looked positively splendid. This morning dressed in an immaculate black coat, tight-fitting buckskin breeches and with the breeze fanning his dark hair as he strode towards her, she thought he was the handsomest man she'd ever seen.

'If you'll excuse me, my lord, I am trying to win a wager.' She drew a deep breath and tried to hold the pistol straight. She'd show him she could shoot. She jerked the trigger. A bang but the bottle remained. Tears pricked the corners of her eyes.

'I find it best if I keep my eyes open when I shoot,' he drawled and winked. 'It helps with the aim. A wager, eh? I'd have thought a card game would be a more appropriate wager — for a lady.'

'I wanted to prove to Charles that I could do it. It looked simple when you two were practising yesterday.'

'Well.' Viscount Fordingley fingered his

2

chin. 'I suppose it is a useful . . . accomplishment for a lady . . . a girl, being able to shoot a bottle at sixty paces.'

'My heart is quite set on it, sir.' How dare he call her a girl! She was seventeen. She thrust her chin in the air. 'I am quite determined to show my brother I can do this. And I have a pair of silk dancing slippers riding on it.'

'Dancing slippers, eh? Now it becomes clearer. Let me give you some pointers. Charlie deserves to lose every now and then.'

'Would you help me? Charles has said how you are one of the best lieutenants he has ever had the fortune to command, that your skills are second to none.'

He gave a gallant bow and took the pistol from her hands. Her fingers tingled where they had brushed his. Her heart raced far too quickly. They were actually having a conversation and though the house was only just behind them they were quite alone.

'You may call me Tony, Miss Cullen. Charlie is like a brother to me and therefore you and I are nearly related.'

Tony? Jemima rolled the word around silently on her tongue, let it settle in her mind. It suited him with his laughing eyes and devil-may-care smile.

'Why can't I hit the target?' she asked,

hoping he'd think the crisp morning air had caused the flush on her cheeks.

'Firstly, you need to secure your feet more firmly, like so. And when you grasp your pistol, hold it tight. I have never seen one bite yet.' Tony demonstrated. 'Now you try.'

Jemima wiped her hands on her trousers and took the pistol. She looked at the bottle and then at the gun.

'Is this right?'

'Your hands are too low.' He placed his fingers under her elbows and lifted them. Jemima's mouth went dry. Which was worse — trying to hit the target or having Tony standing only inches away from her?

'Now, take a deep breath, keep your eyes on the target and fire.'

She could feel the warmth rising from him, enveloping her. As if in a dream, she pulled the trigger. The bottle shattered.

'I did it.' She let the pistol drop into his hands, knew she was shaking but didn't care. She clapped her hands together and twirled around. 'I really did it. The ivory slippers will be mine.'

'Yes you did it. I shall bear witness to it.' Tony's face was wreathed in smiles. 'A first rate shot.'

Jemima stared at the shards of glass on the ground and wondered whether she would be able to do it with Charles watching and without Tony's firm hand steadying hers. 'Do you think I can do it again? In front of Charles?'

'Your brother will take my word that you fulfilled the terms of the wager.' His voice sounded smooth and easy, and she wanted to believe him.

'Thank you,' she replied after a pause.

'I'll make sure that rascal pays up before tomorrow night's ball.' Tony tucked the pistol away in his pocket and pulled his jacket straight. Could she ask for the pistol back? She wanted to keep practising. Now that he'd shown her — 'You will save a dance for me, won't you? It will be my last ball before the regiment sets sail for Portugal.'

'A dance?' This morning had gone from disaster to perfection in a moment. 'I'd be delighted to . . . Tony.'

'May I escort you to breakfast, Miss Cullen, and then we shall make sure Charlie coughs up those dancing slippers?'

He offered her his arm and Jemima rested her fingers on it, felt the taut muscle beneath the cloth of his coat. He could keep the pistol — for now.

1

The evening of 19 January 1812,
Ciudad Rodrigo, Spain

A wood splinter pricked the palm of her hand. Jem Riseley gripped the ladder more tightly and ignored the pain. It mattered not, because within minutes, an hour at most, she would be dead.

Already her lungs ached from the cold air with each breath she drew. The trooper standing opposite her shivered uncontrollably and he had a sick, green look in his eyes, yet his taut white knuckles gripped the ladder as surely as hers. He knew his duty.

Being a frozen corpse with a wood splinter in her hand was better than a dancing death at the end of a hangman's rope. There was honour in dying as part of the Forlorn Hope.

'Soldiers! The eyes of your country are upon you.'

Jem shut her eyes as Major General Crauford's words pierced the darkness. 'Be steady, be cool, be firm in the assault. The town must be yours this night.'

Silence, eerily thick as the uncertain

shifting of dozens of boots was muffled by the rocks and snow. Jem blinked and willed the rocket to go up now. She wanted the assault to begin, and for everything to be over.

Lieutenant Gurwood, his eyes flashing with the prospect of glory and promotion, stood with his sword raised a few paces in front of her. Ready, waiting, his shoulders were stiff yet even he could not suppress a shudder as the minutes dragged on.

There was a good reason why the men she was with, who had volunteered to be the first to go into the breach, were called the Forlorn Hope. And she was counting on her own kind of glory in meeting death and the enemy head on.

The church bell in Ciudad Rodrigo began to toll seven o'clock.

'Sergeant Riseley, good luck to you,' a low, familiar voice whispered, close to her ear.

Jem shuddered as the razor-sharp rasp of the major continued. He must be standing right behind her, where she couldn't see him, yet only a foot or two away. She felt the hairs on the back of her neck bristle under the stiff leather of her stock. 'I hope to see you after this battle, Riseley. You and I have much to talk about.'

She wanted to gulp, run. She couldn't. Did the major — *know?* During the past few weeks since Bessie and Sergeant Thompson's death from fever, she had never felt as exposed. She had seen him glance more than once in her direction. Rather than staying in the shadows as Bessie had always made her do, so that there was nothing to distinguish her from the next trooper, she had been promoted. Despite making sure she pretended to shave, never putting a foot wrong in drill and playing cards with the best of them, the major's hooded gaze was acute, his eyes questioning, pensive. A cruel man. No one in the 95th could forget what he'd done to those three camp followers last October.

If he discovered she was a woman . . . Jem forced her spine straighter. No, he would not find out until she was a corpse on the ground.

'See you, sir,' Jem muttered, her words cut short by the crack of the rocket that blazed through and illuminated the dusky sky like a meteor.

Lieutenant Gurwood's countenance was expressionless but his eyes flashed in anticipation. Then he flinched and stepped forward, and everyone was on the move.

Jem knew exactly what she had to do and could do it without thinking. She hoisted the ladder on her shoulder and quickly walked towards the small breach in the city wall. The rest of the Hope jostled along with her, their impatience palpable, yet trying to swallow their fear. Jem ignored the faces of the other troopers and concentrated only on the looming stonework of the city walls ahead, and the task that lay before her.

No one spoke. The sound of boots and breathing laboured on, waiting to be interrupted by something, waiting for the first response from the French.

There was nothing.

Where were the French?

Jem felt her ears tense, ready to hear a cry that had still not come. She was only fifty feet from the wall. Perhaps their luck would hold and they would be able to scale it before the French responded?

Then it came. A lone voice pierced the early morning more surely than the most virile of cockerels.

'*Les Anglais! Les soldats anglais avancent!*'

The wall erupted in a hailstorm of fire. The sky above the wall erupted into orange. A cacophony of musket and cannon. Jem plunged forward with her long ladder.

The trooper right in front of her fell with an agonizing cry as she raced to cross the ditch. There was no time to help him. No time to do anything but get on with what she had to do.

Jem heaved her ladder up against the seemingly endless wall and started to climb.

★ ★ ★

The distant roar of the cannons echoed five miles behind the lines where D Company of the South Warwickshire regiment were bivouacked.

Captain Anthony Dorrell turned his head slowly to one side, pressed his lips together and then stared at the piece of Spanish ground at his feet, a warm yellow colour by the light of his lantern but five miles from where he wanted to be.

'The assault has begun, Cap'n Dorrell,' his sergeant said, ambling up towards him and scratching his grizzled chin.

'Indeed.'

'Think of 'em poor devils on the ladders now, sir.' Sergeant Masters shook his head. 'Half of 'em blown to bits within minutes.'

Tony did not answer for a moment. He had attempted to volunteer for either the storming party or the Hope. Colonel Garroway had given him short shrift, refused to countenance the request and ordering him instead to guard the baggage trains.

A necessary duty, but any fool could guard a baggage train. Wives, camp followers and

11

deserters were no match for regular troops even when they were as raw and untried as these ones.

Tony glanced over the mess of soldiers, supplies and equipment that passed for winter quarters. His gaze settled on a trooper standing some twenty yards away, a tin mug in his hand from which some liquid dropped to the frosty ground as the soldier gave an almighty yawn. Unshaven, the trooper's red jacket was slung carelessly on, with every button undone. Tony felt his jaw tighten, the only small salve being that the lad certainly wasn't from D Company.

Was he deceiving himself? Half of his lot were probably hunkered down in their beds.

This was what happened when supplies were short and new recruits arrived with no real idea what was happening around them and had nothing substantial to do. Some action, a victory was what was needed. Before the boredom started to eat at his bones.

'Are the men ready?' Tony asked, instantly regretting the harshness of his tone. Masters could not be expected to work miracles. 'Do they understand what could be expected of them?'

'As ready as they will ever be,' Masters replied laconically. Masters knew as well as he that the troopers of D Company were engaged in a variety of activities, of which not many were directly related to the war effort. 'Why don't you join us for a game of cards later, Cap'n Dorrell? Passes the time.'

Tony felt his forehead crease as his eyes narrowed. 'Sergeant, a part of me, a very small part, would be happy if the attack today fails. Because, at least, then we would see some action.'

He heard the sharp intake of breath.

'Sometimes, sir, you worry me.'

'It won't come to that.' Tony clapped Masters on the shoulder. 'But perhaps they will have to call us in on reserve, to save the day. It would be a chance to make up for that incident at El Badon when we were nearly routed by the French.'

Tony paused. The sky was a heavy, dark, grey but in the distance there seemed to be a glow of orange. Perched up on its seemingly impenetrable hill, the town of Rodrigo must be burning. Who knew what turn next the Peninsula campaign would take, how quickly they might be all in Paris, because if they could crack Rodrigo, the other forts might lose heart and the French would be on the run.

'You weren't to blame for that, sir,' Masters said.

Tony ventured a smile. His men were loyal,

which in his book counted for a lot.

'You and I know what happened, Masters, but I fear Picton and Wellington blame me. I've not been given command of a decent mission since.'

'You will, sir. There's plenty more to come. Besides, storming a city . . . '

Masters' voice faded, as if in reverence for his colleagues, as the noise of the cannons suddenly became louder.

★   ★   ★

Smoke filled Jem's nostrils. She could taste gunpowder on her tongue. Below her lay the bodies of soldiers, either writhing in agony or still in death, and at any moment she could be down there with them. She pulled herself further up her ladder. Its top rung was level with the breach. If only she could get to the top before —

'Up the ladders, men! Not a moment to lose!' Lieutenant Gurwood shouted, and then there he was, level with her on the ladder beside hers, waving his sword like a madman. 'We can do it. For God and King George.'

Gurwood pressed on upwards, and reached the top of the breach. Jem pulled herself higher as out of the corner of her eye she watched the lieutenant grapple with a defender before arching backwards off the ladder and falling to the ground. Jem swallowed.

Jem tightened her grip on her rifle. She could do it, she could swing herself on to Gurwood's ladder. She was next in command, she had to take charge. They had to make good the breach.

In the distance she could hear cheers, and British voices.

'Picton's men are beating us, lads. Are we going to let them?' an officer shouted in crisp tones.

'No!' the troopers chorused back as one. 'The Ninety-Fifth! The Ninety-Fifth!'

'There's no denying, brave boys!'

The Ninety-Fifth, the Ninety-Fifth, Jem repeated to herself in her head as she began to swing her body to gain momentum. She lunged forward, gripping Gurwood's ladder with everything she had. Her foot slipped, and she slid down, but only a rung before regaining her balance. The Ninety-Fifth, the Ninety-Fifth, for the Ninety-Fifth, and for England, she could do it.

She scrambled up the ladder.

Half obscured by smoke, a dark metal mouth gaped open. Jem stared as the smoke swirled around it. Her mind numb from the ringing of musket fire, took a moment to register its significance. Her heart stopped. A cannon!

A French face shone white at the flare of a torch being lit. When the time was right, he'd put the torch to the fuse and the cannon would fire down and across the breach, obliterating the storming party.

Jem started to climb across the ragged stones of the breach, her hands groping for finger holds as she levered her body and her rifle up the broken wall at the breach's edge.

Her hand slipped and she skidded back two feet. Her legs dangled over the precipice. If she let go, she'd die, broken on the rocks. But how many more would die if she failed?

Jem drew a deep breath that seemed to line her lungs with frost. Her time to depart was not yet. She swung her legs over the wall and landed squarely. The French soldier was a dark silhouette with his back to her as he leant towards the fuse.

With no time to load and fire a shot, Jem crashed the butt of her rifle down on the defender's head. He crumpled without so much as a cry, and lay still.

'To me! To me! Ninety-Five! No retreating!' she called, and struggled to turn the weighty cannon. 'The town will be ours!'

A trickle of soldiers started over the wall.

16

Most headed along the ramparts, including the two officers. One officer pushed her to the side and she fell to her knees beside the French gunner.

The world erupted and buckled as an explosion rocked the ramparts. A hail of small pebbles and stones rained down on her. A British officer flew through the air like a cloth doll and lay twisted on the ground writhing in pain.

Jem pulled herself back to her feet and was about to race to the officer's aid but her knees felt as if they were about to buckle again beneath her. She dragged the back of her sleeve across her face, as if brushing away some of the grime would do something.

'Riseley, what are you doing standing there?' Gurwood barked behind her. 'We've got bloody Rodrigo to take.'

'The castle, we need to take the castle,' she said, turning to see Gurwood, his eyes determined despite the blood pouring down his face. Jem caught her breath. 'The French will regroup at the castle.'

'Of course, Riseley. Of course! That's where the governor will be!' Gurwood swiped his sword through the air like a scythe and pointed it upwards. 'Come with me lads, there's glory still to be had.'

With half a dozen other soldiers, they raced

17

through the dark streets. From all around came the sounds of destruction — glass and tiles being smashed, gunshot, fire and screams. Groups of French soldiers stood with their hands held high, as British soldiers fired their muskets in the air. There would be little mercy for French soldiers who contin- ued to resist.

Jem forced her feet to run faster until at last, her chest shuddering with the effort of breathing, they came into the open square where above them the castle loomed, tall, square and medieval, its sand-coloured stone half-cloaked in green ivy and darkness. Suddenly it was as if their group was alone. The shouts and occasional musket fire seemed distant from the immediate silence.

The small door cut into the stout wood of the castle gates seemed to be not quite shut and Jem lunged at it with her shoulder, her rifle ready to shoot. The door swung wide open, the creak of its iron hinges the only sound. Inside, the castle courtyard seemed empty. Nothing stopped them entering the castle. No resistance.

'Damn we're too late, Picton's lot got here first.' Gurwood swore. 'It's deserted.'

'Hadn't we ought to check, sir?' Jem said quietly. 'Make sure the castle is secure?'

'Very well, sergeant, carry on. I'll see what I

can find out here. They may have missed something of value — a snuffbox or somesuch.'

Gurwood began to direct the troopers where they should look.

Jem heard her own footsteps echoing on the stone floors and it did not seem right. Tapers still burned, tables stood firm, the shelves still held their ornaments. Only in the governor's reception room was there any sign of a hasty departure. In the centre of the room, the large dining table held the remains of a half-eaten meal, and a dressed bird still to be carved at the centre. Jem's stomach rumbled.

She moved closer to the table, noting a knocked-over wine glass and the slow trickle of red wine across the polished table, dripping on to the floor. A chunk of white bread lay within her grasp.

Jem licked her lips, tasted smoke and considered it. No one was likely to miss a piece of bread. Perhaps Gurwood was right, perhaps someone else had grabbed the glory and received the garrison's surrender.

She reached across the table towards the platter, and heard a muffled gasp. Jem sprang back.

'Out from under there!' she shouted, levelling her rifle at the underside of the table. 'The town belongs to the British.'

'Don't shoot! We shall come out.'

An impeccably dressed man who had seen too many fine feasts and a woman dressed in a low-cut, red silk gown, her hair tumbling about her shoulders, emerged from under the table.

He clicked his heels, and handed his sword to Jem.

'The garrison is yours,' he said in perfect English. 'I, Governor Barrie, surrender this fort to you.'

★ ★ ★

Later, as the first faint streaks of dawn appeared on the horizon, Jem stood next to Gurwood at the breach as Wellington's representative, Lord Fitzroy Somerset, buckled the sword around Gurwood's waist. In the rosy hue, Jem could see the destruction the night's work had caused. The hastily arranged piles of bodies, the burning houses, the continuing cries of the women.

The British army had won a stunning victory, but she had failed. After this simple ceremony, she would go back, rejoin her company and face the major, if he still lived. There was always that chance, that slim chance that somehow the major had failed to survive the storming party. She might be safe.

She tried to hang on to that thought and pay attention to Somerset's words.

'A capital piece of work, Gurwood. Far fewer lost than I thought might be, and you survived the Hope and captured the governor as well.'

Gurwood preened. 'Ably assisted by Sergeant Riseley. You have no idea how these men have to be directed.'

Somerset turned his piercing eyes towards Jem. 'I have heard of Sergeant Riseley's exploits,' he said in his precise way. 'There is promotion for both of you. Gurwood, you are to captain a company in the Royal Africa Corps and Riseley, you are a sergeant no longer. You are promoted to the rank of ensign.'

Ensign? They were making her an officer?

Jem felt her heart begin to pound. She wasn't supposed to be standing. She was supposed to be among the corpses — here, in the breach of the wall at Ciudad Rodrigo. She was supposed to be dead now, on her way to St Peter. Not here, being promoted to the rank of officer. There would be no hiding from the major in the officers' quarters.

2

In the distance, a single bell tolled for the dead and dying.

Jem shifted the weight of her haversack to the other shoulder and concentrated on walking straight along the path. The ground was stony and uneven and bore the jagged imprints of hundreds of pairs of boots. She nearly slipped but righted herself before she tumbled. Her muscles protested at the violent movement. The adjunct had pointed towards this group of whitewashed buildings being the Casa San Miguel. Not the farm to the left.

She approached the tall central building — the farmhouse — and its carved front door. It was in good repair, every window intact. Only a few miles behind the lines and it was too ordinary, too ordered. A wave of tiredness washed through her as she hoped she'd come to the right place and would find some of her new company here, and their captain. Instead of returning to the 95th, they had seen fit to move her — it was unsettling to the men to see a man promoted from the ranks.

The only thing Jem knew was that she had

hope once again. She could do this. She could be Ensign Jem Riseley. Her other life had ceased to exist. She had been given another chance.

She knocked and nothing. Jem pushed the door open and stepped into a tiled and smoky hall. The warmth hit her, sending a flush to her cheeks. The smell of roasting onions made her stomach rumble. She hadn't seen the inside of a building for weeks, hadn't eaten anything apart from hard tack and the meanest scraps of salt pork.

Strains of Rule Britannia assaulted her ears, coming through a half-open door.

'One last toast before we retire to our beds on this glorious day, this day when we swept all before us. To the brave, incomparable fallen. Gentlemen to Major Char — '

She pushed the door open.

Three officers slumped in wooden chairs and only one was conscious enough to be speaking. He paused mid-sentence and looked up from his glass. His untidy brown hair tumbled forward on to his forehead and unshaven bristles pushed his cravat even more askew.

'Yes, what is it?'

He was staring at her through his bleary eyes. Could he see through her disguise? Jem noticed the jugs on the table and could smell the sweet aroma of wine. She shifted from boot to boot and remained exactly where she was — in the shadows.

'Excuse me, sir. Could you tell me where I could find the Captain of D Company, sir?'

He raised an eyebrow, tilted his head back. Underneath the dishevelment, he was devastatingly handsome. The shadow across his chin couldn't hide the firm cut of his jaw, the perfect symmetry of his features. He was the sort of man a girl might dream about, if she allowed herself to dream. Jem gave her head a shake and tried to concentrate on the wall.

'Might know. Depends on who is asking. If it's m'tailor tell him I sent the bill off yesterday.' He chuckled and Jem's breath halted as she caught the sparkle in his eye. 'If it's a posse of Spanish lovelies come to express their gratitude, well now that's another kettle of fish . . . '

She'd seen that devilish twinkle before, in the eyes of the one man she'd had the misfortune of falling in love with. Viscount Fordingley — the first and last man she'd ever kissed, the man who had broken her heart. Fordingley would have never let himself go for three days without shaving. She forced her breath out. No, she was imagining things.

'Sar . . . ' Jem paused and started again.

'Ensign Jem Riseley sir.'

'What's a Sar-Ensign? Some new sort of half-breed officer?'

'No, sir. I was made an ensign this morning.'

'By whom?'

'By Wellington himself, sir. I earned a battlefield commission.'

'And what did you do? Save the life of Wellie's horse?' He laughed. Jem fastened her gaze on a crack in the plaster above the captain's head.

'I was in the Hope, sir.'

'You survived the Hope?' The captain's countenance sobered swiftly. His hands gripped the arms of his chair and he sat up straighter.

'Not a scratch. I was lucky.' Jem tried not to think of the others who had fallen around her. A foot to the left or the right and she'd have been dead. But they'd missed, somehow. 'General Barrie surrendered his sword to me.'

'Well I'll be . . . A real live hero.'

'The real heroes are dead, sir.'

The captain gave a pained expression, exhaled. 'You can say that again.'

In the silence, Jem stood awkwardly and tried not to think of her brother, Charles. He'd been a hero, a real hero, dying on the Talavera battlefield to save his men.

The captain took another gulp of his wine. His eyes narrowed as they returned to rest on her.

'What are you doing here, Cullen?'

Cullen? Jem felt the blood drain from her face and her limbs freeze cold. There was no way he could know. He couldn't have guessed. She had been Jem Riseley for over a year. Miss Jemima Cullen no longer existed except in her nightmares. Who was he? How could he have guessed?

'The colonel sent me,' she stammered and willed back the tears. Jemima Cullen might have cried but Jem Riseley never cried. 'He ... he assigned me to your company — D Company of the South Warwickshires. I'm your new ensign. Jem Riseley.'

'The devil he did! You're dead, Charlie Cullen. I saw you fall at Talavera m'self. Now get out.'

Jem needed no second invitation. She staggered outside and into the daylight of the yard. She stood, hands on her thighs, drinking in great gulps of fresh air.

She should have died back there. At least there her death would have had some meaning. Unless she did something quickly, she'd be on the first boat back to England, facing a hangman's noose.

'Can I help you, lad?' a voice asked.

26

She looked up into the craggy face of a sergeant. She took a deep breath and stood up, ramrod straight. She could do this. She'd bluff it out.

'I'm the new ensign of D Company. Jem Riseley.'

'Sergeant Masters, also of D Company.' He stood back and leaned on the stout stick he'd been carrying and looked her up and down. 'Welcome, lad.'

The sergeant's face looked kindly enough, Jem decided. He was an older man — the creases on his brow remained even as he smiled. 'The Captain threw me out of his billet. Mistook me for some other officer, I think.'

'Yes, well, a fit of the blue devils, I'm afraid.' Sergeant Masters ground his stick into a hump of icy mud. 'Captain Dorrell wants to be out there leading every charge and this time it was our turn to guard the baggage train. So he's a wee bit upset about missing the action. Ignore it, lad. He's bang up to the mark usually.'

'Captain Dorrell? Anthony Michael Dorrell, Viscount Fordingley?' Charles's best friend — no wonder he'd noticed the resemblance straight away. He was without a doubt the man in this army most likely to see through her disguise.

'Yes, that's him. You must have heard of him, of course.'

'Yes, I have heard of him,' she said, choosing her words with utmost care. 'He's made rather a name for himself and his exploits.'

'Some people say his reputation as a hero is exaggerated, Ensign, but, between you and me I don't think there is a braver officer in this battalion. His storming the cannon at Talavera was magnificent.'

'Were you with him at Talavera?' Jem's heart stopped. Heaven help her if this regiment was riddled with Charles's former brothers-in-arms. Her chest was used to being tightly bound with bandages day after day but now she struggled to breathe evenly.

She might as well go throw herself on the mercy of the colonel and hope the army would understand.

She placed her hand on the edge of the stone trough beside her and lifted her chin. The British army would not *understand* — she'd be sent back to England in disgrace. She would not go back to England.

Nor would she desert. She might be many things but she was not a traitor to Crown and country.

Through the fog, she heard the sergeant say 'Alas, no, none save the captain from this

28

company was there.'

So Fordingley was the only one who could guess. They were not good odds, but she had no choice but to take them.

★ ★ ★

Tony rocked back in his chair, stared at the wooden door as Major Carruthers roused himself sufficiently to pour him another glass of wine. First he missed the real action at Ciudad, and then Charlie's ghost appeared, berating him for not being there.

'How about another song?' Carruthers chirped.

Yes, Tony thought, they'd done it — without him. Taken Rodrigo and had the enemy on the run. For once His Britannic Majesty's Army were moving forward.

'Captain, come out and meet your new lieutenant.'

He'd tell Sergeant Masters what he could do with his confounded impertinence in a minute.

Tony rose and started unsteadily towards the entrance, blinked in the stark winter light. Standing before him dressed in the 95th's green jacket with a trooper's helmet on his head was Charlie Cullen. He'd recognize that straight nose and dimple in the chin anywhere, even after nearly three years.

'Lieutenant? I see no Lieutenant. Don't try to flim-flam me, Masters. Is this your idea of a joke?'

Sergeant Masters held up his hand. 'The colonel has sent Smith's replacement.'

Tony stood up straighter and buttoned his jacket. He passed a hand over his eyes. Still there. The apparition saluted smartly.

'Ensign Jem Riseley, sir.'

Now he might be a trifle disguised but he'd lost it as to why Charlie Cullen was pretending to be his new lieutenant. 'What's the joke?'

'Joke, sir?' the apparition answered back.

'Charlie, I might be a little foxed but if you're not Major Charles Cullen then I'm . . . the Queen of Sheba.'

Charlie took a step forward and stumbled. He was looking a bit pale. Must have had a few too many too. Charlie wouldn't have stood for guarding the baggage train, he'd have managed to persuade the colonel to let him have a slice of the action.

'I'm Ensign Jem Riseley, sir, newly commissioned into D company. I've been transferred from the 95th.'

The lad had a point, Tony thought. He was short of a lieutenant and was expecting one called Riseley to arrive. Distinguished in battle? He'd be useful with his rabble. And Charlie had for three years been pushing up daisies. Where'd all that time gone? He ran his hand through his hair.

'Ensign Riseley, I'm Captain Dorrell, Viscount Fordingley, Captain of D Company. Mistook you for an old pal of mine . . . ' Tony grabbed the doorframe to steady himself. Probably didn't need to really, but just in case. 'Well, welcome to these merry few, this happy band of brothers, Jem Riseley.'

★ ★ ★

Jem stared at the captain, not quite believing her luck.

The captain held out his hand and Jem shook it. Manfully.

'Thank you, sir, and I must say it's an honour to serve under such an illustrious hero as yourself, sir.'

He chuckled. 'Hero, you say? Thought we'd agreed all the heroes are dead. I am just a man doing my duty.'

'And what a duty it is, sir.'

So far so good, Jem thought. Apart from that awful moment when he had thought she was Charles and she thought all was lost.

Captain Dorrell beamed. 'I have a feeling we are going to get on famously, Riseley.'

'If you please, sir, it's been a long two days and I am nearly dead on my feet.'

The captain stroked his chin. 'Did Colonel Garroway say anything particular when he sent you here? Any orders?'

'He said you'd make a gentleman of me, sir.' Jem raised her chin and stared him squarely in the eyes. 'The right person to bring a lad risen from the ranks on, he said.'

'Did he indeed?' The captain clapped her on the back and Jem struggled to keep on her feet. 'A gentleman, you say. Stick with me lad, and I'll make you a man to be proud of. Masters here will show you where to bunk down.'

If only he could make a man of me, Jem thought as she followed the sergeant to a farm building across the yard. It would make life so much simpler.

★   ★   ★

Someone had taken a hatchet to his head. Tony winced as he started to put on his shirt. Each movement of his fingers sent a fresh throb shooting through his head.

Tony gave an uneasy laugh. It was his own fault of course.

His hand brushed against his chin as he finished buttoning his shirt. He needed a shave. It felt like a good three days' worth.

Painful though it was to move with such rapidity, he seized the mirror from the top of the chest and looked at himself critically.

Had he let himself go that long? If Wellington shaved twice a day, there was no excuse. He was a gentleman, not some slovenly shuffling ne'er-do-well.

Tony peered at the bleary-eyed face in the mirror. Would he, if he were Colonel Garroway, give the most prestigious commands to a man *who hadn't even shaved that morning?*

No, he wouldn't.

Was this how they saw him, an officer past his best, fit only for baggage-train duty while others garnered the glory? Content to live on the reputation of past exploits while others continued to risk their lives?

No, not any longer. Not ever.

Tony paused in mid swipe with his razor. He'd been shaken last night when he thought he was seeing Charlie Cullen's ghost.

But it was a most curious thing that a lad who was the very spit of Charlie should turn up to serve in his company. And that this lad should have survived the Hope.

If there was a divine almighty up there, and he wasn't sure, was he being sent something. A sign?

No, an ensign!

Tony winced at his pitiful joke. Even his wit was stale this morning. A smell of something that promised to be fresh pork wafted into his room and his nose. It could prove to be a good day yet.

The sound of musket fire reverberated through the room. Tony's hand froze in mid-swipe. A second round was fired off.

Tony hurriedly wiped his face with the towel, grabbed his pistol and ran outside. All was at peace. Masters stood with his hands behind his back, whistling.

'What the devil is going on?' Tony demanded.

'It's Ensign Riseley. He decided the men needed a bit of target practice, sir.'

'I know, half of our men are raw recruits.' Tony ran a hand through his hair. A drill-happy ensign, that was all he needed. 'But what I want to know is who gave permission?'

'The ensign is a rifleman, sir. When I apprised him about the new recruits, he was concerned about their ability to fire.' Masters maintained a poker face, but his eyes twinkled. 'He said under the circumstances, he was sure you would approve.'

'Damn me if he did. Does he know how early it is?' Tony strode off through the snow in the direction of the musket fire.

'That wasn't quick enough, men,' he heard the ensign shout. 'You'll need to be faster than that. You can have a minute's rest and then we'll try again. Three in under a minute is what the army requires.'

Tony frowned and quickened his pace. He snapped a curse under his breath as he slipped on a patch of ice and nearly lost his balance. He loathed popinjay officers who demanded more of their men than they could do themselves. They were the sort that ordered the lash for any minor error. In his experience it was the quickest way to demoralize the men. Officers should lead from the front.

Tony hastened round the corner. The scene was almost exactly as he'd expected — his men lined up and ready to waste precious powder and shot on the new ensign's whim. The morning light was unforgiving. Most of the troopers seemed all too disinclined to look their captain in the eye. He wouldn't begrudge the men their victory celebrations — there was no immediate danger. The argument he intended to pick was stood before him, still wearing the green uniform of a sergeant of the 95th.

The ensign stood, pocket watch in hand. Tony shook his head. In the broad light of day, it was hard to believe he had ever mistaken the ensign for Charlie. The ensign was at least half a head shorter and slighter. But his face did bear the faintest resemblance and Riseley had curly black hair like Charlie. All things considered perhaps it had been an honest mistake.

He tried to remember if Charlie had a brother. He shook his head. Not a brother, a sister: a small delicate thing who wouldn't say boo to a goose, if he recalled correctly. Often had her nose stuck in a book and was inclined to gaze at him with big, serious eyes. Rather attractive eyes actually — Tony pulled his thoughts back to the present.

'Morning, ensign,' Tony stood tall and held his hands behind his back.

'Good morning, sir.' Ensign Riseley saluted smartly back.

'And what is going on here?'

'Drilling practice, sir. Sergeant Masters said half of the men had arrived within the month from England,' Riseley answered with his chin thrust slightly forward. Again Tony was struck by how like Charlie the lad was. The inflection was close to being the same. A relation?

'And the men's shooting is?' Tony knew quite well what it was like. But the late Lieutenant Smith had thought accuracy ought to be above speed.

'These men can get off less than two shots per minute, sir. If the enemy are at a hundred yards, you need to get off close to three shots or you'll end up with a bellyful of bayonet, sir.'

'Three shots in a minute is a tall order, Ensign.' Tony put his hands behind his back. 'An extremely tall order.'

'I would like to get the men to do three shots per minute.'

'In my company, the officers lead by example, Ensign,' he said in low but firm voice. Riding the men hard was the surest path to surly resentment and the quickest way to destroy the company's morale he had worked so hard to build up and maintain.

'I am not sure I understand you, sir? I don't believe I am asking more of the men than they can give.'

'Can you fire three shots in less than a minute, Ensign, with that rifle? Upon my soul, you are a better shot than I.' Tony gave a barking laugh. The ensign was young, impetuous. This was his first experience at being an officer. Hopefully Riseley would seize the opportunity and back down, a graceful retreat.

'I believe I can do so, sir.' Again the insolent thrust of the chin.

37

'Let's see you do it then.' Tony had had enough of this. If his ensign was insisting he learn the lessons of command the hard way, then so be it. In order to be respected by the men, you had to prove you could do something.

'Sir?'

'I want to see three shots in under a minute. And accurate as well.' Tony looked directly into Riseley's eyes. They were grey like Charlie's. Did the lad understand that he was being given a choice — to become a hero to the men, somebody to look up to, or to back away?

Tony heard a chuckle and shot a quelling glance at the crowd. A couple of the troopers shifted uneasily. Riseley's countenance was white, as if he was about to be sick. It was a baptism by fire, but he'd learn. He had the makings of a fine officer, but there were lessons he had to learn.

'If you will give me a minute, I'll retrieve my rifle.' Riseley rubbed his hands on his breeches. Tony knew if he allowed Riseley to leave the field, the ensign would lose his nerve. He'd seen it before.

'You are not asking these men to shoot with your rifle,' Tony replied quietly. 'You can use one of theirs. And show them how it is done. Trooper Jones, give your musket to the ensign. And ensign, your watch, if you please.'

★ ★ ★

Jem had felt the colour drain from her face and her knees threaten to give way. She wasn't worried about the challenge. On a good day, she knew she could average about fifteen seconds per shot. She held her former company's record.

No, it wasn't the shooting, but the watch. She owned exactly three things from her former life, things that had belonged to Charles — the book he had given her for her seventeenth birthday, a lock of his hair and his watch. And when Captain Dorrell saw the watch, what then? What lie would she tell?

'My watch, sir?'

'I am a fair man, Ensign. As you judged, so shall you be judged.' The Captain held out his hand. 'It is a direct order, Ensign.'

'Very good, sir.' Jem said a quick prayer and handed it over.

She took the proffered rifle and balanced it in her hand. It was an Indian pattern Brown Bess musket. Her shoulders relaxed a little bit. With an Indian pattern, three shots were not difficult; a good rifleman should be able to get off four per minute. With a Baker three

39

shots per minute was about the top of the range. However, an Indian pattern was not as accurate as a Baker.

'What would you like me to shoot, sir?'

'Sergeant, set up the bottles at one hundred paces. There, there and there.' The captain indicated the spots with his hand. 'You will need to hit at least one of the targets.'

Jem bit her lip. It was the exact same exercise Charles had done on his last leave home to demonstrate to her his proficiency. After he had left, Jem had practised and practised in order to show Charles how much she had improved when he came home. Except he hadn't and she had used her skill to secure her place in the army.

'Are you a betting man, Ensign?' The captain's voice pierced her concentration. 'Are you willing to up the stakes?'

'I am not sure what you mean, but I am always willing to take a wager.' Jem's breath caught in her throat. 'What sort of wager did you have in mind?'

'Let's say your watch against a new sword.'

Beads of sweat started to gather on her forehead. 'That I can get off three shots and hit one of those targets?'

'No, let's make it interesting.' The captain took another considered look at the watch, closed the lid and weighed the timepiece in his hand. 'All three targets hit.'

There were murmurings in the ranks. Jem eyed the targets. Could she do it? She knew with her own rifle, she probably could, but with this one? She balanced the Indian Pattern rifle in her hand, feeling its weight. She could hear the men behind her swapping bets. The crowd seemed to swell with each passing second. She swallowed hard.

'If you feel unable to accept the wager . . .' the captain said.

No, she would not lose face in front of the men. She took a deep breath and squared her shoulders.

'Sir, I accept your offer!'

The captain's eyes widened for an instant. 'Very well Ensign. It's your watch.'

'I know, sir and I intend to get a new sword to go with it.'

'Well said, Riseley. Well said.'

Jem set her feet and palmed the first cartridge. The procedure was one she'd done a thousand times before. Hold the musket horizontally in her left hand, cartridge in her right, rip with her teeth, retain the bullet in her mouth, pull the hammer back one notch, prime the frizzen, pour the rest of the powder from the cartridge into the barrel, spit the

41

bullet in, and stuff the paper in after it. To save time, instead of using the ramrod, bang the musket sharply on the ground. Next pull the hammer back a further notch, take aim and fire.

She gave a nod to the captain. 'On your orders, sir.'

He looked at the watch. The seconds ticked past. Sweat started to stream down her forehead, she wiped it away with an impatient hand. Her stomach clenched.

'Go.'

Jem loaded, rammed and fired. She heard the tinkling of glass. White smoke billowed around her, obscuring the view. Her mouth tasted of gunpowder and grease. She loaded, banged with all her might, fired again, taking aim at the second bottle. Nothing.

There was a groan from the crowd.

She loaded, and rammed. All was in readiness. Through the smoke, she could just see the glint of the second bottle. She pressed the trigger. Her reward was the tinkling of glass.

The captain hadn't called time. How many more seconds did she have? Could she try once more? She had to. The watch was at stake. She refused to lose the watch. Not Charles's watch. Why did she let her stupid pride rule her head? She should have never

42

accepted the wager. She had this one last chance.

Jem ripped open the next cartridge, loaded, aimed and fired.

3

The captain's call of time and the shattering of glass sounded at the same instant. The crowd erupted in cheers.

Her legs gave way. She sank on to her knees amongst the slush and ice, fingers tight around the muzzle of the gun. She wiped her hand against her mouth, looked towards the bottles and could only see shards of glass on the frozen ground. She had done it. She had won.

She looked up at the captain, prepared to hate him, but he was smiling. His face transformed by the curve of his lips into one of the handsomest she had ever seen. Her eyes followed the clean line of his jaw and came to rest where the ends of his dark hair dusted the top of his ear. Jem's breath caught in her throat. He looked exactly as he had done all those years ago in England when her heart would have ached for just such a smile.

'Very fine shooting, Riseley.' A warm sparkle in his eyes told her he meant it. 'Four in a minute. There's not many who could accomplish that. You shattered all three bottles. Hell, I should have wagered against m'self.'

He strode over to her and placed his hand on her shoulder. Jem tried to ignore the ripple of unwanted sensation coursing through her at his touch. 'I am glad you had it in you lad. For a moment, I wasn't sure, but that was as fine a show of shooting as I have ever seen.'

'I don't ask more of the men than I ask of myself,' Jem gasped. She moved and he let go of her shoulder. She placed her hands on her knees and drank in great gulps of air, willing her heartbeat to go back to normal.

'I never said you did, Riseley. If you could teach the men to shoot like that, the French won't know what hit them. D Company will be the talk of the regiment.'

'My watch, if you please.' Jem put out her hand. She tried for an insolent smirk, the sort a young lad would make, not the love-struck smile of Miss Jemima Cullen. 'And I believe you owe me a sword.'

'You shall be paid in full as soon as I can arrange it.' The captain ran a hand through his hair. 'An officer needs a sword. And you deserve the best. Not that the French will get anywhere near you.'

'I look forward to it, sir, but right now I need my watch.'

The captain took a long considering look at

the watch and then shut the case with a decisive click.

'It's a mighty fine timepiece.' He tossed it from one hand to the other before handing it to her. 'Not yours originally, I think.'

'I know that. I won it at a card game.' Jem took the watch and stuffed it into her pocket. 'The stakes that time were very high indeed.'

It was truth at least. She had won it. The last night Charles was home, they'd played écarté and she won, claiming the watch as forfeit. He promised her the watch when he returned from the campaign. When the small box of effects arrived back from Portugal after his death, she had taken possession of the watch before her stepfather could get his hands on it.

'A gambler, eh? There is hope for you yet, Riseley. Are you as good at cards as you are at shooting?' The captain watched her with narrowed eyes.

'I try to win more than I lose,' Jem answered cautiously. If the captain wanted another wager for the watch, he'd have another thing coming. She wasn't prepared to take the risk. In fact, she would try to find something else to time the men by. Out of sight, out of mind. Hopefully. 'I do play sometimes, for money.'

'We must hazard a game of Hazard some

46

day soon.' He turned abruptly in the direction of the men. Their muttering ceased. 'Yes, the show's over, but not the drill. Don't slouch, Trooper Hook.'

'I look forward to it,' Jem muttered and tried to keep her voice from shaking and her eyes from noticing how a lock of jet black hair tumbled over his forehead.

She watched his long fingers push back the lock of hair. Then he turned back towards her and the frown on his countenance changed to the grin. He gave a slight bow. Their eyes held for a second before Jem looked away, her heart thumping all the harder. Was there something speculative in his eyes?

'Orders, Fordingley!' The clipped educated tones of the adjunct interrupted. He handed the captain a sheet of paper and then paused, slightly bent, to get his breath back.

The captain snatched the paper and tore open the seal.

Sergeant Masters stepped up next to the adjunct and winked at Jem, nodding towards the captain. She tore her gaze back to the captain and watched his quick eyes read it in a moment. His face broke into an even larger grin.

'At last.' He stuffed the paper in a pocket and rubbed his hands together. 'Riseley, choose a dozen men. The best shots in your opinion. Masters, you can drill the rest.

'The colonel has seen fit to give D Company other duties than guarding baggage trains and foraging the countryside for hidden stores. We leave in ten minutes.'

'Right-ho,' Masters replied and looked at her expectantly.

'I don't understand, sir?' Jem said, perplexed.

The captain grasped both her shoulders. Looking into his eyes, feeling his hands on her was too . . . dangerous. He let her go, and she drew a deep steadying breath.

'Riseley, you and I are about to go hunting for confounded, traitorous deserters. At long last, the colonel has given me something to sink my teeth into. A chance to show him what D Company can really do.'

★　★　★

Tony watched the back of Riseley's head as the horses trudged along the narrow road. Riseley had found an excuse to slip off his horse the minute they had left the camp behind and was now leading it up the steep slope. Tony's own mount, Beacon, was a bit skittish. Underfoot was snow, intermingled with patches of ice. Any moment, he knew he

48

would have to dismount but officers were supposed to ride.

He tried to pay attention to the road, to the mission ahead. But his mind kept circling back to one question. Where had the ensign won that watch? That timepiece had been Charlie Cullen's, he was sure of it, felt it in his bones. He remembered packaging it up and sending it off to Charlie's mother. How had it come to fall into such careless hands?

The times he'd seen Charlie take out the timepiece and admire it; he said it always reminded him of home. Now some wet behind the ears lad had it, and had won it in some infernal card game! Ensign Riseley had no appreciation of what the watch symbolized. It was part of the reason for the wager — to give Riseley one last chance to back down without losing face, and to test if the watch meant anything. Charlie would have wagered his boots before the watch. And he wanted the watch himself, something to remind him of Charlie.

Tony gave a cluck to Beacon and urged his horse forward. Anything to get his thoughts away from the rut they were stuck in.

'The road branches here, Captain,' Riseley shouted.

Tony looked at the simple sketch map the colonel had sent with the orders. 'We take the right hand fork towards Fuentegauinaldo then circle around back to camp, making a clean sweep of the area. We are searching for one deserter in particular — a man who goes by the name of Le Loup. He leads a band of murderous deserters, men who owe little allegiance to either side.'

'Do you think he is there?'

'That is what we intend to find out, ensign, to see if the Spanish guerrillas are giving us accurate information.'

'Pity we are not going to a convent to rescue some señoritas,' called one of the troopers. 'I could do with a bit of gratitude in the night. Warm arms about me to keep the cold away.'

'Couldn't we all, trooper? Couldn't we all?' Tony gave a laugh.

He noticed Riseley remained aloof from the general laughter. If anything, the ensign's back seemed straighter, disapproving.

'Don't tell me the fairer sex holds little interest, Ensign? What sort of a man, are you?'

'Sir,' Riseley turned and faced him, meeting his eye. 'It's just with one thing and another I have not had much opportunity.'

'We must further your education with all speed,' Tony said with a laugh. 'There is one thing above all, Riseley, a gentleman should possess, and that is the ability to deal well with the fairer sex. I look on it as an essential part of your education.'

★   ★   ★

Her face burnt as the ribald laughter swelled up around her. Just the thought of the captain taking her to one of the flesh pots that lay just outside the camp made her squirm. Thus far, she had managed to avoid the women who were available in every town, for a bit of money, by playing cards. She bit her lip. Somehow, she doubted if the captain would take an urgent game of cards as an excuse.

How could she explain her dreams were not filled with ladies, but with men? No, not men, one dark haired man — *him*. Ever since she had first laid eyes on him, three years ago. Jem swallowed hard and dragged her eyes away from the spot where his dark hair met the white of his cravat. She narrowly missed tripping in a hole in the road.

Blast him and his broad shoulders.

'So how old are you, Riseley?'

Jem tried to think. She knew how old Jemima Cullen was — twenty. But twenty was much too old for an ensign with an unbroken voice. She'd have to be younger, much younger.

51

'I don't rightly know, sir. Me ma was never too clear on the date.' Jem exaggerated her accent. 'Sixteen or seventeen by my reckoning.'

'Sixteen or seventeen. 'Pon my soul that's way past the age to be made aware of the joys of a woman with soft lips. You never forget a woman with soft lips.'

Jem glared at him. She was tired of the subject. He had obviously not thought her lips soft enough three years ago last Christmas. She had thought she'd died and gone to heaven when he caught her under a sprig of mistletoe. His firm lips seeking hers. Within an instant, it was over and he loosened his arms, stepping away from her. Her dreams had flared like candles, until she heard Charles enquire about Dorrell's intended — a Miss Arabella Triptree. She then had the utter mortification of hearing Dorrell describe the woman as a paragon of virtue, an angel beyond compare. The lady he was about to ask to marry him, directly after he finished his visit with them at Cullen Park.

'Are you married, sir?' The words tumbled out before she could stop them. She had to know. Had he done as he had said?

'Married? Good God, no.' The captain gave a great guffaw. 'Never have been leg-shackled, and not bloody likely to be either. Nearly was once though, but the lady in question decided she had other . . . obligations 'fore I had a chance to ask her.'

'And so it is not a state you'd recommend?' Jem tried to keep her heart from thumping and her eyes on the road. The thought that the captain had not married Miss Triptree — had not even asked her — gave an added fillip to the day. Her poor bruised and battered heart of three years ago need not have been. Over her shoulder, she saw the captain give her a queer look. Hastily, she added, 'The idea had crossed my mind once or twice. I understand the Portuguese ladies can be very accommodating wives. Something to keep the chill away on a cold winter's night.'

That should do it, thought Jem. That should end any talk of consorting with loose women. It would be easy enough to invent some Portuguese sweetheart whom she was pining for.

Why hadn't she thought of it before? Jem clicked her heels with a little swagger.

'Ensign, marriage is beyond your purse.' The captain drew level with Jem and looked her in the eye. His face creased with concern and his mouth tight with some emotion. 'Not on your pay. So get the idea straight out of your mind. There's many an officer I have seen ruined by a precipitous marriage to some ambitious person of the female persuasion.'

'Just curious.' One more idea gone wrong.

'Female company is all well and good, Riseley, but marriage.' The captain seemed to be warming to his theme. 'Well damn me, if it doesn't make me shudder. I'd rather face a whole garrison of Napoleon's finest than spend five minutes with a lady with marriage on her mind.'

'Very good, sir, I'll try to remember.'

'It is one of the reasons I go down on my knees and thank the good Lord every night he saw fit to make me a younger son. No need to reproduce or to do my duty by way of the family. No, I serve to remind my father of the joy he takes in the appointed heir. Women, Ensign, are well and good in their proper place, but you can't beat a good adventure.'

'Amen to that, sir.' Jem tightened her grip on her horse's reins and attempted to lead the horse up the steep slope without hesitating. She was Ensign Jem Riseley, not some weak-kneed female who blushed at a roguish smile from the captain. Adventure is where her mind should be, not on the shape of his lips, and hankering after another taste of them.

The column continued for some miles in silence, the only sound the crunching of the snow underneath the boots of the soldiers. Off to the right, Jem could see a farmhouse with several buildings. The first thing that struck her as they drew near was the absolute stillness of the place. Not even a cow lowed. Then she saw it.

'Should we investigate, sir?' She pointed to the rising column of smoke from one of the buildings.

'Well spotted Riseley.' He pulled out his small brass telescope and examined the farm for several minutes. Jem waited and wondered if she should have said anything. Was she being too jumpy? Too over eager?

The captain collapsed his telescope and motioned to the rest of the squad. He dismounted, handing the reins of his horse to a trooper. Within moments, someone had handed him a stick and everyone had crowded around. He drew a diagram in the snow, showing where the different structures and possible places to hide were.

'I want the buildings entered at the same time,' he said, tapping the stick on the ground for emphasis. 'If there are any damned deserters there, I want them caught like rats in a trap. Jones, Riseley, come with me. The farmhouse shall be our search area. On my signal.'

The men of D Company rapidly got into position. Jem's heart hammered. Before with the 95th, she had always known where the enemy was or should be — now it was a guessing game. Which door, if any, held the deserter? She primed her rifle and waited.

The captain, with an intense look on his face, motioned to one trooper to move to the left.

Sweat started to trickle down the back of her neck.

Would Captain Dorrell ever give the signal?

He raised his sword above his head and then dropped it to his side, kicking the door as he did so.

Jem rushed in behind him. The sparsely furnished room was a mess. The table had been turned upside down. Two wrought iron candlesticks, painted crockery and a set of rosary beads lay scattered on the floor amongst the puddles of red wine.

'It appears someone has been here before us,' the captain said through gritted teeth. 'The question is, have they gone?'

A faint noise, like scratching, came from above. Then a muffled cry — a woman's cry.

'It appears your question has been

answered. They are still here, sir,' Jem said in a hushed voice.

The captain's gaze flickered from her across the men. He nodded towards the stairs. 'Up you go, Riseley. Time to earn your spurs. I'll be behind you, covering your back.'

Jem started to mount the stairs, two at time. Each footstep seemed to take a lifetime, each creak of the stair boards seemed to be too loud. Her mouth had gone dry, but she refused to stop. She had to go, to see, to find the deserters, the animals who had done this.

The whitewashed hallway was deserted. A wooden crucifix hung lopsided on the wall. There were two half-closed doors. Jem plunged forward, pushed the nearest one with the end of her rifle.

The room was empty. There was a bare bed, a wooden wardrobe and a poorly fastened shutter creaking in the wind. She glanced out in the deserted courtyard. Jem forced her shoulders to relax.

A floorboard squeaked. Her every muscle froze.

Jem kept her back to the wall and inched along the corridor towards the next door.

Another muffled scream. Jem covered the remaining two feet in a single step. She kicked open the door, brought up her musket and prepared to shoot.

On the narrow bed, a man in a light pink jacket fumbled with his patched breeches while a young black-haired Spanish woman cowered, terror etched across her white face. The man glanced over his shoulder at the sound of the crashing door. His face contorted by fury, lust and something more. The jagged scar running from his temple to his chin and his pointed ears gave him the appearance of something more beast-like than man. Jem knew she should pull the trigger but froze.

In the blink of an eye, the deserter grabbed the woman and swung her in front of him. His face broke into a mocking grin.

Jem's stomach turned over. The woman was in the way. She had to be sure of her shot. Her split second hesitation had caused her to miss her opportunity. There again, she had blocked his only means of escape.

Images blurred as her recurring nightmare began to engulf her senses. Was it a deserter with his hideous scar standing before her or her stepfather? Both faces contorted with the same mixture of anger and lust. Was she here or back in England, just after her mother's funeral, turning back to the drawing-room to find her stepfather, standing there with his breeches half-unbuttoned, beckoning to her, and reaching out for her? It was the same look, the same taunt. What are you going to do about it? — as her stepfather pulled his breeches down with one hand and while the other pawed at her breasts, holding her tight. Where was the candlestick, the candlestick she hit him with to escape the last time? There was nothing over the fireplace in this room. She could never find the candlestick . . .

She heard the woman scream. '*Madre Dios*.' Mother of God.

The room reeled then righted. Jem found her gaze staring at the broken chair in the corner and pulled it sharply back to the deserter. This was no nightmare. She was not alone. There was no candlestick but she had a weapon — a weapon that could kill.

'Unhand the woman or I'll shoot.'

The man laughed and his expression changed to a lip-curling sneer. He tightened his grip on the woman's shoulders. She gasped and her eyes seemed to plead with Jem to hold her fire.

What the devil was she going to do?

Jem felt a movement beside her. Her eyes were glued to the deserter and his captive, but her heart gave a leap as she heard the captain draw a breath. His warm hand lightly touched her shoulder.

'Don't even attempt it, Jem lad. That's an

order. Think of the girl.'

Jem gave a brief nod to show she understood but kept her finger tight around the trigger.

★ ★ ★

'It seems you are outnumbered, traitor.' Tony looked at the deserter with his threadbare coat and patched breeches.

The deserter's eyes narrowed.

'English, are you? Which regiment? Or French?' Tony said as the idea struck him. The man wore a British army coat — even though its regimental insignia was missing, and he could have picked it up anywhere.

The man thrust his chin in the air but kept his lips pressed tightly closed.

Tony glanced at white-lipped Jem. What could be bothering the lad? He had survived the Hope only a few days before. This was nothing compared to that.

'When you have a clear shot, take it,' Tony muttered under his breath. Jem gave another nod but Tony could see his fingers trembling.

'Release the girl, or — ' he began.

The deserter swore as the woman sank her teeth into his forearm — swore in French. He staggered back a step and the woman threw herself on the floor, covering her head with her hands.

'Now, Ensign. Take your shot now!'

The musket fire reverberated throughout the room. Too late. The deserter hurled himself out of the window. Tony swore and rushed over in time to see the man picking his way too fast across the roof of the outhouse below.

'Riseley, quick. Your second shot!'

Tony heard the ramrod clatter to the ground.

He primed his own pistol; he wanted to give the ensign the chance to redeem his mistake but there was no time. Tony marked the deserter.

He fired.

His shot ricocheted off the tiles. Missed — the man had jumped down on to the ground and out of the way just in time.

He picked himself up from the cobble-stones and headed around the corner and out of sight with a distinct limp.

Scarred face, a limp and French — without a doubt it had been Le Loup, Tony thought with a grimace.

'Do we go after him?' Tony saw the ensign's hands were shaking.

'No.' He banged his fist on the wall. 'Too late.'

The woman started sobbing in the corner, great gulping sobs that tore through men's souls.

'I missed sir. I don't know how I missed, but I did.'

'Don't be so hard on yourself. It was a hard shot to take.' Tony laid a hand on the ensign's shoulder. The lad reminded him of someone. Not Charlie Cullen, but himself. Over eager and not inclined to accept mistakes. Isn't that what Charlie had said on the last day? The day when they quarrelled and Charlie stormed off towards the cannon and death, accusing him of insubordination. He had never had a chance to apologize, to make things right.

The ensign flinched under his hand.

'The shot was there for the taking and I missed. It is a hard thing to forgive.'

Jem Riseley had to learn that life continued after one bad shot.

'You'll have others and make them. It's the thing about war — where there's fighting, there's shooting.'

'But what about the men, sir? Will they think less of me?'

'You have a duty, Ensign, not to let your own feelings of inadequacy show — one of the best officers I have ever met told me that. The men will see what they want to see, what you let them see. You saved the girl. Be proud of that.'

'But I shouldn't have missed.' Ensign Riseley kicked the floor with the toe of his boot.

Tony gave a nod to the girl who had recovered some of her composure and clothing. She was looking at Ensign Riseley with eyes of longing. 'You saved the damsel in distress. She might be grateful, very grateful indeed.'

'I wouldn't know, sir.' Riseley's ears turned nearly as red as the rawest recruit's coat.

Tony frowned. Something had to be done about the lad's education. Or otherwise Riseley would be prey to every petticoated poppet with an eye on his pay. And he'd be leg-shackled to some unsuitable female in the blink of an eye.

'We ought to get the lady away from here, and back to safety behind the British line.' He glanced out the window. 'It is not a total loss. We shall return victorious. We have captured some of the deserters. You take half the squad, the prisoners and señorita back to headquarters. Wellington can deal with the deserters as he sees fit. A pit in the ground is too good for them, but I don't envy the men who have to shoot in cold blood.'

* * *

Three days later, Jem was trying to forget the pink-cheeked smiles of the señorita as she rode back to camp perched on Jem's horse and the jokes at Jem's expense from the entire squad. It had been with great relief she'd delivered the señorita to a nearby convent and the watchful eyes of the nuns. The last thing she needed was women becoming love-sick over her.

Jem breathed on her hands, trying to warm them up. Thankfully, the captain so far had not made good on his promise to further her education as a gentleman. She hoped he'd forgotten the idea of visiting fleshpots and cantinas with her.

She had concentrated on drilling and improving the men of D Company's battle readiness, trying to forget how his hand had felt burning into her shoulder at the farmhouse. Or the way the timbre of his voice sent shivers down her spine. Given half a chance, she'd start acting like a love-struck female herself.

The captain had been on two other missions looking for deserters in general and Le Loup in particular, but he left her behind. Obviously he hadn't been too impressed with her ability under pressure.

Jem kicked the ground. She should have made that shot. If not the first time, then when the deserter was running away on the cobblestones. There was no excuse for her dropping the ramrod.

'There you are Jem lad.'

Jem turned and saw the captain striding towards her with a huge grin on his face and his hands behind his back. No man had the right to look that good. She paused, collecting her thoughts before she handed the command of the squad over to the sergeant and strode towards the captain.

'You wanted to speak to me about something, sir?' She tried to ignore the way the afternoon sun highlighted his eyes.

'Ensign Jem Riseley, this is your lucky day. Your damned lucky day.'

Jem's heart sank to her boots.

What was he talking about? Surely not his promise of introducing her to the cantina? How would she bear watching his hands on some black-eyed Spanish woman as they slowly danced the fandango?

'Riseley, you are an officer now, and the colonel said I could make a gentleman of you and, so help me God, I intend to.'

Jem's heart skipped a beat, but she tried to tell herself not to panic. He was being kind to a junior officer. To refuse his offer would alert his suspicions and cause more problems than it solved. She bit her inner lip, thinking quickly. She had to find an excuse, any excuse, to avoid being taken to the cantina to find a woman.

'I have a bit of free time,' the captain continued. 'And now is the correct moment, I believe, for you to start your education, to learn from a master.'

4

Tony waited for the ensign's answer; he waited to see the pleasure explode on the ensign's face when he realized the treat in store for him.

'Sir? I am awfully busy at the moment,' Ensign Riseley said, gesturing to the line of soldiers standing in perfect formation, with their shoulders back and muskets gleaming at their sides. 'The men are improving and the fire rate is now a consistent two rounds per minute. Not good, but we should be battle ready soon.'

Tony frowned. 'Sergeant Masters has already informed me of your excellent progress, Mr Riseley. This is something that concerns you as an officer and gentleman.'

'Sir, it is my opinion the men should be drilled a while longer.'

'That may be so, Ensign, but I require your presence at another task. Something I am sure you will find much more pleasurable.' Tony rubbed his hands together, enjoying himself. The look on Riseley's face. Pure trepidation. What did his ensign think was going to happen? A lesson in carving for the table?

'Sir, I am at your disposal.'

'Very good, Riseley,' Tony said. A small quirk of a smile may have escaped but he resisted the temptation to laugh. The lad would be like a child in a sweet shop once he realized the pleasures of using his sword properly. 'I intend to make sure you are well educated in the art of swordsmanship. It is all in the thrust you know.'

'The thrust? Are you sure, sir?'

'I do know what I am talking about Ensign,' he barked with some impatience. If he had had a senior officer taking such an interest when he was a newly commissioned officer, he would have been hardly able to contain his excitement. Riseley displayed as much enthusiasm as if he'd just ordered an all night march. 'I have a certain reputation in the area, and perfection in swordsmanship is what every officer should aim for. It is the mark of a true gentleman.'

The poor lad developed a greenish pallor. Tony ran his hand through his hair. He would have expected the boy to be champing at the bit, eager for the experience.

'It isn't often I have the time to give lessons, but I think they will prove useful, particularly after that little incident a few days ago. You can watch and learn the importance of the first assault, the opening and the all important final thrust.'

'I am sure the lessons will be very useful, sir.'

'If you had your sword at the ready then, I am sure we would have caught the bastard.'

'My sword, sir?' Riseley cocked his head to one side.

Tony swore. 'Ensign, did you think I'd forget a wager? I told you then I would get you a sword with all speed and I have done so.'

'Oh, that sword.' The look of relief on the ensign's face was clearly visible. 'I had forgotten the wager, sir.'

'A gentleman always pays his debts.' Tony brought the sword from behind his back. 'A light cavalry sword, Ensign. To suit your height. I have had your name engraved on it.'

'Thank you, sir. When you said education,' Jem said, turning as bright red as a newly arrived officer's coat. 'I thought . . . well you meant . . . with the ladies.'

'Ensign, those displays of swordsmanship are strictly private.' Tony gave a barking laugh. Mystery solved. It was too amusing. The poor lad actually thought . . . Tony sobered. 'And I never would be so bold as to claim prowess in the bedroom sport. No, for those sorts of lessons, you need an experienced lady of the night, not a captain in the Light Infantry.'

'I'll try to remember that, sir, when the time comes.' Riseley's whole face was a beacon of colour.

'Don't be overly concerned, Jem my boy. When the time comes, you will find everything will turn out to your satisfaction.'

★   ★   ★

Jem gripped the sword tightly in her hand and tried to forget the double meaning she had been attributing to the captain's words. It was the bout that was important.

The weight of the sword brought back so many memories. Her throat constricted as they assaulted her. How Charles had taught her some basic manoeuvres after she had spent weeks pestering him. And the fencing duels she'd watched that Christmas season between Charles and the captain. Charles had never allowed her to fight the captain, saying it wasn't suitable . . . for a lady.

She was a soldier now with no pretensions. She reckoned she still had it in her, still could fence.

'Well at least you have the grip correct.' Tony stepped towards her. 'It's a start. You're a natural, Riseley.'

Would Jem Riseley have the faintest idea of

what to do with a sword?

Jem was supposed to be from the streets, brought up among people who would never have seen a sword, let alone known what to do with one in the normal course of events. Jem fumbled and let the sword slip into a more dubious grasp.

'Do I, sir? Must be beginner's luck. Is that how you hold it correctly?'

Jem felt the tingle of his fingers on her hand and warmth begin to spread up her arm as he showed her how to hold the sword. The scent of soap and something indefinably him enveloped her senses. If she tilted her head, she'd look up directly into his eyes. She knew she'd be able to see each of the impossibly long eyelashes and lose herself in his dark eyes.

Jem swallowed hard and tried to drag her mind back to the present. Such thoughts belonged to Jemima Cullen, and Jem Riseley didn't have the luxury of thinking them.

The captain's eyes narrowed. He gave her a curious look. Jem blinked and it disappeared. Had he felt it too?

'I think I have the idea, sir,' she said, keeping her voice steady. 'I am ready for my lesson, sir.'

'No, no, Ensign, in fencing, you begin in the en garde position, with your blade in

71

front of your face.'

Jem kept her gaze trained into the middle distance and away from any chance of meeting his. It was too . . . dangerous. Her heart was beating too fast, resounding in her ears. She copied his stance but made sure she held the sabre awkwardly. 'You mean like this?'

'Hmm, yes. It will do for now, but with practice you will improve.'

Through the corner of her eye, Jem could see some of the men gathering around, faces curious. Amusement for the troops? She thought not. Her display of shooting combined with surviving the Hope had made her notorious enough.

'Captain?' Jem gave a nod towards the ever-increasing crowd. 'It appears we have an audience.'

'Ensign, I think we had best continue this lesson elsewhere, out of sight of the men.' The captain leant towards her and she made the mistake of catching his eye. She looked to the ground in confusion but he'd held her gaze just a moment too long. He stood up straight and sheathed his own sword. 'There is no need for you to become less in their eyes.'

Her heart skipped a beat. He had noticed her discomfort. This exercise had more to it than just feeding his ego. She should be thanking her lucky stars he'd interpreted her desire as fear.

'Very good, sir.' Jem turned to Sergeant Masters and gave orders to continue drilling the men.

She watched the captain's back as he led the way to a more suitable place. This was the one man she ought to fear above all others. He had nearly seen through her disguise once, and he might do again. One word from him and her next trip would be back to England and the gallows. And yet, she longed for him to pull her into his arms, to touch her and to be attracted to her as a man is attracted to a woman.

★   ★   ★

Tony led the way to a deserted piece of scrubland behind the Casa San Miguel. There was nothing stopping the morning sun and the gravelly ground was free of ice. Perfect.

'This will do I think, Jem lad.' Tony gestured with his arm. 'Private and yet enough space to move about it.'

Jem nodded, his face white lipped. Tony found himself frowning again. He didn't want to humiliate the lad. He wanted to help the boy, so Riseley could hold his own

73

in any fencing bout.

Too often Tony had seen other officers use men risen from the ranks as the butt of their jokes. Already Lieutenants Ashton and Pemberton had made disparaging remarks about the ensign, and how they wanted to see if skill with a rifle translated into skill with the true gentleman's weapon of a sword.

Tony knew what they were planning. And he refused to let it happen to any officer under his command. It was hard enough to command the respect of the men, without having to worry about being stabbed in the back by a bunch of half-wits who had no appreciation of military skill or tactics. Officers such as Ashton and Pemberton were only in the army because they were younger sons who emerged out of Eton or Harrow fit for nothing else and had fathers with deep pockets who purchased commissions. He'd like to see Pemberton face down a French general and survive.

Jem had proved himself with the drilling of the men. He'd done more in three days to improve the men's skill at firing a rifle than Ensign Smith had done in two months. About the best thing that had happened to Smith was shooting himself in the foot and having to retire to England.

'Jem, you will have to do better than that,'

Tony said, noticing the ensign held his sword like a pikestaff. 'You held it correctly the first time.'

'Sorry, sir.' Jem wiped the back of his hand across his brow, squinted and adjusted his grip.

'Now to every fencing match, there are certain parts — the attack, the parry or defence. The riposte is an attack after a parry and the redoublement happens after an attack was missed or parried. I'll attack first, and you see if you can block my attacks with the strongest part of your blade. Now, shall we begin?'

'I think I understand what you just told me.'

Tony started with a few simple cuts, something for Jem to defend easily. The first cut, Jem blocked. But with the next, Tony sent Jem's blade spinning through the air.

'Ensign, watch the blade not the man. It is that you are trying to block.'

'Right, sir. Blade, not man. I'll try harder, sir.' Jem wiped his hands on his breeches and went to pick up the fallen sword.

'Again, Ensign if you please. Are you ready? On your guard.'

This time, Jem seemed to improve. The lad was a natural, Tony thought as Jem blocked yet another of Tony's attacks. A few lessons, a bit of practice and Pemberton would have no reason to be smug.

'Right now, I want you to go on the attack, Jem. Advance slowly. Picture in your mind where you want the blade to go.'

'Like this, sir?'

Tony only had a split second to react but managed to parry the blow and send the ensign's sword spinning once again out of his hand. 'That's the general idea, Ensign. But let's try it one more time.'

★　★　★

Jem wiped her hand across her mouth and stared at the captain. This was the fourth time in six engagements he'd sent her sword spinning out of her hand. She'd hoped if her technique was bad enough, he'd leave her alone. But no, it seemed to make him more determined than ever. Her arm and shoulder ached. It might only be a light cavalry sword but every time he sent it flying out of her grip, it jolted and pulled her muscles.

Her mind was distracted by the way the sweat collected at the base of his throat, the way his white shirt clung to his chest.

She swallowed hard and ran her tongue over her parched lips. 'Don't you think we've practised enough for today, sir?'

'I am not going to give up, Ensign. This is something you must learn, if you ever want to be an officer who commands respect from both his men . . . ' Tony's expression looked very serious. 'And his equals.'

'I'll give it one more go.' Jem held the sword firm. The nearness of him was so distracting. She kept concentrating on the line of his jaw, the movement of his lips, and not his sword.

'That's the attitude. Never say die. Now this time, Jem lad, don't go for the obvious. Try to think of where your opponent might be weakest. Look to the opening.'

'Understood, sir.' Jem swallowed and gave a practice swish with her sabre. This time she'd show what she could do. She was past caring that Jem Riseley wasn't supposed to know how to fight. She only knew she wanted to wipe the grin off his face. She either took him on, or she quivered like a silly woman at his handsomeness. If she could concentrate on beating him, she could stop thinking about the proximity of his person.

'We begin again. This time see if you can knock my sword out of my hand.'

Jem took her position and allowed the captain to attack. Their blades met as she blocked the first blow. He retreated, she attacked but he easily deflected the upward thrust.

'Will you give quarter, Mr Riseley?'

'No, sir.' Jem answered. The captain was not going to be as easy to defeat as she hoped. 'No quarter.'

He grinned. 'That's what I wanted to hear.'

Around and around they circled.

Jem wanted to end it, to show the captain he couldn't spin the sabre out of her hand again.

The slightest flinch from her and she saw his immediate reaction. Every trick she remembered from Charles, the captain seemed to have an answer for. Sweat started streaming down her face. Her tongue grew dry, her throat sore.

In the back of her mind, she heard Charles's voice — *Tony is a master with the sword without a doubt, but he has one weakness.*

'Nearly got you that time, Jem lad,' The captain's face was alight with pleasure. 'Remember to watch for the counter feint.'

Jem had it. She had remembered. She made as if to drive to the right side with her sword, but instead attacked the left and at the last moment, she engaged the captain's blade and swept it around in a full circle. The captain's weapon spun out of his hand and hurtled to the ground.

The captain's eyes widened, and then he swept into a small bow. 'I believe this time, Ensign, honour is to you.'

Jem sheaved her sword and placed her hands on her knees. 'Thank you, sir. Will that be all?'

'For the moment.'

She drew herself up, caught his eye. He was watching her intently. His dark eyes and lashes flickered as he took in every nuance of her movement and Jem had the sense he was staring at her from depths far beyond those of a captain to his ensign.

Lazily the fingers of his right hand came up and brushed the curve of his jaw. Then his eyes came back and settled on her exactly, and Jem's breath stopped.

The sheer masculinity of him would have physically shaken her had she still been Miss Jemima Cullen, a young woman barely out of the schoolroom. The British army had taught her something useful — how to hold her own when everything around seemed to be crumbling, how to hold her own against men such as him. She could hold her own against him.

Jem thrust her chin in the air and let a smile play on her lips. 'It was an honour to learn from such a master, sir.'

'Upon my soul, no one . . . ' He paused and shook his head as if to clear it. 'No one since Charlie Cullen has been able to knock the sword from my hand.'

She must pray what she saw was the shock of surprise defeat and nothing else. 'A lucky blow, sir.'

'No it was more than that. You were waiting for me to overstretch m'self. Who in the name of all that's holy taught you? I have only known one other person to make that move, use that particular feint, and he's dead, died at Talavera.'

'It was a happy accident, that's all, sir.' Jem reached over and handed the sword back to the captain. She knew it had been a mistake to make the move. She had wanted to deflect attention from herself and the only thing she had done was to remind him of Charles.

'Suppose you are right. But you have talent lad, and talent will take you far. A few more lessons and you will be able to hold your own in any fencing match.' He had looked away, lightened his tone.

The last thing she needed was the captain watching her every move. She was going to have to be extra careful to be Jem Riseley through and through from now on, give him no reason to suspect anything. The perfect soldier in all things. God forbid he found out

80

who she really was. He'd send her straight back to her legal guardian, to her stepfather.

'Thank you, sir.'

'We might as well pack it in.' He cast his face to the sky and squinted. 'It looks like it's about to snow again.'

★　★　★

Tony glanced out of the window and saw Ensign Riseley standing in the slush.

'Sergeant, get those men lined up and keep their heads down,' Ensign Riseley shouted in his usual no-nonsense tone.

Riseley knew his stuff and was exemplary at getting on with the job, thought Tony with a small swell of pride. It was a lucky day when the ensign had arrived in D Company. Not a gentleman, so it would make promotion all the harder but there was always the possibility of brevets for the most outstanding officers who lacked the necessary ready cash to purchase their way up the ranks.

Over the past few days, he'd begun to notice there was something not quite right about the way the ensign held himself, wondered if his instincts were deceiving him. He had thought he must be going mad. He'd be damned if he would develop a *tendre* for another man! Hell would have to freeze over

81

first before he would consent to be one of those men who . . . He'd felt it most strongly during the fencing lesson yesterday when their breath had intermingled and he had the overwhelming desire to taste the ensign's lips.

His hands paused in straightening his cravat.

'Pon his soul, he had been too long without a woman.

'Andrews, the new ensign is a very pretty lad, isn't he?'

'I can't say I noticed much, sir. I believe the señorita you rescued was quite taken with him, cried when he left her at the convent.'

Tony sighed and tried again to fasten his cravat but a vision of Ensign Riseley bending over to pick up his sword danced before him and his loins tightened.

'Andrews,' He took his time over his words. 'How long have you known me?'

'Ten years, give or take. Your father, the Earl, hired me.'

'And in all that time, have you ever known me to be interested in boys of any sort?'

'Boys, sir?' Andrews nearly dropped the clothes brush. 'It's skirts you chase. Always have. Are you feeling entirely well, sir?'

'Thank you for reassuring me, Andrews.'

His instinct was right. He could feel it in his loins. The ensign was a woman.

Tony looked at the way her breeches caressed her shapely bottom as Riseley bent down to pick up a dropped rifle. She had been in the army for at least a year, surely someone else would have noticed before now . . .

'Anything to oblige, sir.' From Andrews' tone, Tony could tell his manservant was not entirely satisfied with his state of mind.

Tony stroked his chin. He could confront her right away of course. Formally denounce her. Or would it be better to have a quiet word with the colonel? He rejected the thought. Garroway was a damn fine commander but goodness knows how he would handle it. D Company and the entire regiment would be a laughing stock if it got out. A petticoated ensign.

Now, what the devil was he going to do about her?

He had so many questions to put to her, starting with why. Presumably, she had joined the army for a reason. That one incident at the farmhouse aside, she was such a superb shot and dedicated . . . Was it possible a woman would want to make a career as a soldier? No, impossible. Tony raked his hand through his hair.

If she wanted something to do, perhaps he could find a place for her in Lisbon.

Somewhere small, somewhere easy to visit. A smile pulled at the corners of his lips. Now, there was a very pleasant prospect.

But why was she here? Did she have a more sinister motive? Who had helped her? He needed answers and he needed them fast.

'Andrews, how quickly d'you think you can get your hands on a cask of brandy?'

'It might take a little time, sir.'

'We have precious little time. I need to know before the army begins its move to the south, before it is too late.'

'What are you planning, sir?'

'I need to gather some more information first before I will be certain how to proceed. Brandy — good for loosening the tongue, don't you think?'

'Yes, sir. I'll get on to it right away.'

He would have to remain sober, although he would appear drunk to allay her suspicions. The plan was very simple really. He would get her tipsy and then he'd confront her alone and find out what the devil she was all about.

Tony glanced through the window one last time at Jem Riseley drilling the men. Entirely satisfactory as an ensign, entirely appealing as a woman. What a confounding contradiction!

5

The rain ran down the back of Jem's neck, soaking her cravat even in the short distance across the yard from her billet to the farmhouse of the Casa. There was little point in trying to improve the men's shooting in this weather. Firing in heavy rain was impossible. No, today was a day for doing not very much of anything. The sort of day she hated. And now, the captain had called a meeting. Jem hoped there would be something to do, some action to take to keep her mind off her increasing propensity to lapse into daydreams about the captain.

The fire in the wide hearth was blazing. Jem tasted the warm humidity on her tongue and saw the steam rising off the other officers' woollen jackets. She pressed her cold fingers together, savouring the warmth.

The briefing followed the same lines as the other briefings — the same complaints about lack of food, problems with foraging and desertion. Jem pinched the bridge of her nose, trying to stay alert as Lieutenant Ashton droned on about the importance of a spotless uniform. Jem gave a short report on the battle readiness of the men, then lapsed into silence hopeful that the meeting would end before she fell asleep.

'One last thing,' the captain said to the assembled company. 'My man Andrews has come by a cask of fine brandy the French kindly left behind for us at Ciudad. You'll all join me this evening here in a little celebration designed to keep this bloody awful weather at bay.'

'Bravo,' Ashton said and there were general mutterings of approval.

'Right gentlemen,' the captain said. 'I suggest we start the celebrations at about six o'clock? Right now it's time to get cleaned up, eh?'

'And the señoritas?' Lieutenant Pemberton asked.

'Señoritas appear to be a might scarce on the ground. You may have to be content with brandy, Pemberton. Come on then, you rascals, look lively.'

★   ★   ★

She was back at the captain's billet prompt at six o'clock but the captain was nowhere to be seen. Jem allowed a long breath to escape her lips. It was going to be a hard evening watching the others drown their sorrows and frustrations in drink when she had to remain sober. The risk of becoming tipsy was too great. Her mind was filled with daydreams of the captain as it was. If she was drunk, she might be unable to keep her hands off him. Jem forced the thought from her mind.

The long table at the Casa San Miguel shone and on it stood proud were brass candlesticks with beeswax candles, instead of the usual mixture of cases, papers and spare equipment. Jem fingered her tin mug, as she looked at the gleaming silver and pewter cups the other officers would use, far more expensive than she could ever afford — even on an ensign's pay. She knew she didn't belong here — either as Jem Riseley or Jemima Cullen.

'On time, Ensign? Jolly good!' The captain gave a barking laugh as he entered the room. 'This French brandy is fine stuff. Now where's Andrews got to? He's been guarding the confounded cask all day. I tell you I'm looking forward to this.' He rubbed his hands together.

Jem tried not to notice the gleam in his eye, or the close fit of his immaculate breeches on those long legs. She should have declined the invitation. She should have invented some-thing to do, something urgent that required her attention elsewhere, but the desire to spend every moment possible in the captain's company had consumed her.

With any luck after an evening watching him get into his cups, she would stop these foolish fancies and she'd begin to forget all over again that she had once been Miss Jemima Cullen.

More voices and footsteps were coming from the corridor. Jem hurriedly took a place at the far side of the room, in the shadows away from the captain.

Within an hour, the captain seemed to have drunk a gallon of brandy but was still perfectly lucid. 'A toast, my good fellows in arms,' he said raising his glass. 'To D Company.'

'Hear, hear!'

After another hour, things had deteriorated. The candles were spluttering and Jem was the only one of D Company's officers not to be slumped over the table, engaged in a battle with consciousness.

She carefully tipped the remains of her brandy into Pemberton's silver cup and then held out her mug to be refilled. Pemberton started to sing 'Adieu you Spanish Ladies', then forgot the second verse and contented himself with singing the chorus again.

Jem started to scrape her chair back. She'd

make her excuses now.

This was an experience never to be repeated. Every nerve was over-stretched as it was.

The captain began to sing. 'When I was a young girl at the age of sixteen, far from my parents I ran away to serve the King. The officer enlisting me said I was a nice young man . . . '

Jem froze. She knew the song, the one about a girl who had joined the army and become a drummer. It made her still with fear every time the troopers sang it.

'In pulling off my red jacket it often made me smile,' the Captain sang. 'To think I was a drummer and a maiden all the while. And a maiden all the while . . . '

'Dash a point, whereza señoritas?' said Pemberton trying and failing to raise his head. He sent Jem's mug flying across the table in his struggles and Jem watched the steady drip of the brandy on to the floor. 'Still at least they ain't Miss Garroway with marriage on their mind.'

'Hold your impertinent tongue on the colonel's daughter, Mr Pemberton,' said the captain.

'If only I could, sir,' Pemberton leered.

The captain frowned but didn't rebuke him further. Jem sighed. He must be far gone to allow Pemberton to so slander a lady's name.

'Keg's empty,' said the captain. 'There might be another bottle or two of something. I'll go and see.'

Ashton started snoring.

Jem watched in agony as the captain stood up, swayed before inevitably collapsing. 'There's a thing. Can't seem to find me legs. Give us a hand, Ashton.'

No reply but a gentle snore.

Jem's stomach turned over. There was no one to pick him up unless she did it. None of them even seemed to have noticed.

Her every muscle tightened. Her mind told her to stay where she was.

'Give me a hand will you, Jem lad!' The captain opened a bleary eye and stared at her. Hard. 'You're the only one who is half way sober.'

All eyes seemed to be on her, even Pemberton lifted his head. Everyone would notice if she did nothing. Jem pressed her palms against the table. She had to do it. She had to help the captain. She walked over to the heap sprawled on the floor.

'Much obliged,' he said as she pulled his arm over hers.

His scent was pervasive, despite the stench of spirits. She swallowed hard and tried to take control of her emotions. She couldn't

90

want the captain, not like this, not in this state.

She pulled him upwards until he was standing and leaning against her. His chest touching hers, his thigh brushing hers.

'I suppose I should take you to bed,' she said and regretted the unseemly thoughts her own remark provoked in her mind. 'It's where you need to be.'

'Pity you're not a señorita.' The captain's breath tickled her ear. 'Forgive me but there is too much male company here.'

Jem bit her lip as she wrapped his arm around her shoulder to support his weight better. He was quite right, she'd spent too long in male company. Her thoughts bore little resemblance to a lady's. Where was the properly brought up Jemima Cullen when she needed her?

'One foot in front of the other please!'

She tried to keep her voice efficient and brisk, the perfect ensign's voice.

'As you desire. I aim to please.'

The effort it took to get him up the stairs made Jem want to scream with frustration. Halfway up, she stumbled. They slid down three stairs and lay there, limbs entwined.

She gritted her teeth and tried again. Nothing. The captain couldn't be found like this — arms wrapped around an ensign. The

91

resulting scandal would lead to her certain unmasking.

She redoubled her efforts, righted the captain and shoved him up the stairs.

The captain appeared to have passed out. He felt heavier and leant hard on her shoulder. Her knees buckled under the weight as they entered his room.

She shuffled forward. Her foot hit the stead of the bed with a painful thump.

Jem swung him around, used all her strength to push him on to it. She unbalanced herself and fell on top of him, his masculine body touching her in so many places. And his lips no more than three inches from hers.

She hesitated, unnerved by the experience, yet wanting more, before beginning to rise off him. His strong arms enveloped her and pulled her down again.

'Not so fast!'

He held her fast, pulling her against him, her chest pressing against his. Desire leapt in her, fluttered, banged in time to her racing heart.

'Let me go, I beg you.' She turned her face away and his breath fanned her cheek. She could taste the brandy and citrus smell of him as intimately as a kiss.

'Come here and let me feel your lips.'

His hands found her face, the pads of his

fingers cupped it, pulled it closer, deftly lifted his mouth to crush hers before she could protest or draw back. At the first touch, all sensible thoughts vanished. This would be the first and last time she'd kiss him like this.

That kiss she had enjoyed before under the mistletoe, when she had thought it was the place that the Heaven met the Earth, was nothing compared to this siege.

His lips pushed hers open, invaded, plundered. And she felt her body melt back into that of a woman.

And she was no longer in Spain in a farmhouse but anywhere or nowhere. Cullen Park in Warwickshire, England, and in a feather bed. Yes, that was where she would be for now and she was enjoying this moment as Miss Jemima Cullen, kissing the one man she had thought during those long past days was a nonpareil. She thought she would never meet another to match him.

She never had.

She ran her fingers through his hair, sculpted the contours of his face, pushed her hands backwards, over and around his neck and teased under the folds of his cravat. His arms moved from around her face down-wards, feeling the buttons of her jacket.

Jem started back to reality, to Spain. She

tried to push against him.

'Who are you and why are you here?' he demanded. 'You're a woman dressed in a soldier's jacket. You have stolen into my chamber in disguise!'

'Let go of me, I'm not . . . ' Jem fought against the bands of iron that imprisoned her.

'Methinks you protest too much, my lady fair. No honest woman wears a soldier's jacket.'

'Please let me go. I only wanted to help. The ensign needed help and I . . . ' Jem tried to think, she needed to come up with an excuse, something a drunken man would understand. Her blood ran cold. He sounded remarkably sober for a man who had drunk so much brandy —

'The ensign isn't here? Where's a candle?' The captain sounded surprised. 'I could have sworn . . . '

'No, no. He fell and called out for help. Don't you remember? You slid down the stairs — you and the ensign. I could not carry you and a candle.'

Jem tried to ignore the feelings that were building within her. She had to keep her wits about her.

'No, I don't remember,' he said, a light rasp to his tone.

'I came to your rescue as it were.' Jem

94

forced the words out, hating the necessity of lying. 'Otherwise you both would have been passed out on the stairs. But now I am wanted elsewhere. I need to leave.'

'And I need your mouth against mine.' He wound his fingers around the back of her neck, teasing into her hair. 'I want to feel all of you. You have been driving me mad . . . You are driving me mad.'

This time the kiss was even more dangerous. Every colour under the sun danced across her mind, blotted out the reality, drew her in deeper, deeper into him.

He drank her as though she were a bottomless flagon. He moved his hands down her back, and then around to the front, and back to her buttons.

She shivered with excitement. Then her heart stopped. No kiss was worth discovery.

Jem jerked away, upwards, pushed herself away from his grasp, but he was too quick for her, recapturing her waist, holding her abdomen against his so she could feel the hardness of his body.

'Get off me! I'm not some, some . . . lightskirt. I came to help you, not to consort in bed with you.' She beat her hands against his chest.

'You're in my arms, willingly in my bed, pressing your body against mine. It is all the invitation I need.' His questing lips murmured against her neck. 'And you shall tell me your identity. Who are you?'

Jem bit her lip, a bit too hard and tasted the blood. She had to remain calm.

'Sarah Brown, sir. I arrived this morning with my lady and her major.' The lie rolled off her tongue without a second's hesitation.

'How exactly did you get into my chamber, Miss Brown?'

The captain's arms loosened ever so slightly.

Now was her chance.

She made one last effort, pushed with all her might against his body. She made a bolt for where she thought the door was, hit the wall but feeling along it found the door handle, pulled the door open, a sliver of moonlight came through but he was out of the bed too, hurtling towards her.

Hating herself, she swung around, brought her knee up to meet that part of him least able to deflect a blow and he collapsed on the floor and cried out. She grabbed the chamber pot and smashed it on his head.

She flew out of the door, slammed it shut behind her.

She didn't look back.

★   ★   ★

'Here we go.' Sergeant Masters placed a small sack of onions on the table.

'Hard tack and onions today, then,' Jem looked up from where she sat, oiling the dark brown wood of her musket. Her stomach rumbled in complaint. And not so long ago onions had seemed a delicious luxury!

'Seems there's a rumour flying about.' Masters dusted off his hands. 'Seems there's a woman about.'

Jem stopped polishing her rifle and tried to look unconcerned. 'Good. Perhaps she can rustle up something delicious from just onions?'

'There's a woman *in the camp.*'

'There are lots of women in the camp. The place is riddled with them. Wives, camp followers . . . What sort of woman did you have in mind?'

'Corporal Bell said he overheard Andrews talking about it this morning.' Masters tapped the side of his nose. 'There's a woman dressed as a soldier.'

Jem forced a breath from her lungs. Her heart pounded in her ears.

'The captain said so,' Masters continued. 'I'd wager it's a French spy or an officer's mistress.'

After all this. One moment of madness on her part, and she'd be undone, disgraced and

97

sent back to face the gallows for what she had done to her stepfather. Would anyone believe she was trying to protect herself from rape and she hadn't meant to injure him, only to warn him off? And if her stepfather wasn't dead, what then — prison?

'What utter rubbish!' Pemberton exclaimed, appearing in the doorway, his shirt half fastened and a jaded look to his eyes. 'As if a pea-brained woman, one of the fair and gentle sex, could do the things a soldier could. She'd be smoked out in less than half a minute. Where has she been hidden all this time? The last set of reinforcements arrived well before Ciudad. Masters, I am surprised at you for repeating such ridiculous gossip.'

'Only saying what I heard, sir.'

'Captain Dorrell was a bit foxed last night,' Jem said carefully.

'Ahem, yes, there is that.' A smile played on Masters's craggy features. 'A little bird told me you lot were all passed out around the table.'

'I wouldn't know anything about that.' Jem developed an interest in a spot on her rifle. 'I left quite early, as you will recall, Mr Pemberton?'

The lieutenant squinted and placed the palm of his hand on the side of his head. 'Did you? It is all a distant blur.'

'Yes I did,' Jem said firmly. 'We had a discussion about it. I spent the afternoon supervising the delivery of supplies for the men and was exhausted. You were to give my compliments to the captain when he came to.'

Her heart skipped a beat. Her only hope lay in convincing the captain she had departed. The woman in his bed was some unknown person.

'You may be right. I am a bit hazy about last night's events.' Pemberton conceded. 'My head feels like I drank twice as much brandy as normal.'

'I have a perfect recollection. I don't much care for French brandy.' Jem stared at the lieutenant and willed herself to forget the brandied taste of the captain's lips. Jemima Cullen was going to be kept under lock and key from now on. She'd work until she was so tired, she wouldn't even dream.

There was a knock on the door and Ashton poked his head around it. 'I'm alive,' he said, grinning. 'The sun is shining . . . '

'Unless you've brought a hog we can spit roast you can go and take yourself off somewhere else,' Pemberton snapped.

'No, a message. Pemberton, Riseley, Captain Dorrell sends his compliments and requests you attend him in his billet as soon as you are presentable.'

The curl of his lip indicated he had doubts on the subject where Jem was concerned.

6

The Casa San Miguel was a very different place this morning from last night. Only a faint odour of brandy lingered. Jem steeled herself not to think about the stairs rising to the shadows and the bedroom beyond.

She concentrated her vision on the map spread out on the table, instead of the immaculately dressed man bending over it.

'Good morning, Ensign Riseley.'

He looked more handsome this morning than she thought she had ever seen him. Was that because the memory of the taste of him was still fresh, and the warmth of his masculine touch? Her breath caught in her throat. 'Good morning, Captain Dorrell, sir.'

She hoped the dim light hid the heat of her cheeks. She thought he was about to say something as his eyes raked her up and down. He turned back to his conversation with Lieutenant Ashton. Her heart began to pound again. She was safe. Her lie had worked . . . too well. A pang of disappointment coursed through her. He had never questioned the story. She studied her hands confused. Surely, this was something to

101

rejoice? She swallowed hard and tried once again to look at the map.

The captain began the briefing to the assembled officers. All the officers from three companies. There was a comfort of sorts in a crowd, Jem thought. He could hardly accuse her of being a woman in front of the other officers without being certain.

'You may wonder why we are here,' the captain said with a gleam in his eye. 'We are going to have an unexpected treat.'

'Another keg of brandy, sir?' called Lieutenant Pemberton.

'Alas, no. My head is just starting to recover from yesterday.' The captain gave a rueful smile. 'But if you come across another one, Mr Pemberton, please be so good as to inform me.'

'*Touché*, Captain.'

The captain waited for the general laughter to die down. 'As pleasant as drinking brandy is, this war is about other things. Things with a higher purpose. The reason we serve in this army. Today is not a day for making merry, it's a day for action.'

'Are we hunting deserters again, sir?' Jem asked.

'Not deserters, Ensign, but the French.' The captain banged his fist on the table. 'South Warwickshire may have missed out on

102

Ciudad Rodrigo, but there is still fighting to be had until we rid this country of Boney's men.'

Jem found it difficult to join in the general cheer. She had seen enough of fighting for a lifetime. Death held no fear. But how could she do her job when every second she'd be worried the captain was about to be shot? She fingered the hilt of her sword and tried to get hold of her emotions.

'As you know,' the captain continued after the cheering had died down, 'the French are out here to the west of us, and they think the next attack from our forces will be towards Salamanca. And it is our job to make them think they are right.'

'I am not sure I understand you, sir,' Jem said. 'Three under-strength companies to take on the entire French Army?'

'Of course we're not going to be taking on the entire French Army, Ensign!' Ashton called out.

'Quiet, Mr Ashton,' the captain snapped.

His expression darkened and a serious hush descended on the room. Lieutenant Pemberton's boots scraping on the tiles seemed suddenly out of place.

The captain leant forward and rested his hands on the edge of the table.

'Sometimes, men, there comes a time to

make a feint. To have the enemy think you are doing one thing and actually to do another.' His voice sounded solemn. The high jinks of yesterday belonged to another man. 'Today I have such orders, directly, and from the very highest authority. Now, what I am about to tell you is not to go beyond these four walls.'

His eyes flickered and his gaze landed on Lieutenant Ashton who nodded very slightly. Then he took the time to look at each of his men in turn until finally his gaze came to rest on Jem.

His dark brown eyes looked directly into hers. Unwavering. Prepared, she stood at attention and did as the others had done, nodding very slightly, imperceptibly to anyone not looking for it.

'Do you speak French, Mr Riseley?' She heard his voice from a long way away.

'Me, sir?'

'Is there any other Ensign Riseley in this room?' The tone was impatient, belonged to a man not prepared to suffer fools.

Jem thought quickly. Jemima Cullen spoke perfect French. She had had a French governess until just before her father's death. But Jem Riseley had had none of those advantages. 'I know a phrase or two. Thought it might be helpful with the ladies when we reach France, sir. Parley voo and Mad is my dame Sal.'

She heard a chorus of snickers. Jem relaxed her shoulders. A few more choice phrases and no one would ask her to speak French again.

'I know French,' Ashton said. 'If it will be any help. I learnt it at Eton. I think my accent is a bit better than Riseley's, if you need any help, sir.'

'Did you indeed, Mr Ashton?' The captain stared at him for a long time, piercing him with his eyes. 'Damn me, I hadn't realized you had made it as far as Eton. It does warm the cockles of my heart. I shall remember that.'

It was Ashton's turn to grow red. 'I only meant to help. Riseley is from the ranks, sir.'

'Mr Ashton, you seem to have a keen sense of the obvious this morning.'

'Beg your pardon, sir.' Ashton muttered under his breath to Jem, 'Captain Dorrell appears to be nursing a sore head and I didn't think he had much brandy last night, scarcely seemed to touch a drop.'

Jem closed her eyes. He had to have been drunk, blind drunk. She had seen him merrily singing away. He needed her help up the stairs, had just fallen in a pathetic heap. They had had two tries of mounting the staircase. And the stench of brandy on his clothes.

For the rest of the briefing, Jem kept her eyes firmly trained on the map and tried to concentrate on exactly what was being said.

'Right you slovenly lot, get out of my sight,' the captain said at last. There was a general movement towards the door. A weight rolled off Jem's back. She was free. She had escaped. He didn't know. She added a swagger to her step. 'Not you, *Mr* Riseley.'

She stopped in her tracks. The back of her neck prickled. The door and freedom were ten more steps.

'Very good sir,' she said.

The captain was taking a keen interest in his newest ensign, it had to be that. Like when he gave her the fencing lesson. She willed her heart to keep pounding, her lungs to keep filling with air.

The others filed out leaving them quite alone. The captain didn't speak but seemed content to fold up the map. Jem stood to attention, didn't so much as flinch even though sweat cascaded down her back.

'It has come to my notice there may be a woman in the camp masquerading as a soldier,' the captain said at last. 'She could be a spy and dangerous. I wondered if you were able to shed any light on the matter?'

'Me, sir?' Jem tried to think. The only thing she could see before her was an image of a hideous black gallows. 'I haven't seen a woman dressed as a soldier.'

The captain regarded her for a long moment. 'I thought you might have. You were the most sober of us last night?'

'I left quite early, sir, before the singing started.' Jem kept her gaze firmly on her boots. More lies, but her life was a lie. 'The strains of it followed me back to my billet. You were in fine voice, sir.'

The captain's brow creased. He paced the floor over to the high window and leaned his elbow on the sill. He gazed out before turning back to face her. His expression was softer.

Her shoulders started to relax. He believed her story. 'Lieutenant Pemberton will be happy to confirm that. We spoke about it this morning.'

'Riseley is correct, sir,' Pemberton drawled as he re-entered the room. 'Ensign Riseley left just after we bid adieu and farewell to the Spanish ladies if memory serves. Sorry, sir, forgot my shako.'

Pemberton picked up his black shako from beside the table and left the room. Jem wanted to fall on her knees and bless whoever had sent him. Surely his testimony had to sway things in her favour.

'Very well, as you and Mr Pemberton are

so precise on the timing. I had thought it was later.' The captain ran his fingers through his hair. 'Ensign, if you see anything suspicious, please report back to me.'

'Yes, sir. I will,' Jem said and waited. Would he say anything more? The silence grew and stretched as her heart thudded in her ears. 'Sir, can I go now? I have to prepare the men.'

'Yes, what are you waiting for? We leave in a half hour.'

Jem needed no second invitation and ran out of the door.

★　★　★

Tony thumped his fist on the table. How dare she spin him some nonsense about Pemberton seeing her leaving early! Pemberton might be lacking in the mental stakes but he was a loyal servant of His Majesty, King George. He hated the French as much as the next man.

What sort of fool did she take him for? He'd held her, tasted her — just the confounded sight of her this morning stirred his blood. If anything, the kisses they had shared last night had increased his desire for her.

He ought to denounce her now, leave her

behind in chains to await shipment to England. But he needed Ensign Riseley's expertise. He trusted Riseley to be able to get the job done, unlike that self-appointed fashion critic Ashton or that imbecile Pemberton who failed even to remember where he had placed his shako.

More importantly, the men trusted the ensign; they were willing to follow the ensign and obey orders without hesitation. If D Company acquitted itself well, a promotion was in the offing.

Tony sighed, weighing up the options. There was a slim chance he had been mistaken. He needed the ensign.

The woman could wait.

'Put one foot wrong Miss Who-ever-you-are and you'll hang as a spy, I promise you that 'pon my honour,' Tony muttered before bellowing for Andrews. 'Saddle up Beacon, Andrews. We are going to war!'

★ ★ ★

Tony skirted round so he was in the thick of his men. It had been an easy ride. Beacon was in fine fettle and his great coat had kept him dry but he pitied the troopers who had come on foot. Trampling through the cold sticky rain and thick mud, now they crouched behind this hillock. It was inadequate for cover but the landscape provided no other alternative.

Tony relaxed his grip on Beacon's reins. The fresh air had helped his temper somewhat and the prospect of actually *doing something* was sending familiar trickles of excitement through his veins.

There was nowhere he would rather be . . . except perhaps a soft feather bed in Lisbon with Ensign Riseley.

He had been too long without a woman. Tony pressed his knees into the saddle and refused to allow his gaze to fall anywhere near the ensign.

'Right men, you know why we are here? We have the fortunate honour of being a diversionary tactic. Throw the French off the scent, so to speak. I expect each man do his duty to the best of his ability. Carry on Sergeant Masters. Ensign, a word.'

Beacon snorted and shook his head. Tony wanted to scowl but he kept his expression even as Ensign Riseley scurried up. It was a pity the ensign's career was going to have to come to an abrupt end. Exactly how he would deal with her he would worry about after this was over.

Right now, he needed the best, and Jem Riseley was his best hope. But he also had to keep her alive and the idea of having to watch her lay explosives was unthinkable.

Tony spoke quickly and did not allow his gaze to linger on her serious eyes.

'Captain Raglan is going to take his party over the other side of the river and reconnoitre to spy out if the French have started to move.' He pointed towards a small stand of trees on the other side of the river. 'I am staying here on this side of the bridge to supervise the laying of explosives. I am sending you and a group of sharpshooters over to the other side to provide cover.'

'Understood, Captain.'

'Riseley?' Something seemed to have stuck in his throat. Tony put his fist to his mouth and coughed to clear his throat. 'Remember you remain under my command, not Raglan's. I want you back before the bridge blows. Report back to me directly on your return.'

'Sir?' A line had appeared between her brows.

'Must I repeat the orders? This is not a time for heroics, Riseley. Wellington needs live soldiers, not dead heroes. Look out for yourself.' Tony attempted to stare over her shoulder, not to look in those big eyes looking up at him. By all that was holy, he was taking a chance with Riseley but his instinct told him she was not a French spy. 'That'll be all, Ensign.'

★ ★ ★

Jem hurried off. Ever since the expedition had started yesterday, his eyes had watched her every move.

Why play this cat and mouse game with her? This was worse than the conversation with the major just before Ciudad. Then, she had not welcomed the attention, and now . . .

She marched over the bridge with a small squad of men towards Captain Raglan, a tall, sharp-faced man but a man well thought of. Camp gossip was that when the opportunity to be promoted to major came up it would be between Raglan and Captain Dorrell.

Raglan and his half dozen men were grouped behind a small clump of trees ready to march over the bridge. The faces of the men looked pale and resolute. No French had been sighted, but there was always the possibility. One trooper with a lilting Irish accent repeated his Rosary in a hoarse whisper.

'Ensign Jem Riseley reporting as ordered, sir.' Jem slid her rifle from her shoulder and held it across her chest. The rest of the men followed suit.

Tears pricked Jem's eyelids.

The men were good men. In a few short weeks, she had transformed them from recruits to sharpshooters, men who could on a steady basis fire more than four rounds with an India Pattern and hit more than the side of a barn.

Raglan's narrow eyebrows buckled. He looked her up and down. 'I hear you're a good shot, a marked man, Mr Riseley.'

'I am proud of my ability. I consider all the men in my squad to be marked men.' Out of the corner of her eye, she noticed the men stand a little prouder. 'I reckon we can take just about anything the enemy throw at us.'

Captain Raglan nodded, his eyes assessing Jem. This is it, Jem thought suddenly, if this is the day I must go, then I want to die with my face to the enemy, not with a bullet in my back like a traitor. Out here, with the wind lifting her hair, she could forget about Anthony Dorrell and Jemima Cullen.

Out here, it was just her against the enemy.

'The situation is this, Ensign.' Captain Raglan squatted and drew a brief diagram in the dirt. 'My men and I are to advance, to see if there are any enemy troopers about. When we have gone a bit, and if all is clear, I want you and your men to double back and tell Dorrell to lay the explosives. Next you and your squad return to other side of the bridge to provide cover for the bridge, until we arrive back.'

Basic. Simple. With little chance of actually firing a shot.

'Understood, sir. My men and I will provide cover.' She glanced towards the horizon. 'Do you think there are any French, sir?'

'Heavens knows, but Ensign, if there are, I want you to be the last man across the bridge. Captain Dorrell must be given time to set the explosives, do you understand?'

★   ★   ★

Jem pushed her shoulders back and concentrated on putting one boot in front of the other as if she hadn't a care in the world, as they marched across the bridge. She kept her eyes on Captain Raglan on his mount in front of her and refused to let her gaze flicker to Captain Dorrell who was standing on the bank of the river and directing the laying of the explosives.

Her hand gripped the strap of her rifle. She looked around her. The river was too open but the pine trees and thicker forest behind them could hide French troops. The forest was dense but it might be possible to enact a

114

skirmish from there.

It was not a large bridge, with just two arches, but it was made of stone and was going to need an enormous amount of powder. Jem had counted over twenty barrels on the cart. The bridge crossed the river Yeltes at a bottleneck point where it ran fast and furious underneath. It was the vital link from Ciudad Rodrigo to Salamanca.

Without the bridge, the French would find it much more difficult to move troops and equipment towards the south and Badajoz where the main attack would surely be.

Raglan ordered a couple of men to skirt to the south and join them later while the rest of the party stayed together on the main road heading upstream.

The river quickly widened and ran a smoother course but looked far too deep and dangerous to swim across.

After they had marched over a mile, Raglan halted. 'Ensign Riseley, go back and give the order to lay the explosives. And get your men in position. Once Dorrell begins to lay the explosives, they will be sitting ducks for any French scouts.'

'Yes, sir,' Jem replied and turned her heel and sped back along the muddy road and was quickly back at the bridge.

Captain Dorrell had been standing near the

middle of the bridge and looking over the side assisted by a man with a knotted length of rope. He stood up tall at her approach.

The way he fingered his strong chin just drew her attention to the handsome cut of his features. Rather than sitting up on his horse and directing, he was down amongst the men, checking the charges. A light breeze fanned his hair.

Pull yourself together, Jem told herself, and reported to him succinctly.

He smiled and rubbed his hands together, then shouted, 'Nearly there, men! Carry on, Sergeant Masters.'

At once, they leapt to finish unloading the last of the barrels of gunpowder from the cart, rolling them along the ground, tying them into the net of ropes that had already been laid out.

Jem watched as a barrel was lowered carefully over the side of the bridge, was conscious too, of the captain also watching with bated breath.

One of the men shouted the barrel was in the correct position. Jem thought she heard the captain's sigh of relief. He turned back to her.

'Riseley, you had better send one of your men to tell Raglan to stop the fishing expedition. It doesn't seem like the French are going to come out to play. All is ready to go.'

Jem crossed the bridge again and sent Trooper Hook out in the direction of Raglan. Within fifteen minutes, he had returned with the news Raglan and his men were not to be seen. Jem swore under her breath. She refused to leave Raglan trapped on this side of the river. She shouldered her musket.

'Very well, trooper, I will have to do it myself. You and the rest of the squad get back to Captain Dorrell when he gives the signal. I will see if I can find the missing captain.'

After about half an hour, when she had gone further than she had been with them originally and with still no sign she felt a twinge of unease. Where were they? She had thought Raglan would not go on much further. She must have been wrong.

She diverted from the road one way and then came back and tried the other. She pulled Charlie's watch from her pocket and consulted it. Too long. She'd been away over an hour. Had Raglan somehow returned some other way? It seemed the only solution. She retraced her steps along the road quickly back towards the bridge.

Tony stood on the bridge looking up the road willing Riseley to come speeding around the corner. Raglan and his men had arrived back but where was Riseley? Raglan had said he hadn't seen him but then he had diverted his men a different way back, wanting to check the lie of the land to the west. Riseley would have missed them.

'Sir?' asked Masters, wrenching him momentarily from his thoughts.

'Five minutes,' he replied.

It was a bloody nightmare.

Something gripped his gut. Anger he hoped. He wasn't about to go soft. There was duty to think about. The men were ready. All he had to do was give the word and the bridge was history. They'd done a damn fine job of arranging the powder, the fuse had been unrolled and he knew Masters was itching to light it. Every second they delayed, the French had a chance of spotting them. The life of one ensign was not worth as much as the destruction of the bridge.

But this was no ordinary ensign. She was a woman. Could he give the order for the bridge to be blown knowing she would be stranded on the other side of the river with a hell of a long way to get back to the British camp?

Five minutes passed. Six. Seven.

It was not as if they had spotted any French in the vicinity.

Eight. Nine. Ten minutes passed.

It was no good. They had to blow this bridge. He turned on his heels, cursed the ground. Walked slowly back towards safety. Kicked a stone on the way, watched the mud splatter from it on to his boot. They had to do it now.

To Masters's expectant gaze he said quietly, 'Light her up.'

'Sir!' A shout from one of the men. 'Riseley, sir!'

Thank God, Tony thought as he saw in the distance strolling up the road his ensign. He bellowed, 'Ensign, bloody well get here, quick!'

Riseley made no move to increase her pace. She'd never make it. She'd be stuck on the other side. All because of his damnable desire for promotion.

'Masters, belay that order. Hold fire. Don't light that fuse!'

'It's already lit, sir.'

'Bloody well put it out!' He started to sprint.

She'd seen him running towards her, and also broke into a run. 'I'm coming, sir!'

Tony had crossed the bridge, was well up the road when they met, bent over, resting his hands on his knees. 'Thank heavens for that. We were about to blow the bridge up.'

'Sorry, sir. Captain Raglan appears to be missing, sir.'

'No matter, lad. He went home by another way.' He winked. If he showed his easy demeanour, maybe he'd believe it himself. 'Come on, we'd better be back. Got a bridge to send sky high y' know!'

Riseley shifted her rifle slightly as they trotted side by side, skidded on a patch of mud, just before the bridge. Tony caught her, steadied her.

The earth buckled under his feet and a roaring filled his senses.

7

The sky went orange and then black with thick choking smoke. Tony's body ached in places he had forgotten he had muscles. He was unsurprised when he noted he had just flown through the air and hit the thick trunk of this tree to break his fall and with Ensign Riseley on top of him. Clouds of dust rained down on them, covering them in dirt and pieces of stone.

The bloody fools had blown the bridge up!

His last words to that idiot Masters were to stop the fuse. Masters had singularly failed to do so. Tony loosed a volley of curses.

'Ensign?' No response. The ensign felt like a dead weight on his legs. Tony peered at the ensign, covered in twigs and dust.

'Ensign? Riseley?'

Nothing.

His left hand screamed with pain as he moved it, but he managed to push Riseley off him and scramble to his knees. Ensign Jem Riseley's eyes were closed, a nasty cut to the temple.

'Ensign?'

Tony flexed his fingers, trying to get the

121

blood back into them. There was a heartbeat anyway. That was something. He bent over, heard the faint breath.

Riseley was alive.

Tony frowned as a feeling of joy swept through him. It was only his ensign after all!

Riseley's eyelashes flickered open. Long girlish lashes framing grey womanly eyes.

He wanted to throttle her and kiss her at the same time. Tony drew in a long breath.

'Tony?' She tried to prop herself up on an elbow.

'I am Captain Dorrell to you.'

She closed her eyes for a second — her face became as pale as the stone dust covering her uniform. Tony thought he'd lost her. Then he heard a low voice say 'I'll remember that, Captain.'

A brief silence.

'The fools blew the bridge,' Tony said, drawing back. 'And we're on the wrong side of the river with sun sinking fast. We need to get moving.'

Fear and confusion flitted across her eyes before they blanked and shut again.

The blasted woman had a concussion!

Other than the tree, there was little cover. They had to move and move fast. He regarded the semi-conscious woman. A tall order unless he carried her.

Tony got up on his feet, walked a few paces. He could carry her for the few hundred yards required, picking his way over the rubble of the bridge.

He took a closer look at the remains of the bridge. The bridge was impassable — where its two arches had been were now wide gaping holes. And the waters of the river were swollen to the point of flood.

On the other side of the river gathered Raglan and the remainder of the expedition, and he could see Sergeant Masters waving. Tony waved back, cupped his ears and was unable to hear anything over the roar of the river.

Masters, then Raglan, made extravagant gestures upstream. Raglan mimed walking and drew a large half circle with his arms. Tony frowned and then smiled.

According to his map that sat snug in Beacon's saddle bag, there was another bridge further up the river but it was a deuced long way away. Twenty miles at least, with French troops reputed to be patrolling the area. But it would be suicide to try and cross the river here.

He bent down to pick up his ensign, her knapsack and rifle and hoisted her over his shoulder. He half-dropped her and the agony ripped through his hand as if the muscle was being ripped apart. He gritted his teeth. He held her in place with his right arm and let his left dangle.

Captain Raglan raised his arms in the air in a gesture of — 'what are you doing?' Tony raised his eyes heavenwards. They could see he had the ensign on his back.

He took a few paces forward and they seemed satisfied. He watched Raglan begin to muster the troops together to head back on their own long trek back to the camp, watched until they had begun the march back to headquarters.

Tony clenched his jaw, shifted his burden slightly and started to march in the opposite direction. Only hell knew when he would get back there.

★   ★   ★

The light had faded. Jem realized suddenly what she had been staring at for rather a long time was a simple frame wooden ceiling, the individual beams becoming less and less precise in the gloom. Her body lay on a thick layer of straw. It was warm and more comfortable than beds she had slept on but every bone and muscle in her body ached.

It seemed this was a cowshed with a crib in the corner. Stone walls and a wooden roof but empty of animals. She had no memory of walking here. Ignoring the splitting pain slicing through her brain, she cocked her head to one side and listened. A fire crackled outside.

Whatever door the building had had was gone. She peered outside and her eyes were immediately drawn through the dusk to the bright orange of the fire. Beside it stood Captain Dorrell with his jacket unbuttoned and his shirtsleeves pushed halfway up his forearms. His back was towards her. He selected sticks from a rather makeshift pile and fed them one by one on to the fire.

'Ah, you are awake.' There was something very hard to his tone.

'Yes, sir,' Jem said and swallowed hard and tried to concentrate on the fire, not the ringing in her head. She could feel the heat radiating out from it and took a step nearer. 'I'm afraid I don't know — '

He turned and his eyes blazed with savagery. 'Don't play the innocent with me! By rights I should have run you through, and would have, were it not for the fact you are . . . a woman.'

Jem stumbled backwards, and put a hand on the doorpost to steady her. This was some kind of nightmare.

She shook her head to clear it, but the

images remained, fixed.

It made no sense for the captain to be here, alone with her. She searched her memory but came up against a blank wall. The last thing she remembered was turning back after she abandoned her search for Captain Raglan.

'Please, Captain Dorrell, tell me what you mean.'

'Parley voo and Mad is my dame Sal, indeed! D'you think I am a complete fool? Come on, I am waiting for some answers, Riseley. Or Rizley.' He pronounced the name for the second time with a French accent, mockingly. 'Or whatever your damn name is.'

Jem shut her eyes, the full horror washing over her.

In the dusk, she fancied she saw a rope hanging from the tree, just beyond the fire. A hot tear coursed down her cheek and she swiped it away.

'Did you think I wouldn't notice my new ensign was a damned, infernal woman? Especially when she jumps on top of me — on my bed!'

No, he was anything but a fool. She was the one who had been a fool. She tried to speak, to say something, but found no sound came, noticed she was shaking and her stomach felt as if it was trampled on by a phalanx of Polish hussars.

'Come on, what's your real name?'

Jem breathed again, taking great gulps of cleansing fresh air as a sliver of hope seemed to appear. He knew she was a woman, nothing more. And if he had told anyone else, she would not have been allowed on this expedition.

The knots in her stomach started to ease. He had to have had a reason for keeping his suspicions quiet, a reason she might be able to exploit if she kept her head. She'd do anything. Anything was worth a shot.

She looked at his fierce countenance squarely.

'Yes, Captain Dorrell, I am of the female sex.' And just in case he had been more sober than she thought that night, 'My name is Sarah Brown.'

'Sarah Brown! Woman, no more lies!'

He took two paces towards her, his brows knotted. She stiffened her aching shoulders. She had never run from the enemy before.

She would stand her ground.

Jem crossed her arms and stared back.

'How many times do I have to repeat my damned name before you believe me? Sarah Brown! Sarah Brown!'

He flew forward, pounced, had her struggling beneath him on the floor in a minute, his body pressing heavily into hers, his breath meeting hers. 'You're a disgrace to the fairer sex! How dare you swear at me! I'd rip your pantaloons off and have you in skirt right now if I had one to hand and it wouldn't put you in further danger!'

Wouldn't put you in further danger?

Jem froze. Her heart stopped for a second and then began to thud in a steady beat. He did have some fine feelings. If she could only persuade him to keep her secret, make him understand.

'Sir . . . ' she said keeping her voice steady, refusing to think of his hands holding her or of what would happen when they made it back to camp.

'Sir! How dare you call me sir — you, a traitor to Britain and her Empire!'

The captain dropped her on to the hard ground. Free of his grasp, the cold air whipped about her. Jem drew her knees up to her chest and hugged them tight.

'As I said.' A muscle in his jaw jumped. 'I'd have already run you through for being a spy if you were a man!'

For what felt like an eternity, she sat there, head resting on her knees. Then she decided she must look up, face him. He had walked a few paces away and stood with his arms folded, watching her.

'A spy?' Anger rose up and helped to blind

her to her pain and other emotions. 'I am an Englishwoman good and true. I have no love for the French. You show me one thing I have ever done to help Bonaparte or his men. For the love of God, I led the Hope.'

Silence. He had to believe her.

Jem tasted the tang of the tears as they slid down the back of her throat. She prayed with every fibre of her soul he would believe her but a sinner's prayers counted for nothing.

'Nor do I believe in presuming an innocent man, or woman, guilty unless proven.'

Jem breathed the cold, available air. His warm fingers gripped her wrists and he roughly pulled her to her feet. She swayed and wanted to collapse in a ball somewhere. Hide until the nightmare was over.

Her knees must have given way because he was holding her now. Her head had lolled on to his shoulder. Her limbs felt like lead, her body a sack of potatoes. She must sit or she would fall.

He had his arms under hers. He firmly and without hesitation pulled her to her feet again, turning her body towards him so her chest very certainly met his.

If in this world all that existed was his solid chest, his warmth, the comfort of his arms, then she never wanted to move. She leant her head against his shoulder, breathing in his masculine scent. A lock of hair had fallen forward on to his forehead. The pads of her fingers touched the silken curl, his damp brow.

'Hell, woman!'

His lips were on hers. Greedily. Pulling her face upwards with his free hand so her mouth was better available for his assault.

She let the kiss crush her. Like a spark to dust dry tinder, senses that must ordinarily slumber had been woken by him. What did she care any longer? If not a traitor's death, then she would die for what she had done to her stepfather.

His hand moved up on to her chest and touched her breast. Jem gulped down a jolt of desire. She was under siege and this kiss and whatever might happen next was madness. She must do something before she crumbled, before it was too late.

She pushed with all her might against his chest. She managed to prise his lips from hers.

'Sir, I am not a spy!' She chanced a breath, deeply shocked at her own reaction to his nearness, at the desire curling in her breast. She was behaving little better than the cheapest of the camp followers. 'And I am most definitely not a whore!'

'Damnation, woman!' he swore but his

arms dropped from her.

'Captain Dorrell,' she said in as even a manner as she could muster. 'I am indeed a woman but you do me a great wrong if you believe me to be a spy. I had my reasons for taking the King's shilling and I took it in good faith and swore to serve His Majesty as a good and loyal English subject.'

'It is impossible a woman should have served in the army the way you have! When this comes out D Company will be a laughing stock! In fact the entire regiment will be ridiculed for having petticoat soldiers!'

'Need it become known?' she whispered.

'Madam, Miss, whatever you are,' he said raking his hand through his hair until it stood up on end, 'd'you think for one moment I would knowingly allow a woman to serve as my ensign? Heaven forbid! It's bad enough when the troops insist on having their so-called wives follow the drum. There is no place for the female sex in war. Never has been and never will be. And as soon as we get out of this mess I shall consider it my duty to make sure you are on the first boat back. You should be back in England attending to your family duties.'

Family duties? What family duties? All her family was dead, except maybe her stepfather. Jem moved her foot and sent a stone scattering towards the fire.

She stared at the flames for a long moment, watching them dance.

Something must have shown on her face because his voice was softer. 'You do have a family, don't you?'

Jem stared at the ground. She moved the toe of her boot, where she had been standing on an uneven pebble. If she could get her bearings, she might be able to fashion a story that sounded convincing without relating anywhere near to the truth. Her mind raced but she found no answers, no opening, just a wall of pain. 'Before that, tell me where we are. What has happened? My head feels as if a mule has kicked it.'

The captain fingered his chin. 'D'you remember the bridge?'

She did vaguely but calculated it might be better if she slowed him to think her memory had been lost. She shook her head slowly.

'It was blown up,' he said with a frown and went on to relate how she had been knocked unconscious and he had carried her to here.

Pieces of recollections floated into her mind but it was if it had been weeks ago rather than earlier today. The feeling of flying through the air and then pain as the rock and debris hit her but she had no memory of the journey.

'We have a twenty mile trek before we can cross the river and get back to camp,' the captain finished. 'In the morning, when you are rested, we will begin. The sooner we are through this sorry mess, the better.'

Darkness invaded the countryside remarkably quickly and Jem shivered as the temperature dropped, glad of the meagre heat from the fire.

To have been stranded in the open with only her blanket for shelter would have led to her certain death. Men had frozen to death when they had only had a thin blanket against the elements. She had seen enough of them on the hills outside Ciudad Rodrigo as they waited for the engineers to achieve a breach in the wall.

Jem glanced at the captain's remote face. The distance between them was more than the actual three paces they stood apart. In his eyes, she stood condemned before she opened her mouth. He would never understand what drove her to do it. She swallowed and took a step nearer to him, cautiously. He took no account of it, bent to pick up another stick which he cast on the fire and it was then she noticed how his left arm hung seemingly lifeless by his side.

'Your arm? Is it all right?' she asked.

'Pulled a muscle, that's all,' the captain

said, giving a rueful smile. 'The thing to do I believe is to rest it and it will heal itself.'

'Does it hurt?' She hated to think what it must have been like to carry her from the bridge with an injured arm.

'Of course it bloody hurts!' he snapped. 'Don't come near me with your womanish guiles, trying to play the nursemaid!'

'You are not the only one who has been injured. My side aches and my head feels as if it has been split open,' she said, ignoring him and moving off towards the hut. She grabbed on to the doorframe for support and then sank to the ground, her knees giving way.

★　★　★

Tony stared at her. The infuriating wench. How dare she turn away from him! Anger surged through his body. He had tried to discover why she was here and she had avoided the question.

'The explosion sent us flying a hundred feet through the air, so it is hardly surprising! What do you want? Another medal for bravery?' He spun on his heels away from her.

'Where are you going?'

'To see to the fire.' Tony strode to the other side of the fire without taking a backward glance at her shadowed face. He clenched his fists, counted to ten and then started counting again, forcing his fists to relax.

Never before in his life had he been tempted to strike a woman. But back there within touching distance of that woman, he came close, too close. What was it about the chit that had so got under his skin? He had been tempted to throw to the dogs his birthright as a man of manners and behave in so appalling a fashion? Tony kicked the burning embers of the fire.

If a caustic piece of charring wood chose to burn through his gentlemanly boots and singe his toes, so be it. He deserved it.

He stared at the few remaining sparks for a long time, and not at the woman who had sat in the doorway of the cowshed.

'Oh hell, I swore at a woman! Came within an instant of striking her,' he muttered under his breath. 'Pull yourself together, Fordingley, and remember above everything else you are a gentleman.'

In the distance, he heard the distinctive hoot of a tawny owl. Sound travels far in the cold air, he thought. And light as well. The last thing they needed was a visit from any curious locals.

★ ★ ★

'What were you doing?' Jem asked when the captain's bulk appeared in the doorway.

'Damping down the fire. We don't want every French soldier or deserter in these parts knowing we are here.'

'I agree.' Jem shivered at the thought. Which was worse — facing deserters or facing the captain? The pounding had receded in her head but she was still undecided about the best way to avoid telling him her tale. She kept her face towards the byre as the light from the fire finally disappeared and his footsteps came closer to her.

'Now Miss Brown.' His voice sounded as smooth as silk as if they had just been introduced at a dinner party. She glanced over her shoulder, startled and he had somehow transformed his scowl into an urbane smile. 'Miss Brown, please tell me what your real name is, if you would be so kind. Forgive me but I doubt it is your real name. It bears no resemblance to your name.'

'No,' she gulped, not quite believing he could be regarding her in so soft and gentle a manner. It struck at her every control. 'It is Jem . . . Jemima.'

Jem's heart sank. Now why had she said that! She took a deep breath. As long as she kept her true family name to herself, she was still safe. He would have no cause to return her to her stepfather, the man who was legally in charge of her.

'I used to know a woman called Jemima.'

8

'Jemima . . . sweet thing she was, nothing like you.'

A lump of tears formed in her throat and she found it difficult to decide if she wanted to laugh or cry. She was safe. He had failed to make the connection . . . so far.

She looked at the darkening sky with the last fingers of the sun retreating across the horizon. The cold air bit into her lungs. She could keep her secret, if she played her hand right.

'I prefer Jem . . . Jem Riseley.'

'Jem,' he said as if he was playing with the sound. 'Suits you somehow. Now, I should like you to tell me about your circumstances as you promised. No more games.'

'I am not playing games. I am attempting to survive.'

Her teeth chattered. Without a word, he went into the shed and came out with a blanket. He slung it over her shoulders but left her to pull it around herself.

Inside, she felt an emptiness. She had felt like this for a long while, since she had thrown the candlestick on the floor beside her stepfather's body and ran. As if she had forfeited the right to have finer feelings. She'd buried Jemima Cullen in a past she could never return to.

A sudden spark from the dying fire illuminated his face, kept his features dangerously soft as he spoke. 'You needn't be frightened. I am here to help you. I give you my word on that as a gentleman.'

'I — ' She stopped and pulled the blanket tighter around her body.

He took a step towards her. She should hate him for discovering she was a woman but she couldn't. However, the future looked as bleak as the harshest winter. As Jem Riseley she had had some sort of life. It wasn't much of a life but it had got her through the days, and now it was over.

A sob escaped. Her whole body convulsed. Jem tried to stop it, vexed at her own weakness.

He took her hand in his right hand and captured her fingers between his like a comb, pulling her hand up and turning the inside of her wrist towards him, that point where the inside of her arm ended and her palm began. The touch of his lips jolted her like fire, made her blood run like thick, hot honey up her arm and through her whole body. From one artful kiss.

'Tell me, Jem,' he said. 'I am here to help.'

He continued to hold her hand and drew her very slowly towards him until her body was nestled against his. His chin brushed the top of her head before he let go of her hand and started to stroke her hair.

There was something comforting about leaning into his warm, hard body, something lulling. She must be sure to keep her wits about her lest he somehow found out the truth. It was the sweetest torture. The Spanish Inquisition might have learned something from his methods.

Jem sighed and moved out of his arms. She had better tell him something and hope he would understand and agree to keep the secret of her sex safe. She would tell him about her stepfather, but not the whole of it, not the bit about how she had hit him with the candlestick. It had worked before. Bessie had kept her secret.

'You want to know why I disguised myself as a man and joined the army?'

He gave the faintest of nods.

'When I was seventeen, my father died. The estate was entailed and no portion had been made for my mother or me. We were destitute, living on the kindness of a distant relation.' Jem stuffed her hand into her pocket and touched Charles' watch. Somehow, it gave her strength. 'My mother quickly remarried. She said he was a kind man but I heard the thumps in the night, saw the bruises on my mother's arms and legs. Her face became haunted and she jumped at shadows.'

'And that is why you left — you didn't get on with your stepfather?'

Jem breathed out and tried to marshal her thoughts. He must know what was coming, surely? She clasped her hands together, until the knuckles showed white in the dim light.

'One night he came home in a drunken rage and attacked her, threw her down the stairs,' she said. 'My mother died three days later. He said it was an accident and they believed him. Then after the funeral when all the guests had gone home, he tried to attack me.'

'Attack you?'

'He . . . touched me where he shouldn't.' She spat the words out. 'It was why I froze that day at the farm. It reminded me so much of him, what had happened to me.'

'I want to know about what happened then, back in England.' Jem heard the crackling of the straw as the captain shifted his position. In the starlit gloom, Jem could make out a vague outline of his face. It was impossible to tell what he might be thinking.

'I know what happened at the farmhouse. I was there. I was not there in England.'

'He tried to . . . ' Jem swallowed the lump in her throat as the memory of her stepfather's damp hands grabbing her body overwhelmed her. She closed her eyes and pressed on, willing her voice not to break. 'And . . . well . . . I managed to fight him off . . . enough to break free . . . and then I ran.'

'What happened next?' Tony's voice urged her on away from that awful moment.

She could see it so clearly — her stepfather's body still, blood seeping from his head into the carpet, her torn dress gaping open, and the candlestick in her hand. The words refused to come. She risked a glance at the unmoving face and wished she could discern his expression.

'I ran away,' she said at last, hugging her knees to her chest. 'I had to leave. I was frightened he would hurt me as he had hurt my mother. I didn't know where to go, but I refused to stay there. I went upstairs and grabbed . . . some old clothes . . . some breeches and a shirt. Then just as I was about to leave, I heard a voice, calling, threatening, and telling me I would hang. On the outskirts of the village, I dressed up as a man.'

Jem swallowed. It had been Charles's things she'd grabbed on her way out of the house. She paused as she remembered those desperate moments in the graveyard as she tore her petticoat into strips to bind her breasts, and pulled on Charles's breeches. Her last act as a woman was to place a pebble on her mother's grave. A remembrance of better days.

'Why did you end up in the army? Surely you must have relations? People you could have turned to?'

'When I entered the next village in my new guise,' Jem continued, 'the first people I encountered were a recruiting party, a bit worse for the wear but banging the drum. It seemed like providence. I thought maybe they could help me. Then the leader of the party said I had taken the King's shilling and the others agreed. If I revealed who I was, there was every chance they'd return me to my stepfather or worse. I kept silent and joined them. That night behind the camp, I hacked off my hair. I became Jem Riseley. Jemima was no more.'

Jem shut her eyes, wanted to run again. She'd told her story. She refused to say any more or the next thing she'd be telling him she was Jemima Cullen and . . .

Tears were coming thick and fast now, running down her cheeks. Silent tears. He put his hand up to her cheek and brushed them away, and then the other cheek. A tender gesture that made her want to cry all the more.

'Hush,' he whispered, but there was something fierce in his tone. 'He probably didn't mean to hurt you. He was insensible from drink and grief. Your stepfather had probably forgotten all about it by the following morning.'

Jem nodded. 'Perhaps . . . but I was so afraid.'

'Yes, you weren't yourself when you came face to face with that deserter. You're a fine shot otherwise, quite remarkable for a woman. How did you come to be such a crack shot?'

'I simply practised and practised,' Jem said, trying to still the tears. She gave a shrug. The truth was she'd practised because she'd wanted to show Charles she could shoot too. Men went off to war and she'd felt so useless being a girl. 'My first captain was so impressed with my ability he had me transferred to the 95th.'

'Yet how did you survive? I've often observed this army is full of fools but surely someone must have guessed you were a woman?' Despite the words, the captain's teeth were clenched and all tenderness gone from his voice. 'How long have you been in the King's army — more than a year? It is impossible someone wouldn't have guessed or actively colluded with you. Now, who was it?' His eyes narrowed. 'Were you some officer's light o' love?'

'No! Bessie Thompson, my sergeant's wife, guessed, and then one night I poured out the whole story to her. She promised to help me.' Jem closed her eyes as she remembered the motherly woman nearly as wide as she was tall. She'd have been discovered within a week without Bessie and her many kindnesses.

'If she was so much help, why did you volunteer for the Hope?'

'Bessie and her husband died of a fever and I was made sergeant a few weeks before Ciudad Rodrigo.' Jem tried to keep her voice as unemotional as possible. 'By that time, I knew the ropes. I could cope with anything the army threw at me or so I thought, until we got a new major.'

'Sniffed you out, did he?'

Jem shook her head. 'The new major was a stickler for discipline. He'd had men flogged for nothing, just because they had looked at him. He used to use the men's wives at will, picking and choosing. Who could say anything against him — he was a gentleman and we were common soldiers. I knew if he

145

discovered I was a woman, I'd be . . . raped, or worse.'

She glanced at him but his face was impassive. Didn't he understand what it was like for her? Those desperate days when she feared where the major's gaze would fall next.

'It was then they came recruiting for the Hope,' she said after a long pause. 'I thought it best to die gloriously and for my country. And you know the rest.'

'Damned cur,' Tony swore. 'What is his name? What is the bastard's name?'

'He died at Ciudad Rodrigo.' Her voice was toneless. 'I checked the lists. I never thought to be glad of any man's death, but I was glad of his. I did not bother to find out if the bullet was from the back, but it would not surprise me. He drove men to desperation, the major did.'

'And where did you get your watch?'

Jem stared at him. She could make out the tension in his shoulders. She pressed her hands together. The temptation to tell him the truth was overpowering. He must have half-guessed. The words started to form on her lips.

Unbidden a memory arose — Charles and Tony discussing a case that had appeared in the newspapers about a woman who had murdered her husband, a former officer in the Guards. She remembered Tony saying hanging was too good for her, she had murdered in cold blood.

Her stepfather had been an officer in the Coldstream Guards, a man of honour, with an excellent reputation. Who would believe her?

Jem bit back her words.

If she told Tony who she was, she'd have to tell him the truth, the full truth or he'd return her to her legal guardian, her stepfather and whatever fate awaited her. But if she told him the full truth, the full horror of what she had done . . . any way she looked at it, if she told Tony her identity, she'd hang.

One more lie would not make a difference.

'I won it in a card game.' Jem made sure her voice sounded firm but she could detect a wobble. 'I told you before. I was lucky that night. The cards were with me. I won the watch and five guineas.'

Again a silence.

Tony's eyes assessed her. She forced her gaze to meet his full on, without flinching. He had to believe her.

She refused to dance at the end of a hangman's noose.

'I won it off someone from the 88th,' she said quickly, her words tumbling out faster and faster. 'I don't recollect his name. It was

147

just before Ciudad. He didn't say how he had got it and I didn't ask any questions. I don't think he stole it. Is it important?'

She paused and held her breath, waiting for his verdict.

'Not important. I was just curious and couldn't quite remember.'

Her shoulders sagged. The danger had passed. The tears spilled over her eyelids and she angrily wiped them away.

★　★　★

In the silver moonlight, Tony saw the tracks of Jem's tears on her cheeks. She looked small and vulnerable. What would it be like for a gently reared young lady to be faced with what she had encountered?

A pang of remorse coursed through him.

He wanted to make it up to her, to show her he at least could behave properly unlike the bastard of a major or indeed her stepfather.

'Jemima Riseley,' he said, holding his hand out to her, 'you should know as well as being an officer in the King's army, I am a gentleman and I consider you under my protection for the time being. In fact until any arrangement to the contrary is made. I will wager one hundred guineas you were gently born whatever misfortune has befallen you since.'

She took his hand and shook it, smiling through her tears. Tony wanted to fold her into his chest but restrained himself. He reluctantly allowed her soft hand slip out of his.

Their eyes met for a long moment and he gave a rueful grin. Jem answered it.

'I like you Jem, in fact I like you a lot,' he said, running his hand through his hair. 'I liked Ensign Riseley. I thought at one point I was going insane because I felt an attraction for my ensign. I, who had only ever had an eye for a skirt.'

He held out his arms and gave an exaggerated shrug. Jem tried and failed to stifle a giggle.

'I didn't realize your instincts were that acute. Thank goodness, no one else's were. They saw only the soldier.'

'It was damned hard to get that cask of brandy. And even harder not to drink too much of it.'

'So it was a ruse, I had wondered,' she said, laughing out loud. 'I was certain you were completely foxed.'

'And an excellent one I thought.'

'But you still were uncertain?'

'I know a woman when I kiss her.'

Jem refused to think about his mouth or the taste of his lips that night. She tried to drag her thoughts away from his citrus and sandalwood scent. 'Is that why you were so cross the next morning?'

'I was not. I was perfectly calm and reasonable, under the circumstances.'

'Under the circumstances,' Jem echoed. Then she shivered and the captain drew her close, so they were lying in the straw next to each other. Her heart started to race but she tried to breathe evenly.

'That's better,' he said, running a finger down her cheek. 'No more tears now.'

'No more tears.' She agreed and tried to concentrate on the ceiling, anything but the man next to her.

'Y'know,' he drawled, 'I never thought I would be lying next to a woman in a cow shed in Spain that I wanted to make mine. In fact you might say that passion is overruling my reason and commonsense.'

Even in the darkness, she caught the impending movement of his face towards hers, the inevitable crush of his kiss that had been hanging in the air between them for so long.

Jem shuddered as the pleasure seeped into her, took the heat of his mouth and mingled it with hers. He ran his hands down her side and clasped her buttocks. He pulled her towards him, moulding her into the curve of his form.

The heat from him and from the straw below was making her body feel molten, malleable. If he wanted to make her his, so be it. She wanted to live for this moment and this moment alone.

'Jem,' the word came hoarse from his lips. His arms came round her, and turned her on her back, so she was lying in the straw, looking up at his form.

The scent of his masculinity mixed with straw was as potent as smelling salts, driving her to feel the curve of his broad shoulders, to run her fingers beneath his cravat, pulling it away, freeing his neck.

He groaned, broke away from the kiss so he could work on the buttons of her jacket. He pulled with an urgency that was too slow.

'Is this what you want, Jem?' he asked, his hands pausing on the fifth button.

She pushed herself up, struggled her jacket off. 'Yes.'

His eyes burned like coals. Tentatively he started on her shirt. 'I will look after you y'know. You have my word.'

'I want you, not your word.'

She caught his lips, and tried to lure him closer to her. She needed with the last fibre of her body to have him crushed next to her, wanted his jacket off too; she started to unfasten its collar. She wished her fingers were defter, more skilled.

He pulled back, caught her questing fingers and rolled away from her. She gazed at him with puzzled eyes.

'I mean it, Jemima. You have my word. I intend to look after you.'

'What do you mean — look after me?'

'In England. I'll fix you up with a house.' He then turned on his side and smoothed a hair off her temple. 'Rest assured, you'll want for nothing. I'll have my man of business write out a contract. Your family need not worry. You will be looked after. I will apprise them of the situation as soon as possible.'

'What!' Jem bolted up. She started to pull her jacket on as a violent chill snaked straight down her spine. He meant to send her back to England, to seek out her family. She could never go back! 'I haven't agreed to that!'

Even in this dimness the flash of panic that crossed his eyes was unmistakable. 'Now, come on, I'm not in the market for marriage. The woman I wanted to marry married someone else. Surely you couldn't have expected this would lead to a trip down the altar?'

Did her expression give that impression?

'For crying out loud!' he said. He jumped up standing tall above her, fists clenched.

'I have no desire to marry you,' she said. Her voice sounded distant as if it was coming from somewhere far away. 'And becoming your mistress is something I never considered.'

'I didn't take you for a lightskirt,' he said, advancing.

Whatever he thought she couldn't bear him to think that. Jem drew her knees to her chest. 'I'm not. I've never . . . '

'Let me get this right.' The captain started counting on his fingers of his hand. 'You say you don't want marriage nor my protection either. And you are no lightskirt? So what the hell do you want?'

A lump formed in Jem's throat, making speech impossible. She screwed her eyes shut. When she opened them, he had gone.

'Blast,' Jem whispered, her headache returning with sickening force. She refused to follow him out. No. He wasn't a man to be baited, followed, hung on to like some fawning courtesan. Even if that was what he thought she was.

She got up reluctantly and retrieved the blanket. Wrapped the coarse woollen cloth around her and pushed herself into where the straw was the deepest and willed sleep to come. Somehow in the morning, she'd find a way to convince him.

★ ★ ★

Tony was up before the dawn. A deuced awkward night. Eventually he'd given in, feeling flushed with tiredness and come in from the cold outside back into the cowshed and found a place to bed down. She had been asleep thankfully, or goodness knows what new temptation of the flesh might have assailed him.

His aching arm was only exceeded by the incessant pounding in his head.

In the grey light, she appeared small and vulnerable with her fist shoved in her mouth. He tore his eyes away from her face and pulled the blanket tighter under her chin.

She gave a murmur and snuggled deeper into the straw.

Tony turned his back and forced his feet outside. His gut rumbled. His rations were on the other side of the river but with any luck Jem still had her rations in her knapsack . . .

He shook his head.

The sooner they were back in camp and Miss Riseley was on her way to England, the better.

He started to gather sticks for a small fire.

In the stillness he heard them. Voices on the morning breeze, French voices. How far away? It was impossible to tell, but they sounded as if they were coming closer. They seemed oblivious to his and Jem's presence — chattering and laughing in French.

'Time to get up, Jemima.' Tony reached down and shook her shoulder. 'We need to get moving.'

Her eyes blinked open and she sat up with a start.

'What's going on, sir?' she asked, eyes blinking with sleep.

'The French are coming this way. I don't know how many and I don't intend to find out. Are you fit for travel?'

'My body feels as though it was hit by a bridge,' she said with an impudent grin as she stood up 'but I think I can travel.'

'I'm afraid breakfast will be hard tack washed down with water, if you have your rations with you.'

Jem reached for her knapsack, rummaged a bit and pulled out two pieces of twice-baked rye bread. She carefully wrapped the other few pieces back in the handkerchief before she replaced it next to the salt pork.

'Here you go, sir.' Their fingers touched as she handed him the bread and he drew back as if burnt. The shame of the way she had acted last night washed over her. How could she have behaved in such a wanton fashion, begging him to take her? It must have been the knock on her head. She tried for a joke. 'I don't think it will taste any better in the dirt, sir.'

'Don't call me sir. You are not an ensign any longer, Jemima.'

She bit her lip. Somehow, she had to make him see sense and keep her secret. England was a forbidden place to her and she refused to desert. 'I'm not a deserter. My commission was won fair and square. Wellington handed it to me, himself.'

'I never said you were a deserter, Jem.' He ran his hand through his hair. 'You simply can't be a British soldier. You're a woman. More's the pity. You had the makings of a damned fine officer. You may call me Tony if you wish. Fordingley if you must.'

Jem closed her eyes. In her dreams, she had called him Tony. She swallowed hard. 'I understand . . . Tony.'

He answered with a smile. 'And now Jem, I think we had best get a move on, before we are rudely interrupted.'

'Right behind you, Tony.' Jem shouldered her knapsack and rifle, before taking a bite of her hard tack.

★   ★   ★

They had been walking through the breaking dawn for at least an hour, keeping as close to the river as they dared. The French voices had faded and it appeared they had escaped undetected — for the moment.

Tony shook his head. It was uncomfortably hot for the middle of the freezing cold Spanish winter. He pushed his shoulders back and shuddered at the sticky sweat soaking into his shirt. He tried to remember when he had lasted sweated this much.

He stopped.

His head pounded, aching more with each step he took. And he hadn't been near a drop of brandy in a couple of days. He gripped the tree trunk beside him, the gnarled bark pushing into his hand but he hardly noticed. The ground swam in front of him. Hell and damnation! Sweat poured down his face and yet he froze.

Even biting his teeth together as hard as he could did nothing to correct his errant vision.

'Tony?' he heard a voice call and decided to ignore it. Nobody in Spain called him Tony. If he could just overcome the unceasing pain in his head, he could think. He raised a hand to his brow and it came back covered in water. His knees started to give way.

'What's wrong with you? Captain Dorrell, sir, are you all right?'

Who was calling his name? His ensign? He saw her coming up beside him.

That damned woman! She seemed as fresh as the proverbial daisy. No sweat, not even a glimmer on her brow.

'What? Damn it!' He gave his head a violent shake, attempted to stand straight.

'Captain Dorrell? Are you sure you are entirely well?' Her face faded in and out of focus. His legs refused to support him. The ground was hard but solid. His eyes closed. Just wanted to rest his head for an instant. Somewhere cool. In a stream perhaps, a cold mountain stream . . .

9

Jem stared at Tony, lying crumpled on his side between two tall pine trees.

A startled jay had flown up in the air displaying its pale blue wing patches and white rump, cawing and escaping from the sudden thump of Tony's body as it hit the ground. Apart from that, around them was silence. She could hear her own breathing.

'Tony,' she called softly, 'Captain Dorrell?'

No reply, but the steady rise and fall of his chest. Jem walked over and bent down. She shook his shoulder gently. His skin was burning. She placed her palm on his forehead. It was too hot.

The fever.

In the past months, she had seen so many succumb to it. Jem closed her eyes and placed her hand on her own brow. Cold. She almost lost her balance as the relief washed through her. Fever had not struck her — yet.

But Tony . . .

A lump formed in her throat as she knelt down beside him, placing the rifle against one of the tree trunks. Her eyes refused to leave him. They traced the line of his back, checked his two arms and legs and settled on the mess of black locks on his head. She reached forward and smoothed his hair away from his face. What to do?

Sensibly, there was only one thing to do — leave him. When men were knocked down with the fever like this, they died.

He could be dead within hours.

She could go back to headquarters as Ensign Jem Riseley of the South Warwickshires, her secret safe. She would tell them simply Captain Dorrell had died of the fever . . .

Tony . . . dead.

The body groaned and his arm moved an inch, his fingers splaying out as if he was trying to grasp something more solid than the carpet of dead twigs and pine needles.

Jem moved her hand to still his own and it seemed to relax at her touch.

Not dead yet.

She could . . . what could she do?

Nothing. And the miasma, which caused the fever, was likely here in the sweet, sticky forest air. She should pick up her kit, walk away and save herself.

Jem pushed herself to her feet, eased the backpack higher on her shoulders and picked up her rifle.

She raised her eyes to the clear blue sky as

a hot tear coursed down her right cheek.

The jay was merely a speck in the greenery above. She, too, had this chance to escape. She should take it. Rather than track back to headquarters she should run for all she was worth — desert, seek a new life elsewhere.

And then the risk if he survives and comes back to camp and denounces you will be gone, a little voice said in her head.

Her legs refused to move and her lips tingled as if they were remembering his kiss. Jem pressed her fingers against her mouth and took in deep breaths to steady herself.

He had saved her life back at the bridge and she found it impossible to leave him now. She could not abandon him to an unknown Spanish grave. She swallowed hard. She'd stay and nurse him, try to get him to change his mind about unmasking her, to make him see.

Tony moaned and his eyes flickered open.

'Don't you think about escaping,' he croaked out, reaching out with his hand, his eyes fever bright.

'Furthest thing from my mind,' she replied, taking off her knapsack.

She lifted him to a sitting position, poured water from her canteen into his mouth, and then rested his head against the thick trunk of a pine tree, using her knapsack as a cushion.

161

'Further travel is impossible. Today at any rate, but if we remain out in the open, we will become the prey for any who happen by. I must find us shelter. Shelter, do you understand?'

Tony nodded briefly, then she watched his eyes flutter closed. Droplets of water hung from the bristles that had started to appear on his chin. Jem reached over and dried it with the back of her jacket. She watched him fall asleep before she started to search, always circling back and marking her trail.

She found what appeared to be an abandoned charcoal burner's hut on her fourth circuit — in the middle of a clearing with a good view of the surrounding countryside. The pile of ash and charcoal was cold and covered with dust. Spider's webs festooned the low ceiling and the hut had a dank and unused smell.

She managed to get Tony to the hut through half dragging and half carrying him.

At times, he called her Andrews, at others his mama.

He managed to walk the last few yards to the hut, leaning heavily across her shoulders before collapsing in the dirt. Jem paused, thankful, and rested her hand on the doorpost as she captured her breath back.

'You should have left me there, Charlie.

Saved yourself, not me. I'm not worth it.'

'You saved me,' Jem replied quietly. His face was flushed and eyes unseeing but they suddenly seemed to see too clearly and pierce her soul.

'But I didn't. I let you die. I saw you fall at Talavera. I tried, Charlie. I charged the guns. I would have gone again, I swear it. I heard you cry out but they held me back.'

'I need to get you inside.' Jem forced her feet to move, her body to heave Tony's body forward into the hut.

'Say you forgive me, Charlie.' Tony's face looked quite wild. He gripped the lapels of Jem's jacket. His hot breath fanned her cheek. 'Charlie, say you forgive me.'

'I forgive you, Tony.'

At Jem's words, Tony quietened and his hands loosened. He allowed her to lead him meekly to the hut.

She laid him down on the stone floor with her knapsack for a pillow, and her jacket for an extra blanket. She forced him to drink some water from her canteen before she let his eyes shut and he fell into an uneasy restless sleep.

He had to live, not just for her sake, but for Charles's. Charles had given his life for his friend. She hated to think he had died only so that she should abandon the man he'd lain down his life to save.

Jem sank to the ground, exhausted from her labours.

★ ★ ★

Her eyes opened at the sounds and Jem shook her head and listened. The snap of twigs and then heavy footsteps rang out.

Rough British voices making no effort at silence, laughing and joking.

Deserters.

Jem shrank back against the wall of the hut. Her fingers pressed into the cold stone floor.

'Look Reg, someone's been here.'

'You're imagining things again Stan. Ain't nobody been here. Them all is snug in Rodrigo. We're on the other side of the river.'

Tony began to thrash on the makeshift bed. Jem glanced over as his limbs began to shake and a low moan escaped his throat.

She had thought the fever had broken but obviously not.

Soon he'd begin to call out and then the two deserters would know for certain someone else was here.

Jem pressed her palms into her breeches to dry them. She reached for her rifle and sword, and edged towards the door as she made her preparations.

'Look Reg, a hut.'

Jem nearly dropped the cartridge paper. She forced herself to concentrate on the task at hand — getting her rifle loaded.

'Long abandoned. There won't be anything of use in there.'

'We ought to look, though, eh?'

Jem leaned against the wall and peered out through the inch the door was open. She saw two men through the trees. Both had a lean look about them and were dressed in tattered clothes. They were only about five hundred yards away. From the belt of the taller one swung three rabbits.

'Yeah, in the hut there'll be a señorita ready for the taking,' the rabbit man said with a nasty smile. 'And roast beef, Stan. Whatever you want to imagine.'

Jem swallowed.

Men like these . . . they deserved to die. The rabbit man was most likely the leader of the pair. If she could get him, the other might be easier to take.

She had the advantage of surprise. Jem palmed another cartridge.

Then she saw the third man, hasting at some distance behind the other two.

Three men.

She didn't have time to take out three.

Tony's pistol. Did she have time to find Tony's pistol?

Tony cried out. Jem's mouth went dry.

'What the bloody hell was that?'

'There's someone in that hut.'

No time. She'd have to shoot them. She notched the trigger back, took careful aim at the spot between the eyes of rabbit man. As she pulled the trigger, he stopped to pick something from the ground. Her attempt to adjust her aim was too late.

The shot bounced off the base of a trunk of a tree.

The rabbit man put his hands over his head and looked about. His companion looked like he was about to run.

Yes, run, Jem willed them as she reloaded.

'The shot came from a Brown Bess,' the rabbit man said.

'I don't care if it came from Portsmouth. We're out of shot. I'm off.'

They couldn't shoot her. This was her lucky day. She would bluff this out.

Jem pushed open the door of the hut and stepped outside, raised her rifle to take aim. 'Clear off, this is our patch.'

'Hey, soldier!' the rabbit man called out. 'We're all in this together. We haven't eaten for three days.'

Liar, Jem thought. He'd be getting a good

meal soon enough from those rabbits — if he lived beyond her next shot.

She would not miss again.

She raised her rifle an inch higher and stared down the barrel at rabbit man. His expression seemed to change.

'We're leaving,' he said, raising his hands slightly. 'We're leaving.'

His companion turned on his heel without a moment's hesitation and sped off.

'Wait!' The third man spoke for the first time as he came up to stand beside rabbit man. Rabbit man looked at him, then back at Jem before deciding he wasn't waiting.

Jem's lips turned upwards.

She wasn't doing badly considering all she had to her credit so far was one bungled shot.

She pointed the rifle at the third man.

She froze at the sight of the scar across his face. It was the deserter from the farmhouse.

He raised his hands. His lips twitched before he spoke. 'I believe we have met before, Ensign.'

He spoke English like a gentleman but there was an accent — French.

'From your green jacket,' he said, 'I see you are a sharpshooter. From your captain's uniform, if I remember rightly, you are from the South Warwickshires. You would not shoot a fellow officer?' He waved his hands. 'As you can see, I am not armed.'

'Who are you?' Jem said, keeping her arm and her aim steady.

'Who am I? I go by many names. Names are unimportant. Do I ask you for your name? But Le Loup will suffice for now.'

A cold trickle of sweat ran down her back.

'Now, young Ensign, if you are determined to take me on, I suggest you cede to a gentleman's weapon — swords.'

Half of her told her she should just shoot him now, while she had the opportunity. The aim was clear. He'd raped a woman and was a notorious deserter.

He deserved to die.

The other half tore at her conscience. To shoot a man in cold blood who was in no position to defend himself. Was that right? With swords, she could defeat him with honour, and with impunity.

Jem fired her rifle up into the trees to discharge the shot before throwing it back through the open door.

She grasped her sword and came forward into the open space as Le Loup sped down the forest path to meet her.

He drew his sword from its sheath and, in no apparent hurry, assumed the en garde position with his sword held vertical to the ground.

Jem charged forward.

Steel met steel, resounding through the clearing.

Round and round they circled.

Each feint she tried was matched with a counter feint.

She slashed to her right and nicked him on the cheek. A thin trickle of blood dripped from above his scar.

'You are good,' he said with a chilling smile. 'Better than most but still you will die. I have killed many men.'

He drove forward.

Jem stumbled and fell to the ground.

The steel of his blade hovered above her.

Jem rolled over quickly and sprung back on her feet as he brought the sword down inches from her.

All her muscles screamed in protest.

'Not by your hand,' Jem said. 'You are French.'

'My father was an English lord, but he never married my mother. I am a bastard.'

'You are a traitor.'

'A realist. A Bonapartist.' He gave a Gallic shrug. 'You could join me and save your skin?'

Jem eyed him as they circled each other, wondering where he'd strike next, wondering if she could find an opening.

Her muscles ached and the back of her shirt began to stick with sweat.

How much longer could she hold out? And when she was gone — would he murder Tony in cold blood?

'Join you? Never.'

The swords clashed again. This time Jem was driven backwards until her back touched the wall of the hut.

'My advantage, I believe,' the agent said with a sneer.

With the last ounce of her strength, she thrust her blade towards him and sent his sword arching in the air, as he stumbled and fell.

With three steps, she had reached the sword, pulling it beyond his outstretched grasp.

'I believe it is my advantage now.'

Jem looked at the man on the ground, his eyes full of fear as he stared at her, at his impending death.

She held the tip of his blade at the base of his throat.

Could she do it? Drive the sword through him and kill him? Her hand trembled.

She had to do it now.

A cry rang out.

Tony?

Jem turned her head. Immediately, she felt

a kick to her shins and her legs gave way.

When she was on her feet again, the French agent was racing through the trees.

She stumbled into the hut and grabbed her rifle and ramrod.

The only sign of the agent was the sword which she had thrown on the hut's floor.

Jem rubbed her shin and limped back into the hut.

'Tony,' she whispered and shook his shoulders. He gazed bleary-eyed up at her. 'We have to go, to move now, sir. In case they come back.'

'Andrews?'

'We need to go.' How long did they have? They needed to put miles between them and this hut. 'Now.'

★　★　★

'Rabbit, sir? Do you feel up to eating today . . . Tony?'

That pervasive, echoing voice, a confusion of what was male and female, carried through to his ears. Jolted him awake. His body felt as weak as a newborn kitten though.

He became aware of his surroundings by degrees. The rough woollen blanket. His boots placed side by side. And the dry stone walls of a cave.

Tony pushed himself up on his haunches, allowing the blanket to fall to his midriff as he surveyed the scene. His billet gave him a good view of the aperture opening.

Just beyond the entrance of the cave, Jemima Riseley squatted on her haunches. Her dark eyes had him pinned. Like a rebellious schoolboy, he broke her gaze.

The memory of the fall of her short curls framing that familiar face would not so easily budge though.

She had erected a spit. And on the spit were rabbits.

He could identify the smell of roasted rabbit at a hundred paces. How the devil had she caught them, skinned them and cooked?

This woman was the best shot in his company. Tony winced as he remembered wagering a sword and losing.

Damned, infernal, woman! Rotten waste of a sword too.

Tony laid his head back on its uncomfortable pillow.

Infuriating woman, setting his loins on fire like some Haymarket hussy! He gave a groan.

'Did you call, Tony?'

Tony opened one eye. She was standing there, within touching distance.

'No, I did not call,' he said, turning his

head away from her. 'And who gave you leave to call me Tony?'

'You did, sir. You were quite insistent about it.'

He had the haziest recollection of it. 'Call me what you like. Tony is fine.'

'Was there anything you wanted . . . Tony?'

Wanted, there were loads of things he wanted, starting with her lips against his, but somehow he didn't think that was what Jem meant.

'No, no, carry on with what you are doing . . . Jemima.' He gave a wave with his hand.

'Breakfast will be ready shortly.' She turned on her heel and strode away before he could say anything more.

Tony stared up at the roof of the cave. Next leave, whenever that might be . . . He gave a bitter laugh and tried to remember the time he had last had leave. He should get married . . . to some brood mare from the Shires. It would soon cure him of this damned affliction.

Of course, he could still set Jemima Riseley up in a nice discreet villa in Kensington. His reaction to Jemima was just a symptom. Something he needed to be cured from.

His stomach rumbled again, and sent all thoughts except for the tantalizing smell of cooking meat from his brain. Tony rubbed a hand on his chin and felt the bristles. He was hungry but he was not about to be waited on like some invalid.

He took several tentative steps towards the entrance, hanging on to the cave wall for support.

Jem drew in a breath, took in the sight of Tony Dorrell padding with an air of uncertainty out of the cave and towards her. His skin was pale and his eyes hollowed but there was an alertness to him she hadn't seen since the cow byre.

Her heart leapt.

'Breakfast?' she asked to cover her confusion and hoped he'd think the heat of the fire had caused her cheeks to flame. 'I'm afraid there isn't much on the menu — just rabbit basted in what remained of my salt pork.'

He winced, regarded her closely.

Her muscles tightened because he looked as if he just might denounce her for being an ensign again, a traitor to her sex.

'How long have I been asleep?'

'Two days and a night.' Jem started to take the rabbits off the spit. 'You came over all queer a while after we left the cowshed. D'you not remember? You were burning up with fever. It was lucky I discovered this cave and was able to drag you here. Had we been without shelter, I am not sure you would have survived.'

'Where did you get the sword?' Tony gestured towards the spit. 'Are you using the sword I gave you?'

'I picked it up off the ground.' A half-truth.

'It's French,' He said with a sudden certainty in his voice. His eyes narrowed. 'Nobody discards a fine sword willingly.'

'I fought a deserter — Le Loup — for it.'

'You expect me to believe that. I have no memory of it.'

'Believe what you will.' Jem felt the sudden hot prick of tears against her eyelids. With a fierce hand, she wiped them away. 'The sword is here and you would be dead if I had lost.'

He pushed his lips together and plucked at the sleeve on his jacket before taking a step towards the fire. He stumbled and then righted himself.

'I suppose I should thank you for taking care of me . . . for saving my life.'

He didn't sound as if thanking her was the top of his agenda for this morning but Jem nodded nonetheless.

The silence grew as he sat down heavily on a rock near the fire. A lump grew in Jem's throat. Was that all he was going to say to her? Her heart had hoped for more.

She bit her lip and concentrated on dishing up the rabbit.

'There's only one mess tin,' she said holding out the plate. 'You can use it.'

He rubbed his hands together as if they were suddenly captain and ensign again. 'That rabbit smells heavenly to a starving man.'

He smiled and she was tempted to smile in return.

She placed her share of the meal on a rock and began to pick at it. What had seemed so appetizing at few moments before tasted like dry dust.

He had no such qualms. The rabbit disappeared in a matter of seconds.

He licked his fingers.

'Forgive me,' he said with a contented smile, his eyes crinkling at the corners. 'I'm like a bear with a sore head when I haven't eaten, Andrews always says. I shall be forever in your debt. I only regret I was unable to help in the battle.'

It wasn't much of an apology, but Jem's heart turned over when she saw his little boy lost look.

She swallowed hard and concentrated on the remains of her meal.

'I'm pleased you liked the rabbit.'

'Best I've tasted in goodness knows how

long. Where did you learn to cook like that Jemima?'

'I prefer Jem.'

'Jem . . . I'll try to remember that. So Jem where did you cook like that? Learn at your mother's knee?' Tony gave a laugh. 'It takes a woman's touch.'

'In the army, actually,' Jem said and watched his face redden. 'It is amazing what an empty belly will do for cooking skills. The skinning and cooking of rabbit was not something I had come across before. An old trooper who had seen service in India taught me.'

'Is that right? You live and learn.'

'I would have hardly survived long in the army if I hadn't learnt.'

There was a pause as Tony stood up and walked away from her. Underneath his shirt, Jem could see the muscles of his back and shook herself as a warmth grew inside her.

'Do you feel up to travelling or will you need another day of rest?' she croaked out.

Tony turned around and Jem could see the sweat on his forehead.

'What?' Then he took another step and stumbled. But he shook his head as Jem started forward to help him. 'Perhaps you are right, another day wouldn't go amiss. Is there a stream close by where I can bathe?'

'Down the hill, and turn right. I can show you if you wish.'

'There's no need. I can manage.' Tony paused and gave a rueful smile. 'I appreciate the kind offer, but I hate mollycoddling. Never have been able to stand it.'

'I'm not the best sort of patient either.'

'You wouldn't happen to carry a razor in your knapsack?' Tony fingered his chin. 'M'bristles are a bit much.'

'Funny, you should say that, but I do have one. It helped with the disguise.' Jem went back into the cave, rummaged through her things and brought a cut-throat razor. 'It's sharp. It has never been used. It is amazing — as long as people see what they think they should see, they don't question. It was Bessie Thompson's saying. And as long as people thought I shaved, none questioned me.'

Tony took it and their fingers touched for a moment longer than they should have.

'Jemima,' he said, his eyes looking grave, 'when you go back, you will have to tell them. You will have to go back to England. There is no place for you here.'

Jem felt a stab of pure terror, quickly followed by the quick prick of tears. She refused to go back. 'Why? Why do I have to tell them? You said yourself — I was the best ensign you ever saw.'

'That was before.' Tony tapped the razor in his hand. 'Damn your eyes, why did you have to be a woman?'

'Because I was born that way.'

Jem watched Tony stalk off towards the stream. She bit her lip. Nothing had changed.

10

Tony sat in the mid-afternoon sun, feeling its warmth on his face. Today, he had been able to do more than just shave. The feel of the icy water against his body had helped clear his head.

'Are you all right?' Jem glanced up from where she was roasting two wood pigeons.

Tony winced. It was in her eyes again, the nursing, womanish thing. 'The thing I hate most in life is women fussing over me,' he snapped before immediately regretting it.

'It is lucky for you I remembered about spiders' webs as I was fresh out of James' Powder.'

The line of her mouth was firm. The memory of its taste washed over him, made him long to sample it again. Tony shook his head, tried to hang on to some sort of sanity.

'Spiders' webs? What sort of fustian is that?'

'I heard about it from a Scottish soldier as a way to cure fever.' Jem stood with her hands on her hips looking for all the world like a young bantam. She was supposed to be a young lady. Of sorts. 'I have seen it work miracles. It seemed like a better idea than pouring cold water over you as they do in hospitals. Bessie Thompson was so deranged at the end she let them soak her with the water and be led back to bed by a finger, never murmuring a word. I am convinced the cold water did more harm than good.'

'You fed me spiders' webs?' he asked. The thought was even worse than being forced to swallow a surfeit of lampreys. 'I must have been far gone to eat them. Did you make sure the spiders were off them or were they an added extra?'

'I thought it worth a try. Your fever seemed to break after you ate them.'

'Damn it all, Jemima. Next time, tell me before you start one of your miracle cures.'

'You have to admit, your fever is gone.'

She could be stubborn when she chose. Tony raised his eyebrows. He couldn't fault her logic or the results but it was the idea. In medicine as in everything else, Jemima Riseley seemed to prefer the unconventional approach.

'Did you try the cure with Bessie Thompson as well?'

Jem shook her head. 'No, I only learnt of it later after it was too late to save Bessie and Sergeant Thompson. But when you were ill, it seemed to me to be worth a try.'

'At the moment, my stomach is famished,' he said, 'and perhaps spiders' webs might be a tasty morsel but I think I'd prefer the pigeon.'

Tony listened to her laugh and tried to think of the hunger in his belly and ignore his other hunger, further down. God knew what he was going to do about it, but Jemima Riseley was a complication he intended to do without. His willpower was up to it.

'Tell me about this so-called fight of yours with the deserter,' he remarked, taking a bite of the wood pigeon. 'Where exactly did you meet him?'

★　★　★

Jem sat down on the trunk of a fallen tree and watched the last rays of the sun as they sank in the west. Tonight might be her last chance to persuade Tony. They had been here three days already.

Yesterday and today, he had spent most of the day asleep, recuperating.

She had waited until she had heard snores before taking herself off to the stream to wash. Even in the freezing cold water, it had felt wonderful to bathe without the fear of being seen.

She clenched her jaw. She had to find a way

to convince Tony. She drew a line in the dirt with a stick, her lips curving upwards.

How easy it was for her to think of him as Tony now.

Tomorrow they would shoulder their bags and marching steadily should reach the bridge where they could cross the Yeltes before sundown. Back on the right side of the river who knew when they might run into some of their own and Tony would denounce her for being a woman?

Jem pushed herself off the log reluctantly and stepped back into the cave. Tony lay on the blankets. Without his whiskers, he looked more handsome than ever.

His eyes flicked open at her approach and she saw him regard her steadily.

Jem swallowed hard.

She could do this. She could seduce him into giving her what she wanted — his silence. He wasn't indifferent to her, his reaction to their kisses in the cow byre showed that. She hated what she was doing, what she was becoming, but it was the only way. Otherwise with a fair wind she might be swinging from some English gallows within a few weeks.

Her fingers were numb from the cold but she undid the buttons at her collar and then down the front of her jacket. Her hand trembled on the fourth button for an instant but she forced herself to continue until the jacket hung loose.

All the while he watched her with a dark gaze.

He didn't move a muscle but just watched with an unfathomable expression.

She refused to let it frighten her.

Jem straightened her shoulders and undid the last button. It wasn't going to be as easy as she had hoped, but it was not as hard as she had feared.

She felt a sort of power as her eyes met his and she pushed the material away from her body. Her jacket fell to the floor with only the smallest sound.

The cold bit into her back, sending shivers down her spine. If only behind his gaze she could see some sign of a flicker she could interpret as desire. So far, it was just a stare.

No muscle had moved, not even in his cheek.

Nothing.

She pushed her shoulders back and ran her tongue slowly along her lips as the husband-hunting women at camp did for the benefit of any stray trooper who happened to be passing.

Still nothing.

She reached for her shirt buttons without

looking down. Found the top one. Undid it, and then the next.

The cold air hit her neck and the top of her chest.

Her hand closed around the next button.

'Woman! What do you think you are doing? It's bloody freezing!'

Jem halted, but it wasn't the reaction she was looking for. She fumbled with the button as he stood up. He stumbled back, trying to find his balance. She saw his face grow white about the lips as the button was freed.

Her hand moved to the next.

'D'you want to catch your death?'

Tony stepped forward, clamped his large hand over hers, holding it. The warmth from his hand seeped into hers.

She shivered.

His eyes bore down on her. There was something there — a reaction. Exactly what she could not fathom but he was near enough and his breath was hot enough that she could feel it on her cheeks. He was touching her. Now, if only he would kiss her, she could continue with her planned seduction.

Jem breathed very deeply, looked at him, and parted her lips.

He let go of her hand abruptly and bent down to pick up the discarded jacket. He placed it around her shoulders.

'Oh!' Jem cried out and shook the jacket away.

She had played her last card and it failed. She wanted . . . she wanted to burst into tears.

She refused to do so.

He retrieved the jacket from the floor again and pushed it into her arms.

'Put it on. It's cold.'

'Tony?' She tried to catch his eye but he looked away from her.

All those kisses in the byre, in his room and now he wanted none of her?

'Put it on,' he repeated.

Jem held it fast against her chest.

'Trying to drive me wild with desire, eh? A feint? A diversionary tactic?' There was a sneer to his tone as he looked her in the face. 'Women can be as cunning as the sharpest generals, I know that much. One more button, you with your pretensions towards being gently-born, you'd have been on your back, and to the devil with the consequences.'

She had been that close!

Her heart swelled — with hope. He did desire her. She thrust her chin into the air, let the cold draught hit the curve of her neck — the curve Tony's eyes seemed fixed upon.

'Please, Tony,' she said, wetting her lips and allowing the first tear to glisten in her eye, 'don't reveal me as a woman. If you do the consequences for me will be dire, you must believe me. And, as you said yourself, the South Warwickshires will become discredited and a laughing stock.'

'It is not right for a woman to serve as a soldier. I can't allow it.' His brow creased and his tone seemed to become gentler. 'Upon my honour, I won't allow it.'

Jem stared at him, searching desperately for another way. She had to bargain with him or she would lose completely.

'I promise I will arrange to discharge myself at the earliest opportunity. Just allow it to be a time of my choosing.'

'And you will go back to England?' His eyes narrowed.

That was the last thing she wanted. She would have to lie. She wanted to be honest, but honesty would see her hanged. What alternative did she have?

'Yes, go back to England,' her voice whispered.

He looked thoughtful. His eyes ran over her from head to foot. Jem's breath caught in her throat.

'As a woman?' he said.

'Yes, I will go back to England . . . as a woman, just let me choose the time and place. That is all I am asking.'

Their eyes met and held for only a heartbeat before he broke away and pulled his hand through his hair.

He turned his body away from her, seemed to stiffen and carry an air of uncharacteristic uncertainty. A hope convulsed through her body. Might he be prepared to compromise? It was not much she was asking for — only a small retreat.

The hot, clenching prick of tears stung her eyes. Jem gulped to stifle a sob.

He turned back at the sound.

His eyes were alight. Jem felt herself drawn in, away from the possibility of her own tears.

A sensation began to well in the very middle of her as she regarded the cut of his jaw in the dim light, the broadness of his shoulders, his dark-featured gaze looked as if it wanted to consume her.

Kiss me Tony, Jem thought and wished she dared say it.

'Just how far would you go to secure my promise, Jem?' he said, and placed his hand on her shoulder.

Her shirt was little protection from the heat from his fingers, fingers that slowly made their way closer to her neck.

Anything, Jem answered him with her eyes.

His fingers found her neck, stroked it.

Jem shivered as her desire quickened. His

eyes had become black stone.

'I want you to agree to be my mistress.'

His mistress? Jem drew back, away from his touch. She knew what she wanted. She wanted to crumple to the ground, preferably disappear through it so she forgot she found his offer so appealing. She should reject it out of hand. Her upbringing told her this was what she must do.

'For how long?' she whispered. The echo in the cave seemed to make the words louder.

'Hmm, for how long indeed?' He stepped towards her, his hand slid again on to her shoulder, clasped it gently. 'Here's my proposal. You agree to become my mistress, wholly and exclusively for one year. I will arrange for your discharge, and you will stay in Portugal, behind the lines. At the end of the time, you will have a passage back to England.'

Jem's mind warred with her body. This was not the answer, to become Tony's mistress. But a small voice whispered that if she did, she'd stay in Portugal; she might never have to go back to England.

Her eyes shut. She knew she should tell Tony the truth, but there was the distinct possibility he would turn honourable and insist she return to England, her family and whatever fate awaited her there. If she became his mistress, she'd be outside society, and less likely to meet anyone who knew her past.

Jem swallowed, opened her eyes and let the jacket slide out of her hands.

'I, Jemima Frances Riseley, accept the offer of your protection.'

Tony watched the jacket fall and groaned at the sight now exposed — the swell of her breasts.

She was supposed to refuse his offer. She was supposed to react as a gently brought-up maid, recoiling as she had that night in the cow byre.

He remembered that.

Unfortunately, his body remembered a great deal more — the taste of her lips, the scent of her hair, and the feel of her curves against his body.

'Are you sure you want this?'

'I have accepted your offer of protection.'

She raised her hands and found the top button of his jacket.

'I might turn out to be a cad,' Tony said desperately. 'Don't you want to wait until the contracts are drawn up?'

'You have given me your word as a gentleman.'

Tony thought he might laugh. He wasn't feeling much like a gentleman at the moment.

Desire was shooting through every part of him, prompting an unbearable need to touch her, to make her his own.

Her eyes were wide. Her lips remained slightly parted even after she had finished speaking. She'd tempt a saint.

She undid another button, and another. Her fingers brushed his shirt.

'I promise not to hurt you, Jem.' His voice sounded thick.

This cave was hardly the ideal location. He'd much prefer a feather bed, somewhere warm where he could take his time.

'Why would you hurt me?'

She tilted her face. In the half-light he could read confusion.

Was she really this innocent?

No, he remembered her kisses, and the passion of the other night. His blood surged. It was everything but a virgin's kiss. He only knew at this moment he wanted her.

There was a column at the centre of him, being built up brick by brick. A kiln — that she was stoking with her every glance, every movement. No woman had ever set him so much on edge, had fanned the flames so unbearably.

He'd wanted her since he'd first tasted her. No, before. He stroked her hair, groaned. She quivered and his hands found their way down her back. Sunk into the folds of her shirt as he determined to keep control.

He pulled her towards him so her chest pressed against his and captured her lips.

Something snapped, exploded, crumbled.

His control.

★ ★ ★

An icy breeze whipped at Jem's back, made her realize cold had not caused the goose flesh on the back of her neck. The spinning warmth of his kiss was not enough.

As if he had read her mind, he eased back and found their blankets. He placed one around her and drew her back into his embrace. The blanket and his body entirely trapped her.

He kissed the very tip of her nose, her forehead, trailed his lips down her cheek. A part of her wanted to cry out, to escape but if she did, he would stop and the ache in her middle grew with each passing heartbeat. An ache she instinctively knew, only he could assuage.

'Tony — '

He cut her off with his kiss.

He managed to hold her, and the blanket, and kiss her and still find a way to pull at the remaining buttons of her shirt. Jem gasped as his palm hit her stomach.

He undid the final button and slid his arm around her middle, found the bandages.

'Unusual undergarments,' he muttered. She saw the corners of his lips twitch.

'Let me,' Jem pulled away to give herself a bit of space.

The blanket necessarily fell from one shoulder as he cupped her bottom and pulled her into the curve of him. The heat, the pressure of his hips against hers sent darts of sensation to her middle and threw her thoughts into disarray.

What would happen when he discovered she knew nothing about the arts of love? She must convince him otherwise.

'Tony.' Her voice managed to escape from her throat. The bandages fell away, eased her aching breasts. She moved her hands to the front of his jacket. 'Let me finish undoing your jacket, your shirt — '

'No,' he said, 'there is no need.'

Jem closed her eyes. She had done it wrong. It had barely started and already she was all thumbs and inexperience.

In another moment, he would be ordering her to get dressed again.

Failure.

Her last turn of the cards would be for nothing. She wanted to do this properly, to play the part of the mistress to perfection.

The blanket was behind her, rough wool, but it tempered the cold and hardness of the cave floor. Jem shut her eyes and tried to imagine she was a lady again, a pampered lady in a soft bed, used to the feel of silk against her skin — the sort of lady who would be mistress to a gentleman like Tony.

She did not have to see him to know Tony was bearing down on her, pressing his masculine form against hers, provoking a response from her own body she had never imagined.

He broke off the kiss and she suddenly felt all at sea, vulnerable. He leaned back so he was kneeling over her.

Jem stretched up to try and capture his lips again but he put a finger on her lips, smiled. She kissed his finger and he replied by seizing her hand and suckling on her own fingers. Her whole arm quivered.

It was so . . . wanton. Were ladies supposed to feel such things? A sob welled up. She had forfeited that right.

'Shall I finish the buttons?' Jem whispered, firmly pushing the thought away.

He didn't answer but moved her hand to one side, and deftly pulled the buttons of his breeches open.

Jem swallowed. She was doomed to fail as

his mistress. He would rather undress himself. She had no skill in such things.

'Jem,' Tony croaked as he pushed some hair away from her face, 'there is nothing to fear.'

'I'm not afraid.' Jem swallowed hard and tried to control the knotting in her stomach. She had to do this.

'That's my girl,' he said against her hair.

Jem gave a brief nod and allowed him to recapture her lips.

* * *

Later, Jem watched the sleeping figure in the starlight. Her body ached in places she had not even known existed, but it was a pleasant ache.

'Tony, are you awake?'

He mumbled something incoherent and drew her closer. They had dressed again because of the cold, but had snuggled down together with the blankets as if there was nothing between them. The way his hand clasped her buttocks, she might have still been naked. He gave a contented sigh and resumed his steady breathing.

In the darkness, Jem smiled.

She had done it. She had proven to him she could be a mistress, she could fulfil her part of the bargain. He wouldn't send her away now. Not after he had experienced this. He would want to keep her by his side. She would not have to return to England. They could be together — the captain and his ensign. No one else would need to know. They would go on much as before, except with a few added extras.

She ran her tongue across her faintly bruised lips. He had promised she could inform the colonel at the time of her choosing and as long as she could be by his side, she wouldn't choose it, wouldn't go to England. She wanted to stay in Spain. She was perfectly safe here.

Jem pressed her mouth to Tony's chin. Yes, Spain was where she'd remain, as an ensign. He had given her his promise.

11

Tony woke, shivered and pulled the blanket more firmly around both of them. He looked at the woman sleeping next to him in the pre-dawn light, her body curled to match his.

A thrill ran through him and he wondered what it would be like to always wake up this way with Jem's warmth next to his.

'Incredible,' he muttered and tightened his hold. 'I don't know how the wench has done it, but this is the first time I ever thought of giving up the army and settling down.'

Now more than ever it was important to get her away from here, from this war and back to England. He couldn't bear it if anything should happen to this woman, his woman, for she now surely belonged to him.

His stomach ached as if it had received a blow.

Always before he had lost a good degree of interest after bedding a woman, but now the feelings of protectiveness washed over him. He wanted to make sure Jemima Riseley stayed safe and the other confounded thing was his desire for her had not abated — he wanted her all the more.

She murmured in her sleep, smiling a secret smile and arching her back.

Was she dreaming of him?

It would be good to think that. Tony put his hands behind his head and stared up at the roof of the cave.

Why was it he only had to touch her to be consumed with a desire to fill her?

He gave a rueful smile. He would not rest easy until she was safely behind the lines.

He had thought last night to install her in a house, maybe in Lisbon, where he could visit her. But he knew looking at her bathed in the rose-coloured light of the sunrise that he would not be able to concentrate with worry for her safety.

She would have to return to England and he with her. It was the only way. He had to make sure she was safe.

What if he was killed?

He had seen too many women passed from man to man, having to give themselves to someone just to keep a roof over their heads. Jem was worth so much more. No, he must get her to England, so he could be sure she would be provided for if the worst happened.

He had been the first, the one to initiate her in the joys of passion. That must be worth something. And now he wanted to be the only one. So he was going to have to be prepared to provide for her.

Indefinitely.

He would do it for Jem. If he had thought a month ago he would be contemplating drawing up contracts with a woman he wanted for himself. And forever. This made marriage look easy.

A shudder ran through him at the thought of marriage. He had enough duty in his professional life. His parents' marriage was one of duty and his mother could barely stand to be in the same room as his father.

No, he was much better off acquiring a mistress, than shackling himself to some horse-faced woman whose only advantage was a good breeding line.

He touched her lips with his and her eyes blinked open.

'It's morning, sweetheart. Time to get up. We have a long journey ahead of us.'

She curled an arm around his neck and Tony wanted nothing more than to part her legs and accept the invitation, but he fancied he heard the jangle of a horse's bridle in the distance. Reluctantly he pushed himself away.

'We need to go now.' His voice sounded far sterner than he'd meant.

For a second her face looked confused and even hurt. 'I don't understand.'

'We must get back to camp,' he said, trying

to soften his tone but not weaken. He refused to take the risk after her tale about the deserters. 'We've been gone too long as it is. We must go now. I thought I heard a horse just now, and I don't think we want any uninvited guests.'

Her face sobered in an instant and she struggled out of the blanket and was on her feet. 'We'll leave straight away.'

★   ★   ★

Jem checked and rechecked that all of her belongings were properly packed in her haversack before slinging it on her back. When she arrived here three days ago, she had thought it a mean-spirited cave, cold and dark, but now she thought it one of the most beautiful places on the earth.

Still Tony was right — they had to go back.

She grabbed her rifle and started off down the hill. She refused to be the one to suggest lingering, however much she might wish it.

'I'll carry that,' Tony said and lifted the pack off Jem's back.

'This haversack has been on my back nearly every day for the last year. Why should I not be able to carry it now?'

'I thought to make it easier for you. We have many miles to cover today.'

'It didn't seem to bother you the other days,' Jem argued. Her whole life was in that pack. She felt uncomfortable about anyone carrying it. 'And I don't expect special favours.'

'What sort of favours did you have in mind?' Tony raised an eyebrow, but took the pack and placed it firmly on his back.

Jem scowled as her cheeks began to glow. She wasn't sure she was ready to be teased about last night and what had passed between them. It meant far too much to her.

As she watched Tony stride towards the river, a sudden thought struck her. Maybe their coupling meant little to Tony. He was all efficiency and business this morning. He only wanted to get going, to get back to the camp and to the army.

Was this what life was going to be like as a mistress — waiting around for her man to appear at any time he should fancy?

She refused to let him see how his behaviour hurt her. She intended to carry out her part of the bargain. There was no point risking it through sentimentality.

'I suppose it will be a change to see a captain carrying a pack like a common soldier,' she said, catching up with him and matching him stride for stride. 'I expect it back before we reach the camp. We can't have anyone thinking Captain Dorrell is going soft.'

'Have no fear, when the time comes I will happily hand it back to you. I had failed to appreciate the common soldier carried so much.' He stopped by a pine tree and put a hand on her shoulder. 'You are far stronger than you look. The weight should have damn near killed you. How you managed to carry this for days on end is beyond me.'

'Any time it becomes too heavy for you, let me know.'

Jem stuffed her hands into her pockets and strode off, whistling.

Whistling kept the memories of those dark days when she first joined the army at bay.

It was only by achieving perfection in the drills and never letting anyone see anything was beyond her that she survived. She took a certain sense of satisfaction in a job well done.

Having mastered the art of being a soldier, mastering the art of being a mistress should be easy.

★　★　★

Off in the distance, Tony could see the silver grey of the Yeltes in full flood and the stone bridge spanning it. Once they were across it, there would be no major physical obstacles to their returning to camp.

For once in the journey, they seemed to be in luck and the bridge appeared to be undefended. But he refused to take any unnecessary risks — sprinting out in the open and announcing to every French soldier or deserter in the area they were there.

Too many things depended on getting Jem back to the camp in one piece.

Why was she so reckless and uncaring in her movements?

Tony gritted his teeth.

Had she failed to realize she could come to harm? With every footstep she took, a new danger appeared — the path skirted a cliff or an overhanging rock and he kept thinking he heard the sound of hoof-beats.

And when he wasn't imagining disaster, the sight of her trim behind in her tight-fitting breeches kept attracting his attention.

There was something about a woman in breeches he hadn't considered before. They certainly did make things more . . . exciting. After they got back to England, perhaps he might persuade Jem to wear them on private occasions. So that he could have the pleasure of taking them off.

'Is everything all right? Are we going to have to wait for nightfall?' Jem asked, coming up beside him, and shading her eyes. 'How well guarded is the bridge? What would you like me to do? Should I go down and scout out the situation and then report back?'

'I can't see anyone on the bridge. In fact, it looks remarkably unguarded.' Tony laid face down on the rock to hide his body's response to her breeches and the tantalizing scent of her — soap and something indefinably but unmistakably Jemima. He'd have thought at his age, he'd have more control. 'But more's to the point, it exists and is crossable.'

'We should be back with D Company by tomorrow afternoon,' Jem said and rubbed her hands together. 'Evening at the latest if we keep up this pace. That is good news. A soft bed and some warm food.'

Soft bed?

Tony called a halt to his imagination.

It was too predictable as to where his thoughts were going. This was insupportable. He would not give in to his urges. He coughed.

'Er . . . you're not finding it too strenuous, are you, Jem? Just say the word and we can take a break. I don't want to push you too hard.'

Jem cast him an icy look.

'You forget I was in the 95th, and the 95th walked. Remember the 95th's motto — the first in the field and the last off. It is not a saying but the truth. In order to fulfil our boast, we walked no matter what was in our path, through rain, through puddles, up hill and down without stopping to refill our canteens. And when they buried General Crauford in the breach at Ciudad Rodrigo, the whole regiment wheeled round and walked through a muddy ditch. I was so proud when I heard.'

'Were you always such a hoyden — determined to rough it with the fellows?' Tony laughed. It was a devil of a trouble reconciling his old ensign with the woman he had held in his arms last night. He had to keep reminding himself this woman was the same person who had trained his troops so effectively. It was as if a double existed and the ensign was another person, who sounded exactly like Jemima Riseley. 'Always trying to go one better than them?'

For a second, Jem's eyes took on a far away look.

What was she remembering that caused such a bittersweet smile? The way the corners of her mouth curved, and yet did not curve?

Tony opened his mouth to ask but even as he did so, Jem seemed to rouse herself from the past and come back to the present.

'I'd like to believe I was always like this,'

she said, each word pronounced with care, hesitation. 'But I don't rightly know. My life before the army seems as if it happened in a dream or to another person. I admired my brother enormously. He encouraged me to learn to shoot. He also taught me to fence.'

'You mean you were funning me that day!' Tony sat bolt upright and his mouth fell open. He hadn't even considered Jem might have known how to fence. That explained her sudden improvement. 'You knew how to fence?'

'I rather thought someone from the ranks would be in ignorance.' Jem's eyes had a devilish twinkle and her lips curved most definitely upwards. 'You don't know how difficult it was to fence that poorly.'

'We must have a rematch sometime but this time with épées with buttons on their tips.' Tony hated to think how close he had come to slicing her flesh that day. One careless slip and he'd have scarred her for life. 'Then we can see how good you really are.'

'I'd like that.'

'And,' Tony said, looking at her mouth, 'we shall have to play for slightly different stakes, perhaps a bit more personal.'

'Personal? I rather thought the sword was a personal wager, a hard won wager.'

'Stakes a man might make with his

mistress.' Tony gave a wink and his best leer. 'Perhaps fencing with another type of sword.'

He was rewarded with a blush. His body responded to her smile and he had to fight the urge to kiss her and delve into her sweet depths again. This was not the best order of things, he told himself.

First get the hoyden through enemy territory and then he could devote his full attentions to bedding her.

When they got back to camp, he'd find an excuse for a long leave in Lisbon and spend the entire time in bed with her, initiating her properly into the rites of Cupid, before sending her back to England.

Wagering with Jemima could prove a diverting pastime as they both would win, but now there were more important matters. He drew a deep breath and tried to think about subjects other than the bedroom.

'Are we going to cross now, in daylight?' Jem asked, breaking through his thoughts.

'Of course, if you are not rested . . . '

'Who said anything about not being rested?' Jem stood up and grabbed the knapsack. 'It is not as if I am some young miss who has never taken more exercise than a walk in Hyde Park. I think I will carry this for a while.'

Jem glared at Tony, daring him to take it from her.

What did he really think? That she was as fragile as biscuit porcelain? Who did he think dragged him up the hill when he was insensible with fever?

If he was going to act like this around the men, she might as well go straight to the colonel even though the consequences, at best, would be a short boat trip home.

Without Tony.

Her heart turned over.

He threw up his hands and shook his head. 'You're a strange one, Jemima Riseley. Most women and men would be glad to share their burden but you want to keep it all to yourself.'

Her eyes held his for a long moment. Could she protest in stronger terms? She stood trying to keep her feet planted firm and raised her chin, unsure now what the argument was worth. Not worth losing him.

'I am only doing my duty as I see it. I still have a commission in the King's army.'

'That you do, for now.' Tony closed his eyes and Jem swept her gaze away and over the low ridge in front of them, through the trees and to the river and the bridge some two hundred yards distant.

'That you do,' muttered Tony again. He looked up. 'Now let us hope this bridge will not prove as tricky.'

'See the white stone building,' she said pointing, 'past the copse? And those muskets stacked up outside? Nobody is going to leave a pile of muskets lying about. They are French firearms, not British.'

'Damn their eyes! Just at the moment I think we're due a piece of luck!'

12

'Where do you think they are?' Tony muttered in a loud whisper. They were crouched behind a small hillock close to the white stone hut and the wind carried towards them the faint babble of voices. 'Confound it! We could do without them turning up as we are half across the river, and as easy to spot as Haymarket ware, Riseley.'

'I can't see anyone standing guard,' Jem replied, allowing a wry grin to appear on her lips at the name Tony called her.

'I don't know why you think this is a time for smiling,' he retorted, his voice lashing like a horsewhip, despite its lowness. 'They've got to be somewhere close by.'

Jem gulped and fingered her rifle to remind herself of the seriousness of their situation. She tilted her head and listened to the rise and fall of excited French voices.

'It appears they are busy with other things. Wagering on a card game by the sounds of it.'

'We will wait until nightfall.' Tony fingered his chin. 'Perchance it might be a long game.'

'They are all busy now, and no one is on duty. Come nightfall, one or two may have grown tired of cards.' Jem held the tip of her tongue between her teeth and waited for the response. She had overstepped the mark, but it seemed like the perfect opportunity. 'Yes, the risks might be less at night, but it seems like we have a perfect opportunity now, sir.'

'Don't call me sir.'

Jem looked away and kept her eyes trained on the door to the hut and waited. The first drops of rain started to fall. Jem clenched her fists. They ought to go now when the French would be disinclined to leave the warmth of the hut.

'I think if we go quickly right now, we just might make it.'

'You might be right,' Tony said, putting his spyglass back in his jacket pocket. 'Jemima, try to remember I am no longer your captain.'

'You are my captain until I resign my commission,' Jem replied with quiet resolution.

Tony closed his eyes. 'Have it your way, but you will resign your commission at the first available opportunity.'

Jem's stomach dropped.

Had he lied to her?

She had given herself to him on the premise that it would be her choice when to inform the colonel. She stared at him as if seeing him for the first time. With an arrogant tilt of his head and a curl of his lip, he casually smashed her world to pieces. She dug her nails into the palm of her hand to keep from screaming.

'You said when the time was right I could tell the colonel myself.'

'Jem, time is too precious to argue about this now.' Tony ran his hand through his hair and gave a roguish smile, the sort of smile designed to melt a girl's insides. 'If we fail to cross this bridge all Colonel Galloway will be informed of is that he is missing a captain and ensign. If the French discover us, it will make your time with the Hope seem like a peaceful summer's stroll in Hyde Park.'

'But you promise I can be the one to tell the colonel?' She looked at him intently, her hand tightening around the stock of her rifle until it hurt. She glanced down and her knuckles had gone taut white against the dark brown wood. 'If you refuse, I might as well go over, knock on that door and give myself up.'

'You wouldn't dare. You know what could happen to you!' Tony reached out and gripped her shoulder, his face taking on an intense look that said, *Don't even consider it.*

'Yes, I do,' Jem said quietly, wishing she had not said such a foolish thing, but this was important. She locked eyes with him challenging him to be the first one to blink.

Silence grew between them until a loud laugh from the hut jerked them both back to their immediate dilemma.

'Very well,' said Tony, dropping his gaze and releasing her shoulder. 'You may be the one to tell the colonel. I promise on my honour as a gentleman and an officer in His Majesty's army.'

Jem flung her arms around his neck and gave him a quick kiss. She knew she had been right to trust him. 'Thank you, I won't let you down.'

'You can thank me properly later.' He took Jem's hands from around his neck and put her away from him. 'Right now, we have a bridge to cross. I agree with your assessment that it ought to be done as speedily as possible.'

Jem blinked quickly.

Had she done the wrong thing — kissing him?

She wiped her hands on her breeches. She had better treat him as her captain until that fact changed.

'Shall I provide cover as you cross?' She pointed to a copse of trees on the other side of the hut. 'There is a good spot behind that gnarled oak tree.'

Tony's brows drew together and he gave her a severe look.

'I want you to obey me now as your superior officer. You cross the bridge first and then lie in wait for me. If anything should happen to me, you are not to fire back, not to try to rescue me but to make all haste to headquarters and seek reinforcements.'

'I agree.'

'Damn whether you agree or not! You'll do as you're ordered.' He paused, breathed and then his voice softened. 'When I give the signal and not before, I want you to run like the wind across the bridge. We get as close as possible to the bridge before breaking cover.'

They crawled on their bellies over the uneven ground to within a few hundred feet of the bridge.

The sounds of gambling and card playing grew louder and more boisterous with each passing second.

For what felt like hours, she crouched, waiting for the signal, listening to the rise and fall of French voices.

When Tony tapped her shoulder, she scampered across the bridge with her footsteps echoing in her ears.

Directly opposite the hut, she dropped to the ground and lay hidden amongst a clump of dead rushes. From where she lay, a patch of red cloth was clearly visible.

Jem gasped a breath, then two.

Still no movement from Tony. She raised an arm to signal all was well and watched Tony gesture for her to get lower. Jem crouched further into the mud.

This time it was much harder to watch but she couldn't draw her eyes away. The stakes were higher.

Jem offered a prayer in case God might be listening and inclined to help. She hadn't realized what it would feel like to watch someone you cared about attempt a dangerous crossing. She closed her eyes, trying to push away the feelings she might have for him. For a woman in her position sentimentality was an expensive luxury.

'Come on Tony,' she whispered to the air and shifted as the ice cold mud seeped into her breeches. 'You can do it.'

All was still from where Tony lay. Then she saw a brief movement. He stood up and started for the bridge.

Jem started to rise, to be ready to flee for the next stand of trees. She froze half out of the reeds.

The door to the hut moved.

Tony dived for cover behind a wooden water butt.

A French soldier with a cheroot clamped

between his teeth ambled out of the hut and rubbed his hands down his front. She heard him make a joking comment about his luck to the men inside.

Jem reached down and withdrew a cartridge from her pouch, making as little noise as possible. She fumbled with the cartridge, wincing at the sound as she tore the paper with her teeth. She had to be ready. If the man started towards Tony, she'd shoot. It would give Tony enough time to get across the bridge.

She counted the muskets. Five.

If it came to it, she would hold them off. As quietly as possible, she began to load her musket, waiting and watching after each move.

She stared, willing with every fibre of her being for the man not to go towards Tony. But the French soldier appeared to be taking his time.

He took ten more paces towards where Tony crouched behind the barrel.

Jem levelled her musket, choosing her line.

Five feet from Tony, the soldier stopped, cocked his head and started towards the bridge.

Jem crouched lower in the rushes, following his every move with her rifle. Her finger ached to pull the trigger, for it to begin. She willed it to be patient. She began to count.

A sudden rush of wings and a duck flew up in the air a few feet from where she lay.

The soldier's face broke into a smile and he turned back towards the hut with a shout to his companions to hold the next hand. Jem heard the general laughter as he rejoined them and let out a sigh of relief.

She eased her finger off the trigger.

A trickle of sweat started to course down the back of her neck, and her shoulders sagged with the sudden heavy weight of the musket.

Within a breath, Tony was across and lying by her side. She put a hand out to touch him, to make sure he was real, warm, and not a figment of her imagination.

'That was close.' She bit back the word — sir. 'Thank heavens the soldier failed to spot you. For a second there, I thought our luck had run out.'

'Closer than I would care for.' But Tony grinned, his face alight with boyish pleasure. 'Far too close.'

'You timed your run perfectly.'

'Yes I did. And I'd wager a goodly sum the French have no idea two enemy soldiers have just crossed their bridge.'

'They are more interested in their card game.' A small glow of pride welled within her. Tony had said *two* enemy soldiers.

'If I was their superior officer,' Tony continued and frowned, 'I'd have whoever was in charge's guts for garters. A sentry should always be on duty.'

'Luckily the French seem less by the book than you.'

Jem glanced back at the stone hut. No one had reappeared.

She drew a ragged breath as she relived the moment Tony had raced into the open. Perhaps this was not such a good idea — staying as an ensign. She'd worry every time he did something reckless. There again, if she sat in some house far behind the line twiddling her thumbs, it would be worse.

Out here, by his side, she knew the danger he was in. Back behind the lines, she could only imagine it.

She tried to swallow the lump that had grown in her throat.

★   ★   ★

'The more miles we put between us and them, the better off we'll be.' Jem's mind seemed to be intent on playing the scene with the soldier over as they strode along the road. 'I am prepared to walk all night if necessary.'

218

'You may be, but we'll need to rest soon. Remember I'm recovering from fever.' Tony mopped his forehead. 'Amazing how much strength a fever saps. When you have to do the smallest thing, your body protests.'

'It is hard to recall but how much protesting did you do last night?' she said with a laugh in her voice.

'Just my luck to be saddled with a saucy wench.' Tony gave a roguish smile that held promises her body longed to claim.

'I may be a saucy wench, but at least I can shoot straight.' Jem put her hands on her hips and glared at him, daring him to disagree with her.

'A wench who can shoot straight. What more could a man wish for?'

Tony made a face of mock contrition.

The corners of her mouth twitched. She refused to laugh, despite the look becoming more comical by the moment.

★ ★ ★

Later Jem wondered whether it would have been wise to take shelter in a disused hut they had passed, rather than press on as she had insisted. Then, there had only been a light drizzle falling from the sky. Now, she hunched her shoulders against the driving rain and tried to keep pace with Tony's strides.

The landscape they crossed was bleak, desolate and empty with few trees or houses. Was that a good sign or bad, Jem wondered as they passed an abandoned farm where only a mangy dog sniffed in the courtyard?

Had the bridge blowing feint worked as it had been strategically intended? Or had the French started to marshal their scattered forces elsewhere?

She doubted whether Badajoz would be as easy to take as Ciudad Rodrigo. And it appeared if they were the diversion, Wellington would try for the last remaining French held fort on the border with Portugal before going towards Salamanca.

'It should be a clear run from now,' she said, thinking aloud. 'I would not have thought the French were in this area.'

'Not according to the intelligence I looked at before we left Ciudad Rodrigo, but intelligence is not always correct and we still have the damned deserters to worry about, as well as Don Julian's guerrillas. They lack the discipline of regular soldiers.'

'Are you seriously suggesting they will attack two British officers? If they do, we can always return fire.'

Jem felt Tony's hand on her shoulder. She

looked up and saw his grave face and clenched jaw. It was a complete contrast to the boyish grin of less than two hours ago.

'That is the last thing we want,' he said. 'My only consolation is that traitors are cowards.'

Jem remembered the showdown at the charcoal burner's hut, and how the first two deserters had run away at the first sign of resistance from her. And how the other one — their leader — had escaped the moment she had hesitated with her sword.

'Is there a known problem with deserters in the area?' she asked.

'Nothing to worry your pretty little head about.'

Jem stopped dead in her tracks. She crossed her arms and faced Tony.

'I am a serving British officer, Tony Dorrell, who recently engaged a small band of deserters. I deserve more than pap to be fed to simpletons and half-wits. Tell me the truth.'

For a long moment, Tony didn't answer. The slosh of their boots began to grate and Jem wondered if she should push for an answer.

'There is a theory the deserters in the area are organized and funded by France,' he said eventually. 'Combine that with a group of

Spanish guerrillas who seem more interested in lining their own pockets and terrorizing the local population than fighting the French and you can see why much of my time has been spent chasing these men.'

'And what was the name of the leader?' Jem asked, her blood running cold as she remembered the mocking comments from her sword-fighting deserter, the deserter she had twice failed to kill.

'He is called Le Loup — the wolf. But I have heard conflicting reports about him. He might be a French spy but is fluent in English.'

'Could Le Loup be the man we interrupted in the farmhouse?' Jem asked with a tremor in her voice. 'The man I fought for the sword. The one who escaped?'

'You need to let that go. Stop blaming yourself.' Tony paused in his stride and turned to face her. He put both hands on her shoulders. 'Jem, you saved the girl. That deserter was just one of many thieves and rogues who found British army life too difficult and preferred the life of a traitor. No, that man is probably dead or long gone from this area. As for that man you claim you fought, he will be long gone as well.'

Jem bit back the furious response threatening to erupt from her lips. She had told Tony

222

about the deserters at the charcoal burner's hut and it was clear he didn't believe the whole of it. But arguing with him would only lead to him retracting his promise. She knew the truth of what had happened. That should be enough for her.

'Yes, of course, I will try to let it go, as you say.' She tried to make her voice light, to keep the seething under control.

Tony dropped a light kiss on her nose, the slightest of touches but enough to make her shiver. It was nearly enough to make her want to remain a woman.

'There, that's my girl. Everyone makes errors. A very wise friend told me that once. Learn from them, but refuse to let them haunt your dreams.'

Jem glanced at her boots. If only Tony realized how serious her mistakes were.

★ ★ ★

The driving rain increased throughout the afternoon, until Tony's boots were caked in mud. Andrews would be most displeased, Tony thought skirting around another puddle. Jem, he noted, seemed indifferent to the state of her boots, marching through every pool of mud in her path, keeping to her chosen line.

Every bone in Tony's body ached.

The cursed fever sapped more of his strength than he wanted to admit. The world blurred, before coming sharply into focus.

'I think we ought to stop at the farmhouse up there.' Tony pointed to a group of buildings shimmering in the distance. 'We can get some shelter and food.'

'If you wish, but I could go on for a few more miles, if necessary.'

Jem showed few effects of the long march or the crossing of the bridge. She looked fresh. The rain had soaked her hair so that small curls were sticking to her face.

Drops of water ran from the tips of these curls down, and down her neck. Tony groaned, a different pain overtaking him.

'Jem, we are not in some kind of endurance test. It is better to rest and then start afresh in the morning. How about a bite of warm food and a bit of hay on which to lay my head?'

There were, admittedly, other places he could think of that were even more pleasant to lay his head.

★   ★   ★

About five hundred feet from the farmhouse, Jem turned her head at the whinny of a horse. She looked and then looked again.

'Isn't that Lieutenant Ashton's mare, the one with the three white socks and blaze on its forehead?' she asked, pointing to the horse standing tethered at the side of the farmhouse.

'What the blazes is Ashton doing here? He should be miles away.'

'Looking for us?'

'No.' Tony fingered his chin. 'Captain Raglan knows me well enough to figure I'll turn up like a bad penny, sooner or later.' He shook his head and put his hand on her forearm. 'Something is up. I can feel it in my bones.'

Her every sinew wanted to draw closer to him, feel his embrace, but now they were two soldiers, not lovers.

The air had that heavy oppressive feeling which she always experienced just before an engagement began. But her instincts could be wrong — all seemed at peace in the farmyard.

'What should we do?' she whispered.

'What you should do is to stay put until I give the signal.' Tony leant down and drew his boots backwards and forwards across a large stone to remove some of the mud. Then he stood up straight and fixed his gaze on her. 'If they are chasing deserters, I don't want you becoming involved, becoming a distraction. Do you understand me, Jemima?'

'Why not? I am a soldier. I can assist.' Jem closed her eyes and willed the tears of frustration not to come.

Before he had found out she was a woman, Tony Dorrell would have had no hesitation in sending her ahead. He would have said *Right, Jem lad, off you go and earn your spurs.* Now it was *Jemima, you must stay here, behind, because you are a woman and in case you endanger the men.*

'I refuse to allow you to risk your life.' Tony raised his hand and stroked Jem's hair. She wanted to buckle at the touch. It was too tender; submitting to his authority was too easy. 'If anything should happen to you, I'd find it impossible to forgive myself for putting you there.'

And if anything should happen to you? Jem held back the words with great difficulty.

'I have been in these situations before and have acquitted myself well,' she protested.

'It is something that shall haunt my nights until my dying day. Jem, as your superior officer, I order you to stay behind.' His eyes were as hard as coals.

'But — ' she began, trying to marshal her excuses.

Tony waved an impatient hand, a twinkle growing in his eye.

'No buts, Ensign Riseley. You were the one

who pointed out at the bridge you had not yet resigned your commission. And as such, you must obey the direct orders of a superior officer.'

Jem bowed her head. What a time for him to pull rank.

He had boxed her in very neatly, and she would have to endure another session of torture where she would have to wait for his return.

Helpless.

She would be just a woman waiting to see if her man would make it back from battle. Like the camp wives and followers who crowded around the fires, knitting and twittering the latest gossip while they waited for word of their men. The one thing she could not do was to give Tony a reason for breaking his reluctantly given promise to her.

'Very well, Captain, but I warn you. If Lieutenant Ashton is there, you are to remember your promise. If you wish me to obey your orders, I shall have to remain Ensign Jem Riseley.'

Tony gave a wry smile, kissed the tips of his fingers and pressed them to her lips, which stilled her. '*Touché*, Ensign. I have given you my word and shall not break it.'

Her heart was about to fracture. He could stun her with the senses any time he fancied.

Jem squared her shoulders, stood up straighter and showed she was prepared to follow orders.

There was probably a very simple reason why Lieutenant Ashton's horse was here. But she would have felt better if she could see a member of D Company moving about the place. The farm looked abandoned except for the small mauve curl of smoke from the chimney, and the horse.

She held out her hand as manfully as possible.

'Good luck, sir.' She kept her voice steady.

'To hell with that, Jemima,' Tony said heavily and pulled her roughly into his arms. He pressed his lips purposefully to hers — invaded, stole, plundered — a lightning raid that was over in a moment. Her senses had been stunned and she was left trembling.

Like a love-struck helpless female, as Tony would say.

She raised a hand to his face, and he brushed her palm with his lips.

'That is the sort of thing I need for luck,' he said, striding off. He did not even take one backwards glance, Jem thought, with a pang in her heart.

Jem bit her lip and watched with bated breath as he reached the farmhouse and rapped smartly on the door.

There was a brief conversation with the dark-eyed woman who answered, but Tony did not turn around and beckon to her. Instead, he went inside and the door was shut behind him with a decisive thud.

Jem settled down with her back pressing against the oak tree. She would prove to Tony she was capable of keeping her word and obeying orders. She was not some headstrong flighty female with nary a thought in her head, but a decorated officer of His Majesty's army, equal to any task set before her.

To pass the time Jem reached over to her haversack and pulled out Charles's watch. She opened the timepiece and then indulged herself by rereading the inscription inside. What would he say if he saw her now? She liked to think he'd understand. He had encouraged in her a passion for swords and other boyish pursuits, laughing that she'd need an officer for a husband to keep her up to the mark.

Twenty past four. She would give Tony ten more minutes, and then, if he hadn't returned his orders could hang. She refused to sit here on the freezing cold ground with rain beating down on her head while he was in there in the warmth and light, being offered tasty victuals by the farmer's wife.

She swallowed hard. Was this what being a

mistress was going to be like? Waiting until such a time as he honoured to grace her with his presence, on the sidelines of his life.

The scene swam before her eyes, and she blinked back the tears. Not quite the future Charlie might have envisaged for his sister. But that had been several lifetimes ago.

She stuffed the watch back into her haversack, making sure it occupied its usual place — right next to the book Charles had given her for her seventeenth birthday. Two more minutes. She started to shoulder her knapsack, to make ready.

A movement in the farmyard caught the corner of her eye and she turned her head. Her heart sank to the bottom of her boots. The man boldly striding across the yard was the French agent she had crossed swords with at the hut — Le Loup. The fresh scar on his face was clearly visible.

What the devil was he doing here and where was the sentry from D Company?

13

The French agent gave a low whistle.

At first, nothing happened. Then Jem heard a rustle in the wood behind her. She pressed her back to the tree and crouched low.

Three men emerged from the wood, their faces bearing the hungry look of wolves.

In their hands they carried British muskets, but they wore a variety of rags and cast-offs. One man held a cutlass. Around his shoulders hung the tattered remains of a maroon evening cloak. Jem shuddered to think of what fate had befallen the woman whose shoulders it had formerly graced.

Jem heard her heart pound in her ears. She glanced at the door where Tony had gone in. Did he know these villains were here? Did he realize what was about to happen?

She grasped the hilt of her sword, remembering the orders Tony had given before she crossed the bridge.

In the event of trouble, she was to race for headquarters. Instantly she rejected the idea. If she returned to headquarters for more troops, there was every possibility Tony would be dead by the time she was able to arrive back.

Her stomach knotted and she began her battle preparations.

Her only hope was to create a diversion. She was no fool. The number of deserters meant she had little chance of overwhelming them, but she could at least alert the rest of the company to the danger. If the worst had happened, and they were captured, perhaps her diversion would give them the time they needed to escape.

She drew a deep breath. She was disobeying a direct order. When it was a choice between possibly saving Tony's life and an order given under vastly different circumstances, she knew which she chose.

Jem eased off her haversack as quietly as she could and placed it on the ground where it would be safe. She began to crawl with her musket towards the farmyard to investigate.

She followed the men, keeping cover between her and them. They entered a barn on the perimeter of the farm buildings. Jem slipped in behind them and hid in a stall, waiting to hear what they planned to do.

Cautiously she raised her head and began to count the deserters. Eight.

Jem sank down in the disused straw, making herself as small as possible. Going in like some avenging angel would be suicide. She had to think, to plan — all the while she knew Tony was in the farmhouse either captured or blissfully unaware of what was about to happen.

★ ★ ★

Tony's mouth fell open as he surveyed the scene inside the farmhouse.

Instead of Lieutenant Ashton bustling about or being in the middle of an operation, he sat in an elaborately carved dark wood chair in the house with a wine glass in one hand and a young black-eyed lovely in the other sitting on his knee. Tony counted eight members of D Company besides Ashton who were sprawled about the place in various stages of undress. Several other women were sitting intertwined with them.

Trooper Hook had a bottle of wine halfway to his lips, the wine now poured on to his breeches as he viewed their captain with a dumbfounded expression on his face.

Ashton's eyes widened, his countenance whitened. 'Captain Dorrell, sir!'

The lovely on Ashton's knee stared at him boldly, too boldly by half. She licked her lips and flicked her long black hair, arching her neck as she did so, rustling her skirts even higher above her ankles. A clear invitation.

Tony frowned. He preferred Jem with her chopped hair and in her breeches any day. Actually, he preferred Jem without her breeches. Desire came at this most inconvenient moment and Tony battened it down with anger at the scene before him.

'Mr Ashton, what the devil is the meaning of this? Explain yourself at once!'

Ashton jerked to his feet sending the Spanish señorita sliding to the floor with squeals of protest.

The rest of the soldiers slowly followed his lead, shuffling and trying to tuck their shirts back in their breeches.

'What are you doing here?' Ashton stammered. 'I . . . we . . . thought you must be dead. Colonel Garroway gave me command of the company . . . temporarily.'

Tony watched the men as their eyes widened, fear crossed their faces. Trooper Hook ineffectually dabbed at the spreading red stain on his front. He gave a sheepish grin, gave up and stood gently swaying. It crossed Tony's mind Ensign Riseley would never have allowed such a farce. The ensign always ensured the men were battle ready.

'Reports of my demise seem to be premature,' Tony said and fixed his eye on Ashton. 'I am quite hale and hearty — I can assure you of that. But my question, Mr Ashton, is not what I am doing here but what are you?'

'Looking for deserters, sir.'

Hell, was the man shaking? Tony frowned, searching for a reason.

'And this?' He swept a hand around the room, indicating the empty bottles of wine, the half-dressed women and the remains of a meal. 'This is how you search for deserters, Mr Ashton? Things appear to have changed in my absence.'

'Sir?'

'Is this how you conduct a mission in hostile territory? Consorting with women and drinking wine? Or perhaps in my absence Wellington has decided to move the army?'

He watched with satisfaction as a red flush spread over the lieutenant's cheek.

'No, sir.' Ashton grabbed his jacket from the señorita and stuffed his arms into it, fumbling with the buttons and having to try two before he achieved some sort of order. 'The situation is this. We received information late yesterday that Le Loup was in this area, and proceeded to this farmhouse. After we secured the perimeter and established the fact that Don Julian's intelligence was faulty, the owner invited us in for a spot of repast. He was grateful for the presence of His Majesty's army. I could hardly refuse the invite, sir. We are to maintain good relations with the natives, sir. The deserter has long gone from the area.'

Tony closed his eyes and counted to ten.

'And how many men did you have with you, Mr Ashton?'

'Eight, sir.'

'Exactly how long have you been partaking of this hospitality?'

Tony could see the red spots of spilt wine glistening on Ashton's cravat. Ashton shook not from fear, but unless Tony was much mistaken, his trembling was directly attributable to the quantity of alcohol he had consumed on duty.

'I am not sure, sir.' Ashton swayed for a second and then made a wild grab for the chair for support. 'A while I think. The señorita keeps bringing out more bottles. Not since Lisbon have I tasted such fine wine, sir.'

Tony tried to hold on to his temper, to keep his voice even. It did very little good to shout when a man was as deep in his cups as Ashton. He had always considered Ashton a bit of an imbecile but this was nothing short of wanton recklessness.

Tony counted again to make certain. Eight troopers had been partaking of the wine.

'And who is guarding the perimeter, Ashton?'

Tony narrowed his eyes, and kept his voice ice cold. Ashton blanched, used his finger to count the soldiers and then started trying to count again.

'Yes, Mr Ashton, I count eight soldiers as well.' Tony knew his voice dripped sarcasm. 'I hope for the sake of your future career that nothing untoward has happened and that these people are as you say — being hospitable.'

★　★　★

Jem sat with her back to the barn's wall, one eye on the door and the other on the ever-growing band of deserters; twenty at last count, mostly British but with one or two French to make up the numbers.

The low murmur of several deserters' voices was clearly audible. Where in the blazes was D Company? Surely Ashton was not that much of an idiot? He had to have left someone on sentry duty.

They were at war.

Jem crept out of the barn, looking for the sentry, hoping against hope she'd fail to discover a body. After a quick search of the perimeter revealed no British soldier, she returned to the barn.

More men, deserters, in all manner of dress had arrived in her absence. The barn floor fairly crawled with them.

A whole nest of rats massing for the attack, led by the rat-in-chief, the French agent, the man called Le Loup.

'This is when we teach the British army a lesson. They have captured too many of our friends, men like you and I who only deserted because we had no food,' she heard the French agent say. His accent sounded much less pronounced, almost British. 'How many are in there enjoying Maria's company? Nine?'

'Another one arrived a few moments ago, sor. But to be sure it is no more than nine,' said a swarthy-looking fellow sporting a blue bandana about his neck and speaking with an Irish lilt. His gold tooth gleamed in the dying light of the day. 'We should be able to kill them without any trouble at all. Maria has kept them well entertained, well laced with wine, sor.'

A hole developed in the base of Jem's stomach. She had a sour taste in her mouth. Her hunch had been confirmed. Twice she had missed her chance to finish off Le Loup. This time she would do it. Her moments of hesitation had already cost the British army dear. She would make sure it did not cost any more lives.

'Does anyone know what manner of soldier has arrived?'

'A captain,' came the swift reply.

Le Loup rubbed his hands together. 'Good. I suppose it is too much to hope for that it would be Captain Dorrell. He is one man I most especially would like to see dead. We have a score to settle, he and I. He has interrupted my sphere of operations once too often. Nobody does that without paying the supreme penalty. What do you wager when he dies, he bleats like a stuck pig?'

Jem leant her head back against the wall and tried to breathe evenly.

Ashton, the fool, had walked straight into a trap with his men. With the men she had trained, her men.

No doubt with eyes wide open and spouting pleasantries about the weather as he did so. A great surge of anger welled up inside her. Ashton with his snide comments and his 'oh so gentlemanly' manner had put the lives of all of them at risk.

'Are we all set?' Le Loup growled. 'Shipshape in this man's army?'

'All present and accounted for.' The deserters seemed to think this a great joke.

Jem inched her head around the corner and

counted. Forty men. She could never hope to prevail against forty on her own. But she could even the odds, give Tony a chance to survive rather than be taken unawares. If she could manage to disable Le Loup, perhaps the rest would run, scatter like the cowardly vermin they were.

Her shooting would buy Tony time.

She stood up and raised her musket, her eyes searching for the points of safety, where she would flee to after she had taken the shot and the next one after that. She swallowed hard and tried to get an exact bearing on Le Loup.

She might only have this one chance and she wanted to get him between the eyes.

'On my signal, lads, we attack and show 'em what we are made of.'

'Not your signal, Le Loup,' Jem muttered. 'Mine.'

She pulled back the trigger another notch.

★   ★   ★

'I fail to understand you, sir,' Lieutenant Ashton said and looked like a confused sheep. 'Of course there are no deserters here, Captain Dorrell, sir. I checked . . . in the barns, the sheds, everywhere.'

Tony gritted his teeth and found himself

wishing again Ashton was more like Ensign Riseley. This potential fiasco would never have happened under Riseley. That was the devil of it. Jemima Riseley was beyond a doubt the best ensign he had ever seen except for one thing — her sex. The only thing Ashton had going for him was the fact that he was male. Slow on the uptake and even slower on the execution.

'Drunk on duty is a court martial offence, Mr Ashton.'

'But we had finished the mission, sir.' Ashton raised an unsteady hand, tried to straighten his cravat and singularly failed to do so. 'The señora was most insistent.'

'No mission of this nature is completed until either you arrive back at camp, Mr Ashton, or you are relieved of command by a superior officer.' Tony paused for effect. 'I am relieving you of that command and your conduct will be reported for the colonel to deal with as he sees fit.'

'Sir, I — '

Ashton was cut short by the sound of musket fire and the loud cry of 'To me, D Company. To me. Ambush!'

'I will lead the court marshal myself,' Tony said through gritted teeth as he bodily removed the woman who was blocking the door and yanked it open. 'Go to it lads. No deserter will get the better of the British army.'

'He's just a brown bottle, an ugly brown bottle but a brown bottle just the same, and you, my girl, have shattered bottles before,' Jem muttered her mantra over and over as she tried to take aim at Le Loup.

After her first shot, the area would be covered in white smoke, impossible to aim accurately through.

This first shot had to be accurate.

She had one shot. One shot to save Tony and the rest. One shot to avenge the honour of D Company.

The ragtag army of deserters started to fan out of the barn, leaving by the large doors, preparing for their assault on the farmhouse.

Jem drew one last deep breath. 'I commend my soul to my country,' she whispered. 'If I should fall to rise no more, let it not be in vain.'

She checked her aim one last time, pulled the trigger back and did not wait to see the results.

'To me D Company! To me! Ambush!' she yelled at the top of her lungs and sprinted to her next chosen firing spot.

Through the cloud of white smoke, she saw the deserters start to run. One started to charge towards her position.

Jem rammed the next musket ball home, aimed, fired. The ball hit him squarely in the chest.

She gasped for breath as she heard the shouts and bellows of her men.

Ramming a third shot into her musket, she braced herself, knowing the recoil from the musket would be savage.

Her shoulder was already aching from the first two. The rifle kept hitting her bruises from the bridge explosion.

She fired blindly and prayed it would do some damage.

A shot slammed into the wall inches above her head.

Lucky?

Jem instantly dropped to the ground and took cover behind a cart. She crouched, panting for breath, her lungs filling with the choking smoke swirling all around her.

Her hands trembled as she tried to load the next shot.

Had Tony survived?

She risked a peek at the farmhouse door. Bodies lay littered around it, the bodies of deserters. She tried to take a better look.

The scene was all confusion.

The sound of musket fire resounded from all parts of the yard. Through the haze, she could make out the red uniforms of D Company as they picked their way around the side of the farmhouse. A huge wave of relief washed over her.

The deserter's ambush had failed.

A white hot pain seared through her right shoulder, followed swiftly by a sting in her left side. The world went black for a brief second. She glanced up and through a haze saw a deserter peeking out from the roof of the barn.

She fired her shot.

The recoil from her musket knocked her flat on the ground.

★   ★   ★

Tony strode amongst the debris from the short and bloody battle. He counted the bodies of seven deserters including the leader wearing a bright blue bandana, and none of his men. It could have been worse, much worse.

Without Jem's warning, the deserters would have had the upper hand. As it was, they had only just managed to get out in time. He ran his hand through his hair.

Hell fire, where was Jem?

He had been too busy directing D Company to look for her during the battle. He hoped after shouting her warning, she had hidden somewhere sensible, that she had taken no part in the battle. Tony caught the arm of an exhausted looking Trooper Hook.

'Have you seen Jem, I mean, Ensign Riseley?' he asked, trying to keep his panic from mounting. She must have heard the guns stop.

'The ensign, sir? I didn't know he was here.'

'Who in the hell do you think alerted us to the ambush?' Tony bit out and resisted the urge to throttle the soldier.

'Are you looking for the ensign, sir?' another called. 'He's over here by this cart, but he's been hit and is hurt bad. Saved our lives, the ensign did. You should have seen him fire. It was a sight to behold. If Wellington had a few more like him, our stay here would be short indeed.'

He didn't know how he got there but in less than a moment he was there, kneeling by Jem's side.

He lifted her head into his lap but it rolled slightly.

Tony prayed in a way he had not prayed since childhood, promising God all sorts of things if only Jemima Riseley was alive.

He felt faint at the sight of her bloody shoulder. She'd been wounded badly. He touched his hand to her neck. It was cold but he felt a faint pulse. Tears ran down his cheeks but he ignored them, concentrated on looking at Jem's pale face.

She was alive!

'Tony?' she said, her voice sounded thin and faraway. 'You're alive.'

'Hush.' He put a finger to her lips. 'Save your strength.'

'Had to save your life. It was more important than orders.' She gave a ghost of a smile and her hand touched his cheek before falling back.

'You did well, Jem. You saved more than me. You saved the whole company.' Tony swallowed hard. Even now her life seemed be to ebbing away, her face growing ever whiter.

Why did it have to be Jem? Why couldn't it have been Ashton or some other useless piece of humanity? Tony gritted his teeth. There had to be something he could do, some way he could save her life.

'Ashton, Ashton! Get here now!'

'What is it, sir?' The lieutenant ambled up, swaying as he strolled through the farmyard.

'I want your shirt and your horse.'

'Is Ensign Riseley all right?' Ashton's Adam's apple bobbed in his throat and

246

his pale eyes blinked.

'Give me your shirt! Now.'

Ashton started but obeyed, struggling out of his jacket and flinging it to the ground.

Tony noticed to his satisfaction how Ashton shivered like hell as he pulled his white shirt off.

'Rip it into bandages,' Tony shouted, feeling helpless because he was stuck where he was with Jem's inert head lolled in his lap.

Ashton gulped. 'It's from London, this shirt, sir?'

'Rip it up,' Tony ordered.

'If it hadn't been for the ensign's quick actions,' Ashton said, pulling at the material rather unsteadily, 'we'd all be dead men, sir.'

'Oh for God's sake!' Tony snatched the shirt out of Ashton's hands and began to tear it into strips himself. 'Now go and fetch your horse. Jem Riseley has been shot and I am going to take her to the hospital where there is a slim chance her life can be saved.'

'Her, sir? But the ensign is a man.' Ashton looked at him as if he were touched in the head.

'Like the farmhouse and the deserters, you once again display a talent for ignoring the obvious, Ashton. The ensign is a woman and a finer soldier than you will ever make! Now get me that horse. Her life depends on it.'

14

She struggled but the hands were too strong.

She screamed but no one came.

She shut her eyes but still Jem saw the contorted expression on her stepfather's face as he pawed at her bodice and forced his hand on to her breast. Leering as his other hand pushed up her skirts, his touch like a hot, disgusting rash running up her leg.

She twisted, tried to escape. And there it was again — just like when this happened before — the candlestick. Her hand trembled, poised to grasp, but she hesitated.

If she took it and hit him, she'd kill him. Or she could leave the candlestick where it was on the table and let the monster live and do his worst.

His damp fingers tightened on her nipple, making her cry in pain.

The leer increased.

She had to take the candlestick. She had no choice. She grabbed it and brought it down on the twisted curls of her stepfather's head. He slumped to the floor, the hands fell away.

The motionless body lay crumpled like a discarded doll, and by his head seeping into the carpet, blood. Red, sticky blood that covered her hands, her face, her legs. Her whole body was hot and wet, bathed in blood. Blood everywhere, too much blood. She screamed.

'Give her something for the pain,' she heard an angry voice say. 'Quick, man!'

Tony? He had no place here, not in this nightmare. She struggled, tried to move but she couldn't. Something bittersweet was trickling down her throat. Laudanum? For the briefest of moments, she felt Tony's hands, strong but soft hands, pleasant hands, lifting her and supporting her head.

'I'll look after you, Jemima Cullen, I promise,' the voice said but she didn't know whether she had woken up or was still asleep and dreaming. A new twist on the old.

She swallowed and blackness lapped at the edges of her mind again and she was falling back to the beginning.

Her stepfather coming into the room, towards her and she couldn't move, couldn't run. She was cold as ice as his hateful hands began to paw at her dress.

'You have killed and now you will die,' a rasping voice whispered across the front of her mind.

'Yes, I have. I know I killed my stepfather,' she wanted to say. Her lips would not move.

Cold steel pricked her neck as if someone was holding a knife to it. Her stepfather had no knife. Jem heard a groan escape from her lips, could feel an unquenched pain in her shoulder. Her eyes flashed open.

She found herself staring into the thin, bony countenance of Le Loup.

A malevolent Le Loup dressed in a Spanish priest's garb — black cloak, black hat with the dead eyes of an executioner. She'd killed her stepfather, she'd killed Le Loup and now he too was going to come back and haunt her dreams.

'Say your prayers, little one,' he said and Jem shuddered. 'You have foiled me for the last time.'

The glint of the knife in his raised hand dazzled her. He started to move it downwards.

'No,' Jem screamed, lifted both arms, pressed her hands against his chest and pushed with every ounce of her strength.

He grabbed her wrists with one hand. She twisted, turned, ignored the searing pain ripping through her shoulder. Anything to get away from the knife. A scream tore through her lungs.

'Here, what's going on?' came a loud English voice, familiar. Someone was coming to help her. The knife had disappeared into the swirl of the black cloak.

'*Por favor*,' Le Loup said, releasing her hands and vanishing backwards. Jem collapsed back against the pallet, gasping for breath, and found her gaze looking at a blackened crucifix hung above her on the wall.

'I've been waiting to see you, miss,' came the voice again. It was Sergeant Masters.

There was no doubt now she was awake. The pain was nearly unbearable and the grogginess she felt meant they must have given her an opiate.

The stench of pine fires and illness assaulted her nostrils and groans from other men filled her ears. She turned her head slightly to see.

Sergeant Masters stood beside her, towering above her and twisting his shako in his hands. At her look, he crouched down by her side.

'Masters?' Jem breathed.

'Begging your pardon, miss, but I saw the priest leaning over you, talking to you but you seemed to be trying to fight him off. I thought you might be having a bad dream.'

'It wasn't a priest,' Jem muttered and tried to blink the vision of Le Loup's eyes away.

'There, there,' Masters said, tentatively. 'Some of these black-robed priests do look rather sinister. Them and the nuns are all over this here convent, miss.'

Miss? Masters knew she was a woman! Jem fastened her gaze on the blackened crucifix. She hadn't thought. Of course they must all know she was a woman now.

Masters cleared his throat above the fit of painful coughing that erupted from the pallet next to hers.

'What is it, Sergeant?' she croaked. She had known of the possibility she would be discovered but she had thought Tony would keep his promise. She screwed her eyes up, willing the great hollow in her chest to go away. 'I'm sorry, Sergeant. I ache all over.'

'Begging your pardon, miss, but me and the rest of lads, we've drawn straws, and I came up with the short one.'

'The short straw?'

'Yes, I am the one who gets the honour of asking you for your hand in marriage. Seeing as how you are going to get a pension, the lads thought it could provide a tidy enough sum and you'd need a protector. We drew straws for it. Fairest way.'

'Does the whole company know about me?'

'Yes, miss. The entire camp knows, from Wellington downwards. Somebody overheard the captain telling the colonel . . . '

A bitter laugh escaped Jem's lips.

An offer of marriage from Sergeant Masters and a tiny pension perhaps from the British army! Whatever she needed this fell well short of it. The only proposal of marriage she wanted was from Tony, but that was an impossible dream. All her plans of continuing on as Ensign Riseley, of fighting alongside Tony had been ruined. Everyone knew — courtesy of Tony.

'Thank you for the honour . . . ' Jem faltered.

'Alfred, my given name's Alfred.'

'Alfred,' Jem whispered and tried to choose her words carefully. 'I am honoured by your kind offer, but I am in no fit state to marry anyone.'

His craggy face fell a bit. 'The offer is there — if you should need it, miss.'

'That's very kind of you.' Jem closed her eyes and hoped he'd go away. She just wanted to lie still and sleep until the pain went away. When she opened her heavy lids again, Masters was still standing there.

'Do you know where Captain Dorrell is?'

'The captain? I ain't seen him around lately. I expect the colonel has him busy, miss. There's lots to be done and the colonel depends on him and he was gone awhile with you.'

A hot tear coursed down her cheek.

She hated her weak womanish tears. She had thought he had been here holding her hand but those were foolish fancies caused by whatever the doctor gave her for the pain.

Through the open window, the sound of fife and drum could be heard. He would be there, off on another adventure with no more thought of her. She had served her purpose.

'Are you all right?'

Jem willed her tears to stop and tried to smile.

'Pardon me, miss, but I clean forgot your wound. Hook and Smith swear they would be paying St Peter a visit were it not for you, miss.'

'Thank you, Masters,' Jem said and at last he nodded and walked away. She turned her head, fixed her gaze on the blackened crucifix and allowed the tears to fall. Why had she trusted Tony Dorrell? She should have known he'd have revealed her identity. And now he was off somewhere being the soldier he was. She closed her eyes and tried to sleep.

★ ★ ★

'Jemima? Jem?'

Jem forced her eyes open at the familiar voice. Tony wasn't here, she was dreaming again. Yet a red-jacketed figure was leaning over her. She looked up the smart row of polished buttons, past the stiff cravat, taking in the officer's epaulettes, until her eyes rested on Tony's twinkling eyes and broad smile.

He leant over her, lifted her hand and brushed the back of it with his lips. Her heart skipped a beat. She should hate him for revealing her, but the smile on her face had come too easily. She tried to sit up. Pain shot through her shoulder and she had to lie back down. 'Tony?' she said, refusing to believe the evidence of her own fingertips.

'In the flesh.' He seized both her hands in his and the warmth of them helped distract her from the pain just a little. 'Lie still and conserve your strength.'

'What happened? You must tell me. Le Loup is here, Tony. I saw him.'

'Hush, that's the opiate talking. This is a British hospital.'

'But I — '

'The leader of the deserters is dead thanks to you, Jemima.'

Jem looked up at the ceiling and blinked back tears. There was no anger in his voice. Perhaps he was right — she had been imagining things.

'And . . . the others?' Jem said after a moment.

'There were no British causalities. But enough about that.' Tony put two fingers to her lips. 'Hush now, the priest is on his way. Everything will be all right, Jemima. I promise you.'

Jem started as she remembered her fight with the priest. Real or a phantasm? Her heart pounded at the mere thought.

'I don't need a priest. I'm not about to die and I'm not a Catholic.' She pushed herself upright to prove it.

Her fingers touched her forehead and it was cold with sweat.

Two nuns, whispering together bustled past the doorway, and for the first time she realized she was no longer in the long room lined with dozens of pallets but in a small cell with greying plastered walls, and she was lying on a wooden cot raised up from the ground and the sheet and white linen pillow beneath her felt clean.

'You must not worry, Jemima.' Tony paced the length of the room and back which took him only six strides. Then he came to stand by the cot and again took her hand. 'I am assured it will be a lawful marriage.'

'Marriage?' Jem's heart sank. She had no desire to be a wife to Sergeant Masters. She wanted to be Tony's mistress. She would be safe in her house in Lisbon. 'Whose marriage?'

His frown deepened. 'Our marriage of course.'

Jem wished she could turn her head away, press her face into the cool pillow. He must be a lunatic if he thought she would marry him. If she told him her true circumstances, her marriage bed would be one short step to the gallows.

'I refuse to marry you,' she whispered and her tears started to wet the pillow.

'What the devil are you talking about, Jemima? Of course you will marry me. You have to marry me.'

Jem gazed up at the ceiling where the plaster had discoloured with damp and bit her inner cheek. 'What are you talking about? You never mentioned marriage. You only mentioned protection.'

Tony was silent. 'D'you mean you are married to someone else?'

'No,' she whispered. 'I am a spinster, and we both know I have never been with anyone else.'

'Then, if there is no legal impediment?'

Jem looked at him with narrowed eyes. Once she had imagined a proposal from him, complete with bended knee and hand on heart. But never like this, being informed that a priest was about to appear. He couldn't order her about as if she was still his ensign.

'For one thing, I need to be asked.'

'You were injured and out for the count. How could I ask you?' Tony let go of her hands, stood up, raked his hand through his hair. 'Make no mistake, Jemima Cullen, we will marry.'

Jemima Cullen, Jemima Cullen.

Tony's words seemed to echo through Jem's mind. He had said them before in her dream. She stared at him, trying to fathom how he knew and what else he knew. His hands were clasped behind his back, but his eyes were unreadable.

'How did you find out who I am? Why did you tell everyone who I am?' Jem demanded, hating the sound of her voice. She sounded hoarse, cracked, weak. Exactly like a woman. She stared at the ceiling rather than him.

'I could ask you the same question,' he said peering over her, making it impossible to avoid his gaze. His eyes were as dark as thunder. 'Why didn't you tell me who you were? You agreed to be my *mistress*!'

Jem refused to flinch in the face of the attack.

'Taking you for a mistress would have been insupportable. You should have told me who you were, Jemima!'

'I told you my story.' Jem struggled to keep her voice steady. 'Maybe you had other things on your mind.'

'This is no time for levity, Jemima! You were aware I knew your brother. You must have known from the very first moment when I mistook you for him.' His eyes clouded over. He looked away. 'Hell, Jemima, he was my best friend in the world. Why did you lie to me? Why did you not seek me out? I would have helped you. You must understand that!'

'My shoulder hurts,' Jem managed to say despite the threatening tears. 'Everything hurts. Your shouting is making it worse.'

'Jem,' he said and poured some liquid into a silver spoon, holding it out to her. She swallowed, tasting the bitter laudanum thankfully. 'That's my girl.'

'But I . . . ' Jem began and then forgot what she meant to say as his hand brushed her forehead. How could she want two such opposite things at the same time? Waves of sleep washed over her.

'We'll talk when you are better. I keep forgetting how seriously you were injured. Forgive me.'

'Stay with me, Tony,' she said before the blackness finally claimed her.

★ ★ ★

She must have slept a long while because when she opened her eyes, a blue-grey light streamed into the room. She turned her head and saw Tony standing with his back to her looking out of the small, barred window. The daylight filtered past him, highlighting his hair and the gleaming braid of his uniform.

The bedclothes rustled as she pushed at them to sit herself up.

'Ah, you're awake,' he said turning around. Jem regarded the stubble on his chin, the drawn expression to his face and wondered how long he had been here.

'How is the pain?'

'My shoulder is still aching, but I'm feeling better,' she said, looking into his eyes. 'Soon I will be back to my old self . . . back to being Jem Riseley.'

'You seem to forget, you'll shortly be Jemima Dorrell.'

A throb shot through her shoulder. 'No I won't! I haven't agreed to marry you, Tony.'

He bent down as if to pull something out from under the bed and laid out a blue dress on the blanket. 'I had the devil of a time finding a dress for you. You have the colonel's wife to thank for all this.'

Jem fingered the thin material, muslin, as Tony bent down again and brought up a pile of white cotton — undergarments? And finally, a beautiful, ebony-handled lady's hairbrush.

'Well, aren't you going to get yourself ship-shape?' He stood back and looked at her curiously.

'Now?' Stupidly she had not thought getting out of this cot would mean surrendering her uniform for women's clothes.

'I know I broke my word,' he said with a hard voice and his eyes gleamed flint, 'but in the circumstances I had every right. I have every right. You belong to me, Jemima, d'you hear? Now for heaven's sake, get dressed!' He stepped over towards the small, wooden door.

'I belong to no man,' Jem whispered.

'So you say but it won't be long before the promise you sealed with me with your body in that cave will be witnessed by God. We shall marry. Now put your clothes on. I'll be back in a few moments in case you need any help with the fastenings.' He shut the door behind him with a thud.

Jem pushed the blankets away. It was no good arguing. She had better put on the dress that Tony had found for her. It was slow going, but at last she managed to remove her shirt and breeches and though her legs wobbled, she found she could stand.

She went over to the table in the corner on

which stood a pitcher and a small, earthenware bowl. Someone had laid out her things — her comb and toothbrush — and also a bar of unpleasant smelling soap that she found lathered very badly.

She did her best to wash, avoiding the large amount of bandaging around her shoulder before pulling on the cotton undergarments and finally the dress.

Tony was right about one thing. It would be impossible to reach the top fastenings herself. If her shoulder had not been so stiff she might have managed it.

She sat down on the chair — Tony's campaign chair, she noticed. She resisted the temptation to weep. Tony didn't care for her. He wanted to own her, take what he wanted, regardless of her feelings in the matter. The memory of another man determined to impose his will flashed across her aching mind: the cruel face of her stepfather.

There was a sharp rap and the door creaked open. 'Jemima? Are you ready?'

He stepped inside the room and shut the door behind him. 'Jemima, don't you look a picture!'

She was sure she did — a horrendous distortion with her thick shoulder and this ill-fitting dress that did not even hide the bandaging.

'Y'know your brother and I were great friends,' he said crouching down before her and lacing her fingers with his. His voice was soft, persuading, a gentle caress. 'I think he would have been pleased we decided to marry. Let me do up these top buttons for you.'

'I don't understand.' Jem broke his gaze and stared at the small, barred window. His fingers tapped at the buttons with the lightest touch yet still made her quiver with an anticipation that made her wish he would kiss her. 'Who told you I was Charlie's sister? Nobody knew.'

'Jemima, forgive me but I went through your things and found this.' He pulled a slim, tattered leather-bound book from a pocket in his jacket and placed it in her lap.

A New System of Domestic Economy — she soundlessly mouthed the title without even having to read it.

She'd read it a hundred times, the bold inscription on the frontispiece and now she read it again;

To my dearest sister Jemima on the occasion of your 17th birthday. December 1806. May this assist you to master those feminine skills as well as you can handle a sword. Your devoted brother, Charles.

263

It was clear as the sunlight streaming into this tiny room. Tony was a gentleman, brought up with all the codes of decency and honour, and bound to them. He would have decided to marry her at the point he had found out who she was. Jem snapped the book shut and wanted to do nothing else but weep.

She should have buried the watch and the book in a hole in the ground the minute she had a chance. Like a sentimental fool, she had hung on to them and that weakness had been her undoing.

'Jemima?' He fastened the last of her buttons and she breathed in the smell of his maleness and faint sandalwood and thought how very much she wanted simply to be with Tony. Anything to be near him, to have the closeness of his maleness, the prospect of more lovemaking, which made her feel like nothing on this earth. She took a deep breath and tried to think. They would go wherever in the world the British army sent him, not England. This war certainly did not look as if it was about to be over very quickly. And there would be a strange comfort in marrying a close friend of Charles.

'I came to visit Cullen Park once,' he said pulling her fingers to his lips. The softness of his voice and of his touch threatened to shatter her newly won equilibrium. 'Perhaps you might remember it? You were only young then, hardly out of the schoolroom.'

Jem swallowed. How could she have forgotten the arrival of Viscount Fordingley, tall, broad-shouldered and devastating in his fawn-coloured buckskins and black superfine jacket? It had been impossible to take her eyes off him from the first moment he appeared. Every time she aimed her musket, she remembered how his arms had felt, steadying her as she shattered that bottle. He must have sensed it too, or would the stolen kiss under the mistletoe ever have happened?

'I remember,' she said hurriedly, realizing he was still waiting her answer. 'It was on Charles's last leave.'

'I remember you,' he said and Jem no longer wanted to listen. She knew this marriage was to assuage his sense of guilt, so why did he have to stir up these memories? 'I remember a girl with long dark locks tied back not very effectively with ribbons, and a mischievous grin and with eyes that followed me everywhere. I thought it very fitting Charlie should have such a fine sister because he was such a fine fellow himself. I'm proud to be marrying Charlie's sister. D'you hear that, Jem? Proud.'

He wiped her eyes with a large, white linen

handkerchief. Jem tried for a smile, but what was left of her foolish dream seemed to scatter.

'That's a very kind thing to say,' she said stiffly and with a small nod. 'Thank you for doing my dress up.'

'Kindness has nothing to do with it, Jemima. I intend to behave towards you as I should have in the first place, if I had known.'

'But . . .'

'No buts.'

She wanted to be more than a duty, a debt to the memory of her brother, but what other choice did she have? Sergeant Masters' offer? Or waiting to see what the army had planned for her? A passage back to England, almost without a doubt.

'I will marry you,' she whispered. She was not going back to England.

'Capital,' Tony said with a smile and held out his hand.

She took it, gripped it and stood up and was suddenly awash with a fear that she had made the wrong decision.

'Can you walk?' Tony placed her hand on his arm.

'Yes . . . but I have no shoes. My boots?' Her battered black boots were paired on the floor in the corner of the room.

'Jemima, don't be ridiculous. You're not

wearing those!' Tony scooped her up into his arms before she had a chance to protest. She rested her head against his shoulder as he carried her through the doorway and out into a dim corridor.

'Where are we going?'

'To the chapel, of course. I'll have to find you some suitable footwear later.'

'The chapel?' Her voice quivered.

She saw Tony's jaw just above her stiffen and he seemed to up his pace. The tempo of his boots striking the stone floor increased and each step took her nearer to her point of no return.

'Tony?' she whispered as he stopped outside a door, 'Must we be wed so immediately?'

'Jemima, you are still recovering from your injury and it is to be expected you will be emotional and no doubt still befuddled from the laudanum, but you must keep your mind trained on the simple fact we are to be married now and concentrate on repeating what the priest asks you.'

The door swung open and Jem saw at once the coloured light coming through the stained glass and realized they were here. He didn't put her down on her feet until they were in front of the altar.

Jem looked about her, the stone beneath

the soles of her feet was very cold. The chapel was empty apart from a single nun sat in a chair to the side, her head bent in prayer, a grumbling, hunch-back English priest who looked as if he wanted to be somewhere else and, standing with a suitably expressionless look on his face, Tony's man Andrews.

A hole in the corner affair, and even Andrews knew it.

Above the altar on the back wall was a huge painting, at least ten feet tall. She recognized the scene at once, Mary Magdalene weeping for forgiveness at the foot of the cross. The powerful brush strokes captured every emotion, gave weight to every tear. Mary Magdalene, the repentant sinner who was forgiven despite her heinous crimes of the flesh.

That was what she should be doing, prostrating herself in front of God and asking for forgiveness of all her sins. If she asked, would he listen?

The tears brimmed in her eyes. She was unworthy, and her sins were too weighty to be forgiven. She should have . . . but she didn't know what she should have done, what she could have done. She had made so many mistakes. She swallowed hard and tried to hang on to the thought — Mary Magdalene had been forgiven.

She felt Tony take her hand at the priest's request and knew what she must do. She must ask God now that he might forgive her. So she could be worthy enough to utter those sacred vows in God's presence and became joined to Tony as his wife.

Jem shut her eyes, and willed her thoughts heavenwards. Please father in heaven, accept my repentance most humbly offered and let me be a good wife to this man if that is your plan.

Nothing had changed and yet something had changed. A sort of peace stole over her. She peeped through her eyelashes at Tony. He was staring straight ahead, his gaze improbably blank. When the priest asked, would he say the words?

Through the loud hum of the silence, she heard the priest's voice asking the binding question. 'Anthony Michael Dorrell, wilt thou have this woman to thy wedded wife, to live together after God's ordinance in the holy estate of matrimony? Wilt thou love her, comfort her, honour and keep her in sickness and in health; and forsaking all others, keep thee only unto her so long as ye both shall live?'

'I will.'

Not even a pause, or the slightest hesitation

and yet still he stared straight ahead, unwavering.

Now there was no turning back, she could only go forward, and at least she had saved herself from being shipped back to England. Now she must try to be a good wife to Tony to repay him for saving her.

Jem started at an impatient knocking at the chapel door. Andrews sniffed and left Tony's side to go and open it while the priest hurried through the remainder of what he had to say.

'Damnation!' came the booming voice of Colonel Garroway. 'Andrews, have I missed the show?'

''Fraid so, sir.'

'Fordingley, you wily devil, slipping away to do the deed on the quiet.' The colonel marched down the aisle and the priest snapped his book shut with a frown.

'We are legally wed now, aren't we, Reverend?' Tony asked.

'Yes,' the priest conceded.

Colonel Garroway seized Tony's hand and shook it violently. 'Congratulations, though Mrs Garroway is going to skin me alive. She's been fussing about what to wear for your wedding all day.'

'I did say at headquarters I intended a quiet affair, sir.'

'Yes, but you know women!' The colonel's

laughter echoed up to the high ceilings. 'And congratulations, Lady Fordingley.'

He shook her hand vigorously. 'Thank you, Colonel Garroway.'

'Sir, if Mrs Garroway might be mollified enough to find a pair of ladies' boots or shoes? Suitable for travelling. At least until we get to Lisbon.'

The colonel looked down at her bare feet, now numb from the cold. 'What? Dorrell, there really is no need to resign your commission. I can lose your letter to me on that subject right away and we'll say no more about it. The British army needs men like you.'

The world began to spin.

Tony had resigned his commission?

She had thought, had assumed. She clutched Tony's arm to steady herself.

'My mind is made up, Colonel. My wife and I are to return directly to London.'

Go back to England? Directly?

Her knees gave way, and her hand grasped Tony's arm like a dying man's.

'Tony, I — ' she began in a whisper but the colonel's booming tones cut her off.

'Listen, Dorrell, you are acting honourably towards the young lady. Surely it is all that's required?'

'No. Not a chance in hell.' Tony's voice

271

sounded like a razor scraped over hard skin and cold as ice. Jem shivered. 'My honour demands it. And I'm not sure the army really needs a captain who was hoodwinked into letting a woman serve as his ensign. Let's keep the regiment's reputation intact if we can. With us both gone it should blow over. For the sake of the regiment, we need to put this all behind us.'

'Good show.' The colonel clapped Tony on the back. 'But y'know you're too good a man to let fall for this. We still might be able to patch something up if we can make a hero out of her. A woman hero? Is that believable? What d'you think, Dorrell?'

A single tear rolled down her cheek. She dreaded to hear what Tony thought.

'She survived the Hope, saved my life and the whole company,' Tony said, choosing his words with great care. Jem's face was as pale as snow and her fingers clutched his arm as if her life depended on it. Well, perhaps it did. The law said she was his responsibility to protect now, as well as his honour, and he was not about to have her set up as some travelling circus freak to be gawped at. He shook his head. 'But as to making a hero out of a woman, I don't know.'

'You are doubtless right,' the colonel barked, 'but I would say, if this is what an

Englishwoman can do, I'll be looking forward to the sons you'll have!'

Sons!

Tony swallowed hard. Jemima might already be carrying his child. The things he had done. One part of him hoped and the other was ashamed of the way he acted, slaking his lust on her innocence.

'The aspect never crossed my mind, sir.'

'You look like you've just been made to eat a lime, Dorrell!' The colonel gave a chuckle. 'She is a pretty thing. If I were a younger man in your shoes . . . ' He winked and Tony felt a swell of irritation. 'Think of England, Dorrell, and your duty. Get her back to England and increasing without delay!'

Tony gritted his teeth.

His baser instincts were prompting him to plant a facer at his colonel. But he knew his temper was unreasonable and needed to be controlled.

'On the subject of shoes, we plan to leave as soon as possible, sir,' Tony said stiffly.

'Yes, yes. I'll get Mrs Garroway on to it forthwith. Splendid, splendid,' Garroway seized Tony's hand, pumping it up and down several times.

Tony glanced down at Jemima.

So much had happened so fast, no doubt she was finding it difficult to take it all in. Her face was white, and sweat peppered her brow. He patted her hand and tried to smile encouragingly.

'It won't be long before we are back in England, Jemima, don't you worry.'

'And you will be the toast of society, the belle of the ball,' boomed the colonel.

She gave a faint moan and her eyes closed. Her body started to sink to the ground.

Tony caught her, swung her up into his arms and bellowed at Andrews to find some smelling salts.

15

Jem trembled as she took her first step from the gangplank and on to English soil. All throughout the storm-tossed voyage from Lisbon she had dreaded this. She was desperate to keep the tears from falling, to keep her fear hidden down deep inside her.

Tony had brushed aside her reasons for staying in Portugal, dismissing each of her protests about clothes, illness and damp weather as fustian until she knew she had either to tell him the true reason for her not wanting to come back to England or go with him. And she couldn't bear the thought of the way he'd look at her, if she admitted what she had done. The thought of what would happen when he discovered his marriage of duty was to a murderess filled her with terror.

She shivered and forced her feet to take another step along the stone quay.

Away from the ship and towards the unknown.

Until she knew exactly what had happened to her stepfather, she had to keep the secret hidden. She glanced at Tony's drawn profile as he walked beside her, and her feet stumbled as a pair of dockworkers ducked past her avoiding a large crate to her right.

'Be careful, Jemima,' Tony admonished her in a stern voice, putting his hand under her elbow for an instant to steady her.

She was lucky he touched her at all these days. Not since the cave, not since their marriage, had he even tried to be a husband to her. Kisses, yes, but the kind of kisses a parent gives to a child, not the kisses she knew he was capable of bestowing when desire glowed in his eyes.

'It is just trying to deal with these slippers.' Jem mumbled. 'I found my boots were so much easier to walk in . . . '

Tony chuckled. She stood still and watched as he drew in a deep breath, stretched and looked about the Portsmouth quayside.

'It is good to be back in England. The air is all its own.'

'Smoke from the coal fires?' Jem said, and attempted to keep her voice from quaking.

Tony barked with laughter in reply.

She wrinkled her nose. The saltiness she was used to after being so long at sea, but not the smoke and other thick smells of the various cargos, and the crowds of people! The docks bustled with sailors, workers and women plying their own trade.

Glancing up one of the narrow streets

between the houses, Jem saw a large man approaching, his face in shadow, walking towards them with a purposeful air. She hesitated and wanted to run. Only Tony's fingers on her elbow kept her still and forced her to wait for her fate. She heaved a sigh as a ship's carpenter carrying a new plank across his shoulder came into the sunshine. Not her stepfather or a Bow Street Runner coming to haul her away.

Jem gasped at a sudden movement to their left, but it was a grey cat jumping down from a barrel. She forced her shoulders to relax.

'Where to — ' she began and stopped. Her eyes caught a wiry figure dressed in an immaculately tailored suit and a pit opened in her stomach. She thought he was dead. They had said he was dead. She blinked, staring at the profile of his face. Unless she was mistaken . . .

He turned and she saw his scar, visible under the powder he wore on his face. Then he saw her and his eyes seemed to pierce her soul. He knew and he would come again with his knife as he had done in the hospital. She clutched Tony's arm.

'What's wrong, Jem?' she heard Tony say.

She felt faint, nauseous, unsteady on her feet. Her fingers dug unnecessarily hard into

Tony's forearm but she found it impossible to loosen them.

'Have you done yourself an injury? You look awfully pale. Andrews, Andrews!' Tony's hand came to rest on hers. 'Where is that man when you need him?'

'Look, Tony!' she managed to say in an urgent whisper. 'Over there. That man! Le Loup!'

'What man?'

Jem blinked but the man had disappeared into the crowd. She looked all around for another sight of him, but he had vanished. 'Le Loup,' she gasped. 'What is he doing here?'

'You thought you saw Le Loup?'

'Tony, we must go and warn someone,' she said, thinking quickly. 'The man is a traitor, a spy. What is he doing in England's largest naval port? He must be up to no good.'

'Jem,' Tony said with an edge to his voice. 'Le Loup is dead.'

'I thought he was dead. I thought I . . . killed him at the farmhouse, but I saw him here, and before at the hospital, he tried to kill me. Sergeant Masters saw him . . . ' Tony held her arm back, refused to let her go despite her tugging and Jem stopped speaking. Perhaps she had imagined it. She'd thought she'd seen her stepfather about three times already and they had only been ashore a few minutes.

'Jemima, Le Loup is dead.'

'Are you certain?' Jem stood still and looked into Tony's eyes. 'The man looked so much like him . . . ' She faltered as she did so. His expression seemed so concerned — for her.

'Jemima, I saw the body with my own eyes.'

Jem gave one more glance to where the man had stood, doubting her eyes and her reactions. Tony had seen Le Loup's corpse.

Had returning to England done this to her? If she became a babbling idiot after only moments on shore, how would she react when she went into society? She had to pretend she had no idea about what had happened to her stepfather. It had been a push, and she had not stopped to see . . . Jem forced her thoughts away. She squared her shoulders, lifted her head and met Tony's eyes.

Tony wore an expression of grave concern. She smiled at him, grateful he had held her back before she made a complete fool of herself. Next time, she would do better. Next time she would not flinch in the face of the enemy.

'Thank you, Tony,' she said after a moment as they started to walk up to the row of houses and shops and towards the high street.

Tony grinned and patted her hand.

They paused before crossing the road to allow a group of recruits in bright red jackets and shiny brass buttons to pass. A lump in her throat seemed to grow with each beat of the drum. Already she missed Spain and the army with a fierce longing.

'King George commands and they obey,' she whispered, 'over the hills and far away.'

'Pardon, Jemima?'

'Nothing of any import. I was just thinking of Spain.' Jem glanced up and arranged her face in a smile. What would Tony say if she told him the truth? That her feet longed to follow the drum and go back to the relative safety of Spain. At least she knew where the enemy was there.

'We're in England now. And although *The Courage* was well stocked, I'm looking forward to some decent fare.'

'No more weevil-infested hard tack,' Jem agreed as her smile became genuine.

'Or pork so salty and dried up it might be anything.' Tony pulled a face.

'Or slippery boiled onions.'

'Not in England,' Tony said leading them forward now the soldiers had passed with his chin the air. 'I believe we ought to start for London as soon as possible.'

London! She struggled to take another

breath and pressed the fingertips of her gloves together. Terror washed over her again as the longing to pick up her skirts and run back to the ship filled her. She had trouble keeping her voice steady.

'I thought you intended that we stop in Portsmouth for a few days?'

'Yes,' Tony said as his brow creased, 'but I have a sudden longing for a bed I know to be comfortable, and the dear mama has an excellent chef.'

★   ★   ★

Jem stifled a yawn as she looked around the chamber and realized she was exhausted. Tony was right. Breaking their journey in Surrey was a better plan than arriving very late that night in London. She'd have the night before she had to face whatever lay ahead of her.

He had said he knew The Talbot in Ripley to be a reputable inn. With its well-appointed rooms, it felt more like a palace after the cramped quarters of *The Courage*.

Tony seemed to have vanished. She'd heard him ask the landlady for a cold collation to be sent to their chamber before he had told her, rather sharply, to go on upstairs ahead. It had been over an hour and he had yet to appear.

281

A sigh escaped Jem's lips. Tony had barely spoken to her since they had left the quayside early this morning and hadn't even smiled at her. No, that was not true, Jem thought with a pang. He had been smiling when he had come back from The George in Portsmouth having satisfactorily arranged the hire of two chaises to take them and their luggage to London.

Jem perched on the edge of the large tester bed and thought she would have been happy with even a prod in the back. Better that than being completely ignored by her husband as he had done throughout the journey here. She wanted to know where she stood with him, how much she could confide in him.

A tap on the door and a serving girl entered, bearing a laden tray.

'Oh, thank you. Please can you leave it next door?'

'Yes, Mrs Dorrell, ma'am.' The maid bobbed and disappeared through the connecting door to the adjoining-room which was their private sitting-room.

Mrs Dorrell? Were they travelling incognito now?

Jem found herself frowning, wondering why Tony might wish to disguise the fact he was a Viscount or, more to the point, that she was a Viscountess! If he was ashamed of her now, she dreaded to think how he'd react when he knew the full truth of what she had done. She stared at the door and willed the tears not to fall.

'Upon my soul, if that isn't a solemn face. Aren't the rooms to your satisfaction?'

'Tony!' Her heart skipped a beat as she saw his face wreathed in smiles. He'd swung in through the door without even knocking. 'No, the rooms are lovely, they . . . '

'Have they brought up supper yet?' Tony rubbed his hands together. 'There is nothing like a carriage journey to bring on the appetite. I'm absolutely famished.'

'Yes, it's in the sitting-room next door.' Jem hugged her arms around her. Hunger. Of course, she remembered what he had said back at the cave about being a bear with a sore head. She had been so foolish to think . . . 'From what I could see the tray was full of different things. There should be some-thing to tempt you.'

'Splendid.' He gave a small nod but made no move towards the other room. A distinct gleam appeared in Tony's eye and his gaze seemed to concentrate on her lips. Jem shifted where she sat. She refused to humiliate herself again by begging to be kissed. The memory of what happened on *The Courage* rankled. How she had pressed against him, and he had turned away.

'Tony, the maid addressed me as Mrs Dorrell.'

'Good, I gave our names as Captain and Mrs Dorrell,' he said and took a step closer. His eyes were still focused on her mouth. His hands started to unbutton his coat. 'I intend on having an undisturbed night, my sweet. I have given Andrews the evening off.'

Tony must be tired too, Jem thought. She hadn't even considered the possibility. She had been so intent on her own misery, she had forgotten he had suffered the same journey.

'Shall I get you something to eat?' she asked, trying to keep her heart from racing, trying to maintain her dignity.

'Perhaps later,' Tony began to advance towards her, his gaze narrowing as he undid the buttons of his coat and shook it off, threw it towards one of the chairs where it half landed, half slid off so that one of the sleeves was draped on the floor.

A grin tugged at Jem's mouth. She stood up and reached for the coat. It would be all too easy to imagine Andrews's pained expression in the morning.

'Leave it,' Tony said and moved to stand before her, blocking her path.

'But . . . ' Her hands trembled in mid-air.

284

'It's only a coat, Jemima, and you have far more important things to attend to.'

'Such as?' She tilted her head.

'The rest of my attire.' He thrust his chin the air. 'You may begin with my cravat.'

Jem gulped. He'd never asked her to undress him before. Usually he managed perfectly well himself. She took a closer look at his face. His eyes were sparkling and the corners of his mouth twitched. 'Tony, are you exhausted? Or are you funning me?'

He laughed and swung her into his arms, caught her lips. His lips parted and she tasted the sweetness of his mouth.

She breathed in the musky scent of him, heightened by a day's travel on the road, and something fluttered inside her. Her hands pulled at his cravat. She succeeded only in pulling tighter.

'Not so fast, my sweet.' He raised her hand to his lips and kissed the palm, making her hand tingle. 'You may have some way to go before you become a good valet, but I believe my services as a lady's maid will inspire.'

He pushed her arms away, set to work on her laces and buttons and paused only to finish divesting himself rapidly of his own shirt.

Unable to resist, Jem slid her hand until it touched the warm flesh of his bare chest.

'Jemima, Jem . . . ' he mumbled throatily and kissed her again. He demanded the complete surrender of her tongue, stunned all her senses before breaking away to remove her shift in a lightning movement, so that apart from her stockings she stood completely naked before him.

'Jem . . . wife . . . ' He nuzzled her breasts, sending stabs of pleasures to every corner of Jem's body.

Her knees threatened to give way and she leant into Tony for support, her body arching to his. This was Tony as he had been in the cave, the Tony she had wanted long before, the Tony who had given her something out of this world, despite the pain of the first time.

She froze at the memory.

It was only for an instant but enough to still him. He raised his head and looked at her questioningly.

Jem marvelled at how, without words, he had so quickly sensed something had changed. A lump formed in her throat. What if he should leave her again, as he had on the ship? She couldn't bear that. Not now. She refused to allow it.

Jem pressed herself forward, felt the tickle of his chest against hers; the waves of warmth in his embrace should have assuaged her but they did the opposite.

'Please Tony,' she whispered against his lips, wondering how far she dared go.

He broke away, leaving her cold, exposed, confused. Jem started to tremble.

'Tony . . . you once said you would introduce me properly to the rites of Cupid?' she said, trying to keep her voice from breaking.

'I'm intending to start your next lesson in a minute, but first I want to get m'breeches off.' He gave her a smile as his eyes devoured her. 'If you were being sensible you'd get underneath the covers before you catch your death.'

'I have no desire to be sensible,' Jem replied wondering if she should take her stockings off as she watched him tug his breeches off one leg and then the next.

'Get into bed,' he growled.

'No.'

'Love, honour and *obey* I think it was I heard you say in that chapel,' Tony muttered, walking back towards her — naked, and fiercely aroused.

The glow from the fire danced across his curves. It burnished the curl of his dark hair, all over him, with gold.

'Have it your own way,' Tony said taking her by the hand and drawing her towards him. His masculine form might as well have

287

been a fire. It radiated heat. Jem fell against him, let his body support her. Let her cold flesh splay against him, be softened, as her lips became his again.

Somehow, in an artful manoeuvre, still rested against Tony, she was sinking to the floor, but not the floorboards, not the discomfort of the cave: there was a thick carpet below her and Tony looming over her.

'Waste of a perfectly good bed but . . . ' Tony said nuzzling her neck, moving down to tease each breast in turn as he rested her back gently on the carpet.

'Tony . . . I . . . '

'Hush. Now is not the time for words, my sweet, it is the time when your husband dedicates himself to pleasuring his beautiful wife.'

Jem's breath stopped in her throat as his words sunk in. He thought her beautiful.

★   ★   ★

'Tony.' Jem pushed a lock of hair away from his damp forehead, wondering if she dared whisper words of love in the aftermath of what they had just shared.

Tony shifted, pulled himself up with a groan so he was leaning on his elbows, took a moment to focus his errant gaze on her.

'Jemima . . . you are more than a man might ever expect in a wife.'

Jem closed her eyes and felt a hole open in her heart. He didn't love her. That was too much to expect, but maybe he might come to like her for more than just being Charlie Cullen's sister. She might at least perhaps save him the expense of keeping a mistress. She swallowed hard, too hard.

Tony frowned. 'What is it?'

The thought of him carousing with a painted lady, somewhere, had shaken her like a poisoned arrow through her breast. 'Nothing.'

'You did . . . enjoy it?'

'Yes.' She smiled at him and his countenance relaxed. 'I enjoyed it very much. Tony . . . I'll always enjoy it . . . with you.'

He kissed her on the forehead and extracted himself from her slowly, stood up, and shook his limbs. Jem scrambled to her feet, reluctantly.

'The next lesson will involve the very pleasant feather bed we have at our disposal.' Tony rubbed his hands together. 'But right now I am feeling rather peckish.'

'You are not going to . . . ' Jem said, shocked. He couldn't walk into their sitting-room completely naked as the day he had been born!

Tony grinned. 'My dear, I was most precise when I requested a private sitting-room, I assure you. I also informed mine hosts that we had not been married very long.'

She must have looked as startled as a pheasant with a lamp swung into its face because his brow creased and he leapt over the bed, wrested a sheet from it and wrapped it around her very skilfully into a makeshift toga like the Romans wore.

He played it to her as if he was a footman, bowing. 'Ma'am, your cold collation awaits. Pudding will be served back in here.'

At her laugh, his heart skipped a beat. For about the tenth time in the last half hour. It was just as well they had just made love or he'd have thrown her on the floor right now, and he was starving.

He had waited a long time for this. He had wanted to make sure she was well and then had not wanted the others to hear their cries in the narrow confines of the ship. He wanted her to have no cause to say he had forced his attentions on her. Some days, it had been all he could do to look at her without drawing her into his arms and kissing her.

He took her small hand in his, led her into the sitting-room and had trouble thinking when he had ever felt like this with any woman, anyone. He'd certainly never thought he would be wrapping a woman, his wife, in a sheet to preserve her modesty while they picnicked in a sitting-room of a coaching inn.

She seemed happy. She sat down on the largest sofa and curled her feet up under her. When she smiled, a warmth rose inside him.

Tony turned his attention back to the tray and the platter on it. He took a plate and prepared for Jem a variety of morsels, the best cuts of meats and took it over to her before going back for his own. He wondered if he looked amusing to her doing such a gentlemanly task, as one might for a lady at a ball, but without any clothes on. She was still smiling when he came over with his plate and sat beside her.

'Is everything to your liking, m'lady?'

'Hmmm,' she said. 'Travelling does things to one's appetite.'

'That and other things.' Tony brushed a curl off her neck and tried to fix in his mind the sight of her there sitting contented before firmly turning his attention to his own supper. He tried to quell the rising thought that he wanted her again.

★ ★ ★

Jem reached over and encountered not the warm body of Tony, but a rapidly cooling

291

patch of bedclothes. She blinked in the dim light and sat up.

'Tony?'

'I'm getting dressed, Jemima. I thought to have an early start to London today. With any luck we'll arrive before midday, and have the pleasantries out of the way by the middle of the afternoon.'

Jem blinked back the tears. It was all so reminiscent of the morning in the cave. How could Tony be so warm at night yet so cold in the morning? She had thought they might be getting somewhere, and that she might confide in him this morning about her stepfather.

'How soon should I be dressed for?'

'As soon as possible,' Tony said and came over by the bed, tying his cravat with an expert twist of his hand. 'Don't look at me like that Jem, or else my good intentions will fly out the window.'

'Good intentions?'

'Yes, I refuse to let you divert me, despite your wiles. I have only just got this damned thing tied straight.' Tony brushed the hair off her forehead. 'Jemima, I don't pretend it will be easy, but with my mama's help, hopefully we can avoid the worst of the scandal.'

'Scandal?' Jem pulled the bed sheet tighter around her. 'What are you talking about?'

'The *ton* will be talking about you, once it gets out, about you having been a soldier. But put it from your mind. My mama will help. She can silence the worst and make sure you are received in all the right places. In time, some new talking point will come along, you'll see.'

It was on the tip of Jem's tongue to explain she didn't want to be in society. It was never anything she aspired to.

She sighed and wondered what was going to happen when the full scandal was revealed. She doubted very much even Lady Ardenbrooke would silence the tongues then. There had to be something she could do. She owed him that much.

'If you give me a moment, I'll get dressed.' Jem paused and swallowed hard. Society. The *ton*. She hadn't even considered the expectations of the *ton* when she had purchased her clothes in Lisbon. She supposed she must have been thinking they would go straight to Warwickshire, be immured in the country a good while, not helter-skelter directly to London. 'I hope the clothes we bought in Lisbon will be grand enough for your mother.'

'We'll make sure you are kitted out properly.' Tony waved his hand.

'You don't need to . . . '

Tony cupped her face in his hands and she saw his eyes darken. 'I want to, Jem. You're my wife, my bride. Never did I suppose you could arrange an entire, suitable wardrobe from Lisbon. Everything you want, you need, you shall have. I will look after you *in every way*.'

Jem looked away as the tears gathered in her eyes. She had to do something in return, something that showed how much his words meant to her. She wrapped a sheet around her and padded over to her ridicule. She drew out Charles's watch and held it out to him with a trembling hand.

'This is your wedding present. I won it from Charles . . . in a card game. I know he would have liked you to have it,' she said before her nerve failed her. The watch swayed in her hands.

Tony made no move to take it. He simply looked at her and then the watch. The silence grew and Jem stood, wondering if she had done the right thing. She wished she could unsay the words.

Surely he would take the gift?

He had to understand what the watch meant to her. She placed the watch in his hand and his fingers closed around it.

'Jemima,' he said finally and his voice sounded more like a sob. 'You unman me. I am at a loss for words. I am honoured. Charles Cullen was my best friend. You could have searched the world over and yet not found a more perfect gift. I shall wear it with pride and every time I look at this, I shall remember the debt I owe you and him.'

'I am pleased you like it.' Jem knew if she said any more, she would start crying and her secrets would tumble out in a great rush.

Tony grinned after he placed the watch carefully in his pocket. He drew something out of his inner jacket pocket.

'As we are giving presents, there is something I should like you to have. I bought it in Portsmouth yesterday and forgot to give it to you. Meant to give it you after . . .' He held out a slim leather box and Jem opened it to reveal a necklace of diamonds and sapphires.

'Tony! It is, it is . . . lovely.' Jem wondered where Tony could buy such a thing. Where would she ever wear it? It looked more like something a man would give his mistress than his wife. She tried to smile, but could not help feel it was a bit like a payment, rather than a gift. 'I don't know how to thank you properly.'

'I think we had best wait until later, or we shall never make London. Now, I had best see our transport is in order.'

Jem watched his back, thought about the strange look on his face as he had left her. All she could decipher from his words of duty or honour was that nowhere in between them had been one word of love.

She wrapped her arms about her waist.

She was asking too much if she expected him to love her? He had loved Charlie, and so had she. And the passion they had shared had been real.

Two things then that made this more than just a marriage of convenience. She wanted to trust him with everything, but she also did not want to break this fragile truce.

Jem forced her fingers to pick out her garments and started to dress. Nobody would guess how much she quaked from her attire.

All you need's a brave face as folk don't see beyond the ends of their noses.

Her lips turned up in a brief smile as she remembered Bessie's words of advice. They would serve her again in London as she faced society.

16

The carriage had drawn to a halt. Surely only a minute before they had been whistling through Wimbledon, then Wandsworth? Tony had sat up as they'd bowled past Wimbledon Common and looked out of the window thinking *we're nearly there*. He opened both eyes wide and saw the unmistakable columns of his mama's house. They'd reached their destination — Audley Street in the West End of London.

Now, looking at the fashionable street with its air of superiority over the rest of the neighbourhood, all he wanted to do was sweep Jem up into his arms and carry her off somewhere else, away from all this. The desire to instruct the coachman to drive away from the porticoed frontage threatened to overwhelm him like the vapour that came from the carnage of a battlefield.

It had to be done. Society. Facing it.

Women lived off all the fuss, fustian and intrigues as leeches thrived off a dying man's blood. Within hours of arriving in the country, his mama always wished to be back in London, amongst the *ton*.

He had to give Jemima her chance. He particularly remembered how she had longed for a pair of ivory silk dancing slippers, how she had wagered with Charlie for them and how he'd helped her win them. Dancing must have vanished from her life shortly afterwards. The thought haunted him. He meant to make it up to her, to ensure she had everything she would have had if Charlie had lived. Everything she deserved.

Tony clenched his jaw and, without waiting for a servant to perform the task, opened the chaise's door. The last thing he desired in his marriage was to replicate the war of attrition that existed between his parents.

'Mother's new house. She insisted and papa relented,' Tony said, holding his hand out to Jem. 'My dear mother is very much of the *ton*.'

'Will your father be here as well?' Jem asked as she stepped down, an unease akin to fear flittering across her eyes. Tony forced his arms to stay by his side. Would that he could have hauled her into his arms and attempted to kiss it away! But they were standing on the common pavement of Audley Street.

'Pa stays as far from London and Mother as he possibly can. Having produced the heir and the spare, it is the way she likes it.'

'So it is not a love match?'

'I believe it was a union of two estates.' Tony gave a bark of a laugh. 'Their marriage is one of the main reasons I had resisted becoming leg-shackled. Damn me, I desired never to marry at all.'

'But you did marry.'

'And right glad of it I am.' Tony kept his thoughts firmly away from last night and the way she responded to his every touch. It would not do at all to meet his mother, displaying his affection, his *desire* for his wife. 'I have very rarely had so much pleasure doing my duty.'

Jem's face fell, and Tony noticed the wink of a tear in her right eye. What did she expect him to do — prove his love on the doorstep?

'Lord Fordingley,' the elderly retainer gasped out as the large oak door swung inwards. 'We weren't expecting you.'

'Quiet. Is my mother at home, Grieves?'

'Lady Ardenbrooke is receiving in the morning-room, my lord. Shall I announce you?'

'No. No, I shall do it m'self and beard the lion in the den as it were.'

'Are you home for good then, m'lord?'

'Grieves, the warrior is indeed home.'

Tony started in and then paused and squared his shoulders. He had done what his mother wanted — married a girl with impeccable lines.

He had only deprived her of the wedding itself.

He took three steps down the hall before noticing Jemima was still on the doorstep.

'You don't expect me to go into battle alone, do you?' He said, turning back. He found himself slightly piqued that her lips did not quiver upwards.

'Perhaps I ought to have a few minutes to make myself more presentable?' she said uncertainly.

'Jemima, don't fuss.' Tony beckoned her to come inside. Not that it wasn't tempting to get back in the carriage and head out for Warwickshire — and the devil take society. But he must be patient. His wife deserved her chance to shine. And Mother would take her to a London dressmaker soon enough.

Tony pushed open the morning door, slamming back on its hinges.

'Mother!'

At the sound of a teacup shattering on the floor, Tony winced. Perhaps he should have sent word ahead.

He lifted his hat and nodded at the half-dozen harpies sitting, staring, their fans at the ready and stepped into the room. He'd rather be facing a phalanx of Polish hussars.

'Is this any way to greet your son, home from the wars? Sitting about drinking tea? Where's the orchestra? And the strings of crystal lanterns hung up to welcome me home?'

'Tony, is it really you?'

'In the flesh.'

'You bad boy, how long have you been in England?' His mother rapped her fan against the arm of her chair. 'You might have sent word.'

'I thought you would be pleased to see me.'

'Pleased? Of course I am pleased, but why are you wearing a superfine jacket, and not your dress uniform?'

'I have resigned my commission.'

'*Resigned* your commission? Good lord, you have seen sense at last?' His mother lifted her chin. 'You may come here and kiss me.'

'Mother, it is good to be back in England.' Tony walked over, brushed her cheek and breathed in the familiar smell of lavender. 'I have a few things to tell you.'

'You should have let me know you were coming home.' His mother's eyes narrowed and she picked up a sheaf of papers and shook them at him. 'The Season is about to begin. There are at least two duke's daughters making their debut. There is no reason, *if* you make yourself presentable, why they shouldn't choose you, and — '

'Mother, I am already married.' Tony placed his hands behind his back, clenched his fists, and breathed in the silence, deeply.

'Married? Whatever next! You *can't* have contracted to a gel without consulting your father or me.'

Tony took a moment to stare at his boots and the oriental carpet, as the murmurings and fan-fluttering started and grew.

With slow deliberation, he turned towards Jemima who stood, her cheeks burning crimson, in the doorway.

Something in his chest constricted.

'May I present my wife — Jemima.' Tony gave her an encouraging smile and beckoned her forward. Her arm was trembling as she laid her hand on his sleeve. 'Isn't she a picture?' he said loudly to the room.

Only a single lady dared to give a half-nod in reply before sinking back behind her fan.

'And who *precisely* is Jemima?' His mama's voice was like a hammer against brass bells. Tony stared at her. Her rudeness was insupportable. She should be bloody pleased to see him married.

'Jemima is my wife, and the sister of Major Charles Cullen. You do remember Charlie, Mother? It was my duty and honour to marry his sister.'

Jem wished the floor would open and swallow her.

Lady Ardenbrooke sat, her face chalk-white, as if pinned to her chair. The five other women sat on the edge of their seats their ears pricked for very detail.

Before the day was out her story would be known to the whole *ton* — how Viscount Fordingley, who'd escaped the snares of matrimony for so long, had brought back a wife from Spain.

She had trouble breathing.

Her hopes of explaining to Tony about her stepfather quietly were quashed.

It would be only a matter of time now before he or the law came for her.

She had to do something. Find out what had happened, whether they were looking for her stepfather's murderer, because if they were, she would have to flee. And quickly before she disgraced Tony and his family utterly.

Jem released a breath and felt better. She would try and act as ordinarily as possible until she knew the lie of the land. Then she would decide what she must do.

'And how did Jemima come to be in Spain? Under whose protection?' Jem heard Lady Ardenbrooke ask. 'I seem to recall Major Cullen died a few years ago.'

'Jemima . . . she was in Spain because . . . '
Tony pulled at his cravat as if he was trying to loosen it. There was a brief silence and Jem waited to see how Tony would answer. 'The truth is Jemima and I were betrothed . . . '

'Betrothed! What on earth are you talking about?' Lady Ardenbrooke said, echoing Jem's own thoughts.

'Secretly, in England,' he continued, drawing his chin up and seeming to get into his stride. His arms fell to his sides. 'After Jemima's mother died Jemima was . . . somewhat upset, and . . . and she came to Spain to find me.'

'Fustian!' Lady Ardenbrooke's voice rapped out. 'Do you expect me to believe a gently brought-up young lady was wandering around the Spanish peninsula *quite alone?*'

'Oh my!' one of the ladies said and started to fan herself vigorously. 'A girl wandering alone in that savage territory, that would be . . . Think of the danger . . . to her *reputation.*'

'Fortunately we married in Spain to ensure there was no damage done to Jemima's reputation.' Tony said.

'You poor, foolish girl, losing your mother and feeling yourself quite alone in the world! Tony always could be relied upon to do the right thing — eventually.' Lady Ardenbrooke cast her eyes about the company. 'Don't you all agree?'

The fans stopped fluttering, suspended in mid-air. Then as if on cue, the vigorous fanning started again.

'Of course!'

'What a romantic story!'

'Poor Jemima,' the various ladies cooed in turn.

Jem stared at the richly patterned carpet. Her throat constricted as she came to the painful realization — Tony was ashamed of her serving as a soldier. She was proud of having served as a soldier, and not only survived but been accomplished at it. She bit back the words that threatened to spill out. The last thing she wanted to do was to become notorious — unnecessarily. The story would have to wait until she had found out the truth about her stepfather.

'Now if you will excuse us, I believe my bride is a bit tired from our journey.' Tony gave a small bow.

'Quite, quite.' Lady Ardenbrooke reached over and pulled a bell rope. 'You can stay in your old room and . . . Jemima can stay in the Blue Room.'

'Mother, the Blue Room is on the third floor. We shall require other arrangements.'

Jem watched as the two glared at each

other. Mother and son. She was struck by how like Lady Ardenbrooke Tony looked, especially when both brows were knotted. The fans batted briskly and there was the nervous clink of teacups as the silence stretched on. Her head ached with a blinding pain.

'Anthony, your stubborn resemblance to your father does not become you,' Lady Ardenbrooke said at last. She started to pour herself another cup of tea. 'Jemima may have the Rose Room, and you may take the Green Room. I trust you will be satisfied with that?'

★　★　★

Jem watched the maid carefully unpack her things until she could bear it no longer. She had a headache and she knew she should lie down but she could not. She marched over to the window and looked out on to the smart green lawn of the garden. She focused on the drops of rain speckling the glass panes.

Ordered, symmetrical London with its rules and regulations, its uncrossable boundaries. This house trapped her as neatly as any prison.

She had a day or two at most perhaps where she might feign travelling fatigue. In that time she had to get out and discover the truth of what had happened to her stepfather, whether . . . she choked down a lump in her throat . . . she had killed him.

Jem twisted the narrow band of gold Tony had placed on her finger in the chapel in Spain. She should have told him before and now it was too late.

'Jemima?'

Jem turned to see Tony standing in the middle of the room with a grin on his face. The door clicked as the maid slipped discreetly away. Irritation and frustration swelled in her breast.

'You don't think your mother was taken in by your story?' she said. 'She saw it for exactly what it was — a tissue of lies.'

'Yes,' Tony said agreeably, 'but what my mama thought was unimportant. It was the other tittle-tattlers. I thought it better to feed them something than leave it to their utter discretion to make up. Sympathetic and romantic, it appeals to the female nature. The perfect story.'

'How I was so panting for love that I braved the whole of the Peninsula to search for my betrothed!' Jem waved her arms wildly and started pacing the room. 'It makes me sound like some lovesick fool.'

'Yet you did have a *tendre* for me, did you not?'

How dare he treat her girlish dreams as if they were something to be made fun of! She wanted to slap him across the face. She balled her hands into fists. 'There was nothing about the story I found in the least bit amusing.'

'It was not meant to be a bagatelle served up for the delectation of the *ton*, but a way to forestall questions, questions I thought you would prefer to avoid. Jemima, have some sense! Do you want ladies to draw their skirts away when you walk past?'

'They'll know all about my soldiering ... eventually. It won't be long before the story makes it to England in a letter, on someone else's lips. In the official dispatches, even! And then I'll look twice a fool.'

'Not if you give yourself a chance to be established in the *ton*,' he said. Jem thought she saw a look of hurt in his eyes but it vanished so quickly she wondered if she had imagined it. 'Jemima, do be sensible. You know what people are like! I shall of course inform my mother of the truth at the earliest opportunity. She will be instrumental in assisting you with handling it when the truth does come out.'

'You can't be sure.' Jem glared at him. He seemed so collected while she suspected she might burst out in tears at any moment. Jem drew a deep breath. 'Your mother seemed less than pleased at the news of our marriage.'

Her voice broke on the last word. She had to make him understand this was more than a game.

'Jem . . . ' Tony took a step towards her, holding out his arms.

It took all her will-power not to launch herself on to his chest and weep, to pour out everything. Her head pounded, and her shoulder started to ache. However, the only thing that would do would be to show she was a weak female. She turned her back on him and scrubbed at her eyes.

'The story you told makes it seem as if I am ashamed about what I did,' she said after a moment. 'I am proud of what I did in Spain.'

'Jemima, I wanted to protect you.'

His hand stroked her hair. She twisted out of his grasp. 'Keep your hands away from me!'

'You are quite appealing when you are angry, Lady Fordingley.' The corners of his mouth twitched. 'Very appealing.'

'How dare you make light of this!'

'I am not making light of things. All will be well, I promise.'

'Promise? Why should I believe *your* promises?'

'And what exactly do you mean?'

Jem shivered at his voice, cold and hard as a metal spoon just before being plunged into a pot of boiling fat. His eyes were glinting, dangerously.

The well of hurt and frustration building inside burst and she no longer cared what he might think or how he might react. 'Every single time, you have said 'I promise', you have broken that promise.'

'Which promise?' he demanded. 'Name the promises I have broken.'

'For one thing, you promised I should be able to choose when I informed the army of my sex!' Tears flowed down her face and into her mouth. Jem brushed them away with an impatient hand. 'You gave me your solemn oath, Tony, that I would be the one to tell Colonel Garroway, I would be the one to resign my commission. That we'd go back to England after one year! You made those promises when I agreed to be your mistress.'

'What was I supposed to do — let you die? The surgeon would have discovered the truth sooner than you would have made it to the colonel! Isn't it obvious why I didn't risk any delay to your medical attention? And why should we stay in Portugal after I resigned my commission? Be reasonable, Jemima!'

Jem gripped her fingers into fists behind her back. He wasn't listening *again*, winced as her voice quivered at its unnaturally loud pitch. 'You broke your promise!'

'I don't need to listen to this.' Tony's brow furrowed. 'Jemima, why don't you lie down? You are obviously tired.'

'What are you doing?' Jemima watched Tony stride over to the door. 'Where are you going? We are not finished yet.'

'My dear *wife*, you may not be finished, but I am.' He yanked open the door.

Jem heard the door slam as Tony left the room, sending the china on the mantelpiece jangling. Her insides felt as if they had been twisted into knots. She sank to the floor and hugged her knees to her chest.

'He'll come back and apologize, because I'll be damned if I will,' she whispered to herself.

★ ★ ★

He didn't come back.

She waited.

The afternoon passed with nothing to do but go over her anger and she found it impossible to decide if she should be nourishing her temper or placating it.

When her supper arrived on a tray, she picked at it, then sent it back. The rest of the night, she spent tossing and turning, hoping each creak of the house meant his footstep. Jem watched the morning light grow stronger as it seeped through the cracks in the curtains and shuddered at the prospect of a new day. She pummelled the pillows, lay on her side and then her back staring up at the canopy.

The information she required would mean a trip to Warwickshire, a journey of at least two days. There was no way any excuse of illness from her would suffice. Her absence would be noticed. Someone would have to make inquiries on her behalf. But whom could she trust? Everyone in this household's first loyalty would be to Tony and his mother. She needed someone from outside. But how?

When she could stand her thoughts no longer, she hauled herself out of bed, and rang the bell. Within minutes, a maid had appeared, bobbing and smiling. Jem forced a smile on her face as the maid dressed her hair into a fashionable, flattering style and took inordinate lengths of time perfecting her dress. While the dress was not up to minute, Jem could see from the dressing-room mirror, she was at least presentable. She skipped down the stairs.

Jem pushed the door to the morning room open, fully expecting to see Tony sipping at a cup of coffee, but the only occupant was his mother. Her heart formed a large lump in her throat.

'If you are looking for my son, he has gone out,' Lady Ardenbrooke said. She patted the seat of the chaise beside her. 'Now do come forward, child, I don't *bite*. Sit here and talk to me.'

Jem reluctantly walked into the room and sat down beside Lady Ardenbrooke. She swallowed hard and tried to think of something to say. She wondered if Tony had yet told his mother about her soldiering.

'My son informs me you are tired from your journey, you poor thing,' Lady Ardenbrooke said. 'I swear the boy is just like his father — impossible. He never thinks about the comforts of others until it is too late.'

'He always seemed concerned about the welfare of his men,' Jem said, surprised at defending him so easily. 'In Spain, he insisted the officers never asked more of their men than they were prepared to do themselves.'

'My dear,' Lady Ardenbrooke said and laid a cool hand on Jem's arm, 'that may be true, but it doesn't disguise the fact he has *no notion* where women are concerned.' She shook her head. 'Never has done.'

'I really wouldn't know.' Jem stared into her lap.

A throaty cough and they looked up to see

Grieves standing in the doorway. 'Lady Houndsworth.'

A petite woman swept in. She had a porcelain complexion, blonde curls, and was dressed in the most extravagant green day costume, trimmed with chocolate brown lace, that Jem thought she had ever seen. She paused theatrically in front of them extending her matching parasol out with her right arm so that the point rested snugly on the carpet. She thrust her chin high in the air.

'Forgive me, Lady Ardenbrooke,' the visitor's pert lips exclaimed, 'for calling at this unorthodox hour but I simply had to know if the latest *on dit* was true. Mrs Rundle was so vehement, and I so aghast, and now I even have a wager on it. Tell me it's not true!'

'My dear Arabella, I had hoped you would call.' Lady Ardenbrooke said.

Jem's heart dropped. This had to be the former Miss Arabella Triptree, the woman Tony had once hoped to marry, someone who would know beyond a shadow of a doubt the lie of Tony's story. She listened blankly as Lady Ardenbrooke made the introductions.

'Fiddlesticks! Ten guineas down the drain!' Lady Houndsworth snapped. 'So it's true — Tony's been caught in the parson's mousetrap at last!'

She looked Jem up and down and shook

her head. The back of her neck bristled but Jem resisted the temptation to make a quick retort.

'I have not seen you before Lady Fordingley. From where do your family come, my dear?'

'Warwickshire,' Jem said simply, not about to give anything away about her family she did not have to.

'Indeed you bear a passing resemblance, mostly by way of your eyes and colouring, to a certain gentleman.' A single well-groomed eyebrow was raised. 'The late Major Charles Cullen of Warwickshire?'

Jem tried to ignore the chill running down her spine. 'Major Cullen was my brother.'

'How so very delightful that Tony should chose dear Charlie's sister as his bride, don't you think Lady Ardenbrooke?' Lady Houndsworth flashed the briefest of smiles but all Jem could think was she could hardly bear this woman speaking about Charles in such intimate terms. She would have to deal with this the same way she had dealt with the early days in the army, keeping the current task uppermost in her mind and burying all her emotions deep inside her.

'My dear Lady Fordingley,' she continued, holding out her slim, immaculately gloved hands, 'I am sure we shall become the very greatest of friends. And you must consent to call me Arabella.'

Jem rose and did as she was bidden and pulled Lady Houndsworth's hands, which smelled of roses, to her lips. The gesture was not reciprocated, Jem noticed, though she was rewarded with another of those fleeting smiles as she said, 'Do call me Jemima.'

'Come sit down, my dear,' Lady Arden-brooke said.

Arabella carefully arranged her skirts to show off her figure to her best advantage as she lowered herself to the chaise opposite Jem. She waited with a poised expression on her face as Lady Ardenbrooke poured cups of tea, before saying, 'Where is Tony?'

'Out, you know how he is.' Lady Ardenbrooke waved her fan and turned towards Jem. 'When dear Arabella made her debut she was a diamond of the first water. We had such hopes, Jemima, that Tony might come up to scratch.'

Arabella's eyes flashed a bright spark of green before narrowing as she said, 'Lord Houndsworth was quicker off the mark.'

'That is all in the past, my dear,' Lady Ardenbrooke said with a sigh. 'Now I am particularly pleased you are here, my dear, for I had considered asking you whether you would give Jemima your backing for her entrance into society.'

'Of course! Why ever would I not?' Jem wondered if she imagined the curious flash that passed across Arabella's eyes.

'It is rather a delicate situation.'

'You can trust me absolutely, Lady Ardenbrooke.' Arabella flicked open her green Chinese silk fan and wafted it in front of her face so that Jem found it impossible to see her countenance. 'Why, my poor late mama was your dearest friend and I should like to help . . . in any way I can.'

'We must do everything we can to avert a scandal.' Lady Ardenbrooke said in a low voice.

'What scandal?' Arabella leant forward.

Jem looked from Arabella back to Lady Ardenbrooke. Her heart beat louder than a drum calling men to battle. Tony hadn't told his mother, had he?

'Jemima served in Spain as a soldier.'

17

'A lady soldier! Impossible! I never heard of such a thing.' Arabella's fan stopped in mid-fan. A tiny smile appeared at her lips for an instant before vanishing as her face took on a studied concerned look.

'It's true,' Jem said, suddenly sick of being talked about as if she was not there. What did it matter if this woman knew? The truth would be common currency within days, and Lady Arabella might be a useful ally to have when the true scandal broke.

Jem pushed the thought to the very back of her mind and forced a smile to her lips. 'I disguised myself as a man, of course.'

'Heavens above! How did you ever cope? I doubt I could have lasted two minutes, let alone actually served!'

Arabella fanned herself very rapidly and Lady Ardenbrooke waited with pursed lips.

'Luckily, I was able to serve with honour. Wellington decorated me for my bravery on the battlefield,' Jem said in her sweetest voice. 'Might I trouble you for another cup of tea, Lady Ardenbrooke?'

'Certainly.' Lady Ardenbrooke snapped to

attention and poured another cup of tea. When she was done, she turned to Arabella and said, 'And so where do you think I should introduce Jemima first? I had thought about Almack's.'

The fan stilled and then Arabella placed it down on her lap. 'Leave Almack's to the matchmakers and their insipid wares! And leave Jemima's debut to me. Lady Fordingley deserves to hit society with style and aplomb.' Arabella's face suddenly lit up, her eyes sparkling, and she clapped her gloved hands together. 'At the theatre!'

'I wouldn't want you to go to any — ' Jem started to say.

'Trouble?' Lady Arabella raised a perfectly arched eyebrow. 'It is no trouble at all, my dear. We have a box at the *Sans Pareil* — a week from today. It will be perfect and we must go to my dressmaker — there is enough time to get something made up so you will look completely fabulous. Why, there's not an ounce of fat on you, Jemima! Heads will turn! You will be the talk of the *ton*!'

That was the very last thing Jem wanted. 'Lady H — '

'Arabella, please call me Arabella, my dear. It's the very least I could do — for Tony's wife.' The smile grew on her face. 'I shall take you to my mantua-maker this morning. She will make you up an entire fabulous wardrobe.'

'B — '

'How kind of you, Arabella.' Lady Ardenbrooke interrupted Jem before turning to her to say, 'Tony can afford it, my dear, if that's what's bothering you.'

⋆ ⋆ ⋆

After being poked and prodded for the best part of an hour by the French dressmaker and her assistant, directed at every turn by Arabella, and shown reams of materials, hats, gloves, slippers, all the way down to cotton undergarments, Jem gave up trying to argue what did and did not suit her.

Some two hours later, Jem alighted from Arabella's smart black barouche and breathed the empty, undemanding air of Audley Street before stepping back into the house.

'Tony?' She tapped on the door to his chamber. There was no answer. She knocked harder, raised her voice. 'Are you there Tony?'

Still no answer came. She risked opening the door and the room was empty. Everything about it from the solid canopied bed to the silver-backed brushes screamed masculinity and the air was filled with his scent. She breathed in and realized how much she had missed him, how she'd give anything to unsay those words and have him smile at her again. Only it didn't appear he was going to give her a chance.

Through the half open door to his dressing-room, she spied a dull green jacket lying in the bottom of the wardrobe. She tiptoed in and bent down. Her old uniform! She had been certain that it must have been destroyed. A lump came into her throat. Maybe he had saved it because he couldn't bear to throw it away. She smiled at her foolishness and ran her hand over the faded familiar material. Tony wasn't in love with her. Yes, he desired her enough to ask her to be his mistress but he had married her out of duty.

The more likely story was Andrews had saved it and forgotten about it. In any case, it didn't matter — it was here! She knew what she had to do — the solution to her nagging problem.

She would dress as a man and hire someone to discover the truth about her stepfather.

★ ★ ★

Jem sauntered along Rotten Row enjoying the early spring sunshine, despite the crowds of people on horseback and in open carriages. It only mattered she was outside, not stuck in an hot dressmaker's room being stuck full of pins and having to listen to conversations about whether it was daring or passé to wear a turban or whether the *ton* had yet declared satin or sarsnet to be the more fashionable this year. She was at last taking action and bringing the battle to her stepfather.

Rotten Row — on a day like this there never was a more foolish name for the wide sweeping path that bowled through Hyde Park. A light breeze danced across her face and ruffled her hair. She pushed a strand from her mouth, took a deep breath and decided it was an afternoon where she should be simply happy to be alive. She locked her hands behind her and began to walk briskly down the path.

Out here in the fresh air, it was much easier to think clearly and to plan.

She would sit down and explain to Tony her opinion of society and ask him if he would excuse her from participating in the season. However, he seemed enamoured of London and society. A better excuse was needed. Something that sent her to Warwickshire.

She could pretend to be ill perhaps . . . if she coughed a lot would a doctor put it down to the aggravating properties of the London air and order she be taken to the country? Would Tony come with her? She hated the thought of leaving him.

'Blast his eyes!' Jem muttered to herself and kicked a stone and sent it scattering into a lady's path. The lady turned a shade well matched to her isabella-coloured walking dress. Jem's cheeks grew warm and she hurried on with a mumbled apology.

She must discover what had happened to her stepfather. Jem suddenly felt cold, even with the sunshine beating down on her.

'Sarge? Sergeant Riseley?' she heard a croaky voice call. 'What are you doing here?'

Jem turned to see a one-armed man hurrying towards her. She bit her lip. What now? She looked to the ground but she refused to pretend she hadn't seen the man. He had been under her command in the 95th, until he had been wounded just before Ciudad Rodrigo and invalided home. Jem's stomach twisted. Why had she thought going out dressed in breeches was a good idea?

'Bill Nye, as I live and breathe,' she said, raising her head to meet his familiar round face and matted dark hair with its grey tufts about the ears. 'How are you?'

'Passing well,' came the wheezy reply.

Jem laughed politely at the old joke.

'And you, Sergeant?'

'I received a shoulder wound and have resigned my commission.' Jem waited. Had he heard the full tale?

'Pity you was wounded too. I shall always be indebted to you for saving my life.'

'Think nothing of it,' Jem gave a smile. At least it seemed he hadn't heard. There again, why should he have done? Bill Nye was a working man, not a member of the gossip-ridden Upper Ten Thousand. 'All in the line of duty.'

'I said to our Cathy, Cathy my girl, I wouldn't be here save for Sergeant Riseley.' Nye rubbed his hand across his brow. 'Now if there is anything you wants old Bill to do, you just has to ask. I'm in your debt, Sarge. Mayhap it's providence that's made our paths cross this day? I'd like to repay the debt, if I can.'

Maybe providence indeed or had God answered her prayers? Jem looked at the raggedy dressed ex-soldier and wondered if he had work or at least a reasonable pension. Perhaps he could help her and there could be some coin in it for him?

'Could you find out some information for me?' Jem drew a deep breath. 'There is somebody I lost touch with, somebody I want to find.'

'Could do. I have a mate who was a Runner. He knows who to ask and all that.' Nye squinted. 'It would cost mind. And I'm not working y'see, what with the arm. Is it an old sweetheart you wants to find?'

'No, not quite.' Jem said, relieved to see it was just as she thought. Nye would be doing her a favour and she him. 'I need this gentleman to be found as quickly as possible.'

'And what are these gentleman's particulars?'

'We'll agree the price first, then I'll tell you his particulars.'

'Whatever you say, Sergeant. But is he in London?'

'I don't think so. He could be . . . in Warwickshire. How much will it cost to find him do you think?'

Nye scratched his chin. 'I'll have to ask. Where shall we meet you?'

Jem's heart sank. She hadn't thought. She could hardly invite them to Lady Ardenbrooke's house. It was all too easy to imagine Tony's anger that she had gone ahead and employed a couple of rogues without his say-so.

'Here, tomorrow? At the same time?'

Nye shook his head. 'This is an awful swell place for the likes of us to be standing around doing business in the broad light of day.

Don't you want to find this gentleman on the quiet, like?'

Jem nodded.

'How about The White Bear on Piccadilly? Always busy in there with allsorts. I'll bring me mate and you bring the particulars of the gentleman who wants finding and we'll agree the price.'

★　★　★

By the time Jem reached Lady Ardenbrooke's house, she began to wonder at the wisdom of what she done. She'd agreed to meet Bill Nye and his friend at the tavern he'd suggested. It was too late now, she decided.

She heaved a sigh of relief that no one saw her as she slipped into the house and up the back stairs to change. It seemed a shame to fold away the clothes and put away her boots but at least tomorrow they would have another outing.

'Right, no more lurking in my room, Lady Fordingley.'

Jem stepped out into the hallway and her breath caught in her throat. Standing before her was Tony, dressed immaculately in evening clothes with a stiffer than usual white cravat. He looked as he had done in a hundred of her dreams. She had trouble believing she had ever pressed her lips against his or he had ever cried out in pleasure at her touch. She wanted to ask him to hold her, to show what happened between them wasn't just a dream but his face looked so cold and stern.

'Ah, m'lady, you have emerged. I trust your nap was refreshing.'

'My nap?'

'I looked for you earlier and Mother indicated you were resting after having been whisked off by Lady Houndsworth to her dressmaker's, for an entire new wardrobe. I presume the bill is coming to me?'

His voice was soft, dangerously soft. Jem took a deep breath and tried to keep from snapping at him. She hadn't seen him for a whole day and all he could do was make some snip about a forthcoming dressmaker's bill. This was not how she had planned their meeting.

'Tony . . . I . . . that is . . . perhaps we could have a cold repast this evening, in my room? Would this be possible?' she asked, swallowing her pride. 'Is your mother dining at home this evening and expecting us to join her . . . ? I'm afraid I don't know . . . No one has told me . . . '

There was no answering flicker in Tony's eyes. No roguish smile. Nothing but a cold stare. Jem blinked back the tears. Did he not see she was offering an olive branch?

'I regret I am otherwise engaged.' He gave a slight bow.

'Is there somewhere we are meant to be going?' Heaven help her if she had to endure an evening with his icy shoulder. And she would have to make sure she didn't make any more mistakes, didn't jump in with the unwanted answer. 'Perhaps my blue dress will suffice . . . '

'Not we. I have a prior engagement. I had understood you were indisposed today and you are to make your debut at the theatre next week?'

'Y-yes.'

A vision of long, inhospitable years stretched out before Jem and her heart stopped beating fast and slowed to an indistinct, uninterested rhythm. She had not felt this low, not even when she had volunteered for the Forlorn Hope. They had been married mere weeks . . .

'I won't trouble you further,' she mumbled, blinking back a tear.

Jemima turned on her heel, went back into her room and closed the door with a click. As she did so, she thought she heard a muffled 'Jemima?', but when she reopened the door, he had gone. And only the smell of sandalwood and something indefinably Tony gave a clue that he had ever been there.

The tears streamed down her cheeks. She threw herself on the bed and wept.

★　★　★

The following afternoon, Jem shivered as she strode up Piccadilly in the biting wind. She'd wrapped her neck cloth up very high, so it covered the lower part of her face and she kept her eyes cast to the ground the whole way.

No one assailed her and she reached the top of Piccadilly. She slipped quickly into the stable yard of The White Bear and into the middle of the arrival of a coach from Bristol. Jem drew a breath and squared her shoulders. As far as inns went, The White Bear, under the proprietorship of Mr Webbe as the notice proclaimed, looked at least a half-respectable establishment. A gentleman of meagre means might lodge here, she thought, seeing a gentleman whose dress suggested he was of the poorer sort ask the ostler if there were any lodgings to be had.

Jem dared hold her head a little higher and sauntered past all the fuss of people and luggage. She pushed open the tavern's door and stepped inside. Smoke, the sweet smell of hops and piecrust hit her and she followed her ears along the narrow corridor towards the noise of the taproom.

She rested her fingers for a moment on the door. The enormity of what she was about to do swept through her. She shut her eyes. Whatever arguments she could think of, one thing was as clear as the light of day. She had to know. She opened the door and stepped into the anonymous bustle of men and sprinkling of women of a certain sort.

'Ah, Sergeant, right on time,' she heard Bill Nye say behind her and swung around. He sat at a small table and next to him lounged a shabby man with pointed features which had a distinct resemblance to an overfed rat.

Jem picked up a spare stool and sat down with them.

Nye drank deep into his mug of ale while the rat-man looked her up and down. Fear clawed at her stomach and her fist curled on her lap but Jem forced all emotion from her face.

Nye put his mug down on the table and wiped his sleeve across his mouth. 'This is Alf, who was the Runner. He'll do it. For the right price.'

'Alfred Levington. But you can call me Alf,' the rat-man said and grinned. Jem distrusted his grin, but she didn't have to like it, she told herself. Bill Nye owed her his life but this man would only be in it for the money.

'Pleased to meet you, Mr — '

'Who is it you want found . . . Sergeant?' Rat-man leaned forward and regarded her very closely.

'A man,' Jem said before she lost her nerve.

'And this man you want found has a name?'

'Alexander Cullen.' Jem forced herself to say the words. Since the attack she had thought of him only as her stepfather, not as being related to her by blood at all. In truth he was her father's cousin and had been all too ready to step into her father's shoes — in every way.

'And do you have any idea of where Mr Cullen might be found? England is an awfully big place, and it might cut down on the expense if I had an idea of where to look.' Alf Levington took out a rough-looking notebook and stood poised with a nub of pencil.

'Cullen Park in Warwickshire.'

'And do you want Mr Cullen of Cullen Park to know you are looking for him? Or do you want it on the quiet like?'

'On the quiet.'

Alf tapped his nose and winked. 'Thought so. Didn't we say as much, Bill, on the way over here?'

Nye nodded vigorously.

'Do you think you can find him for me?'

'If he is where you say he is, piece of cake. But it will cost mind, particularly if you want it on the quiet. Him being a gentleman and all. Then there will be expenses. I don't do nuffink without me expenses being paid.'

'How much?'

'One hundred pounds.' The rat-man's countenance did not even flicker as he named his price.

Jem gulped. The sum was much more than she had ever considered. She couldn't think how on earth she was going to get her hands on one hundred pounds.

'It seems an awfully high price.' Her voice faltered.

Rat-man's eyes became narrow slits. 'Do you want the gentleman found or don't you?'

'Sergeant, Alf's the best. He'll do a good job for you.' Bill Nye held up his hand. 'On my honour.'

Jem tried to remember if Bill Nye's honour was worth anything. And what was to stop Mr Levington from going straight to her stepfather and asking awkward questions? She should never have started this, she should have walked away. This scheme had many more pitfalls than she had first considered. However, she had to go forward. She refused to retreat now. She had to trust in providence. She squared her shoulders and stuffed her hands in her pockets to keep both men from seeing the trembling.

'I have ten guineas I can pay you now,' Jem said, drawing the coins from her pocket. 'The balance will have to be paid when you get me the information.'

Rat-man smiled as he took the guineas counting them carefully. He handed one to Nye and placed the rest in his own pocket. 'A trip up to Warwickshire will take a few days. When I'm back, where do I send word?'

At least she had some time to work out where to find one hundred pounds, Jem thought.

'Send word to me at Lady Ardenbrooke's in Audley Street. I have been able to secure a position there. Just leave word for Jem Riseley and I will come and meet you.'

'Mighty quick on your feet, Sergeant, finding a post like that,' Nye said. 'I've been searching for weeks and there ain't much around.'

A trickle of sweat ran down the back of her neck. She listened to the noises of the tavern — the laughter, the clunk of earthenware, and swallowed hard. Nye and Levington's faces were turned towards her.

'A bit of luck,' she said, and thought she

should not have given the name but there seemed to be no choice. She had to hope that they wouldn't ask too many questions.

'I'll contact you when I have some information then.'

'How soon do you think you will know?'

'Two or three days. And don't you worry, Alf Levington will keep to our bargain. Alexander Cullen of Cullen Park, questions on the quiet.'

'Will you join us in a mug of porter?' Nye asked nodding towards the two men who were rolling a fresh barrel into the room.

What was the saying about honour among thieves? Jem thought as she pushed the stool back and got to her feet. She'd given all the money she had to rat-man. She refused to buy them drink as well. 'No, I've got to go.'

She stumbled out of the inn, forgetting to pull her neckcloth up and about her chin until she was half way back down Piccadilly. For better or for worse within a few days, she'd know, and when she did, she would be able to tell Tony the truth and assure him there would be no more scandals; she could tell him that she would be a good and dutiful wife.

Was it wrong to want more than to be just a wife?

Jem put her hand across her mouth as the

nausea rose. The prospect of having to face that ugly pair again was cracking through her skull like shot from an untrained musket. And how the blazes was she going to find one hundred pounds?

★　★　★

Andrews turned the slim box over in his hands, opened it and frowned, and then looked at her incredulously, his expression fixed on the bookshelves behind her. Jem wished they were back in Spain. Andrews was a decent fellow, she was sure, and had she been Ensign Riseley he would be listening to her with an entirely different expression.

As Lady Fordingley, and wearing the brand new buttercup coloured day dress that had arrived today and that Lady Ardenbrooke said complemented her colouring, it was a different matter.

Jem took in a breath. She'd have to try and explain it again. If Andrews refused to help her, there was no one else to turn to. She certainly wasn't going to ask Bill Nye whether he knew a reputable pawnbroker. She knew she should speak to Tony about it, but he wouldn't listen. He'd brush it under the carpet like everything else.

'I need to find someone who can run the

errand for me, discreetly.' Jem held her hands gently clasped in front of her as she stood and hoped it made her look more commanding, in a ladylike way. 'I . . . I can't tell Fordingley . . . yet.'

Andrews exhaled loudly as if he had been holding his breath.

'Please don't say anything to him, will you?' Jem added.

Andrews blinked and shifted slightly, his chin notched slightly higher. 'I'm not sure you've the right of it, m'lady, if you'd pardon my saying. Fordingley is a decent fellow. It seems a might peculiar you should be asking me to help you go behind his back. I'm sure he would give you the one hundred pounds without blinking, without the need for this.'

He waved the necklace box.

Jem gulped. She might have known it was no good asking Andrews to help her. She had no other choice. She put out a hand and grabbed the small marble top table as if to steady herself.

'Lady Fordingley?' Andrews's expression changed to one nearer concern than disdain. Perhaps there was hope?

'Oh, it is nothing.' Jem pulled out the large laced handkerchief from her ridicule, shook it out furiously, sniffed and dabbed her eyes.

With each action, she loathed the playacting more and more.

'I'll see what I can do,' Andrews said frowning.

Jem nodded and sniffed again for good measure. 'Oh, thank you, Andrews. I knew you would help me. And Fordingley will hear the whole of it very soon. It's just . . . ' Jem sighed. 'I wish I could say . . . but I can't.'

'Very good, m'lady.'

Jem sank down into one of the large library chairs as Andrews took his leave. She would get her hundred pounds, and soon Levington would be back from Warwickshire and she would know.

★   ★   ★

Considering they were living in the same house and had chambers next door to each other, she might as well not have a husband for all she had seen of Tony over the past week, Jem thought. At least he was coming with her this evening. It was her debut, at the theatre.

'Jemima cannot be expected to appear in Society for the first time without her husband, or tongues will wag,' Lady Ardenbrooke had said this morning. Tony, who had poked his head around the door of the breakfast room, had simply nodded.

There was a tap, the porcelain handle twisted and the door was pushed an inch ajar.

'Are you ready, Jemima?' came Tony's voice. 'Or we're going to be late.'

Jem swallowed. She hated it when he called her Jemima. It sounded so . . . formal. She took one last glance at herself in the tall cheval mirror. This confection in a lilac-coloured silk that Arabella had encouraged the dressmaker to make up for her fitted revealingly around her breasts, its décolletage daringly low and the sarsnet so flimsy her ankles were showing. Even the snow-leopard pelisse seemed to have been designed to ensure that none of her womanly attributes would fail to be on show. It fastened with a single paste-diamond button on her shoulder. And on her head, she wore a jaunty turban, the height of fashion, but as for the fountain of white ostrich plumes it supported, were they not just a tiny bit over the top?

'Jemima!'

'I'm coming!' Her only consolation was that her white silk gloves covered most of her arms, Jem thought, as she grabbed her beaded ridicule from the dresser and the white, feathered fan. She raised the fan to her eyes and looked in the mirror. She could hide behind it, if necessary.

As she opened the door, her breath stopped in her throat. The black and the white of his evening dress and the well-tailored cut made Tony's shoulders look impossibly broad, the line of his features implausibly handsome.

'Jemima, you look a picture,' he said smiling.

'A fantastical fashion plate from the latest issue of the *Beau Monde*, no doubt, not something actually to be worn by anyone of sound mind.' Yet she could not help giving a small twirl under what she hoped was his appreciative gaze. 'Tony, do you not think this outfit is a little too . . . revealing?'

'In all the right places.' Tony nodded and fingered his chin. 'Come on, the players at the *Sans Pareil* will not wait, not even for you, my sweet.'

He held out his arm. The enormity of what she was about to do washed over her. She had hoped she would have heard from Alf Levington by now, but no note had come. She could do this, but facing Tony now and knowing everything they stood to lose, her stomach revolted.

'You seem a bit pale, Jemima. Is everything all right?'

'I have a little headache. Maybe it's best I don't go to the theatre tonight.' Jem gulped and hoped she sounded convincing.

'Mother will have some laudanum. You can take a couple of drops on the way if your headache is very bad. It would be unforgivably rude to Lady Houndsworth were we to shun her hospitality so late in the day.'

Jem stared at her fan rather than meet his gaze. He was right. She should have thought of a way of getting out of this before.

'Come on, Jemima, you've been shut up in here all week. You led the Hope at Ciudad, you can survive a night at the theatre with a headache. Time you made your debut in society.'

She took her husband's arm. She allowed him to lead her downstairs and out into the carriage and did not allow herself to think what the consequences would be after this evening.

'What is it we are seeing at the theatre this evening?' Jem asked in the carriage as it clattered over the street cobbles.

'A play,' Tony replied, his voice dry as a biscuit, his head lolling against the squabs.

'*Il Giorno Felice*, or in English, *The Happy Day*,' Lady Ardenbrooke said. 'It is a comic operetta.'

Jem spluttered at the irony of it and fanned herself quickly to cover up her reaction.

'You don't have to watch the play, Jemima,' Tony drawled as he stared out of the window.

'Simply sit and look pretty for a few hours. This evening's offering is written by a woman — more's the pity! The sooner they get the new theatre opened at Covent Garden, the better. It'll be some fustian pantomime — '

'Written by Miss Jane Scott,' Lady Ardenbrooke interrupted and rapped her fan on the door handle. 'I have seen several of her works. She is an accomplished playwright. Tony, you've not been in London for years, do be quiet if you've nothing useful to say.'

'How intriguing, Lady Ardenbrooke,' Jem said pointedly, but Tony did not flinch. 'How kind of Lady Houndslow to invite us. I — '

'How is your headache, my dear wife?'

'Quite better,' Jem replied.

'Exactly why Jemima is making her debut at the theatre is still beyond me,' Tony drawled. 'Would not an intimate soirée been more appropriate? I've been getting some dashed funny looks from some people at the club today and I suspect it's around town that the star attractions at the *Sans Pareil* tonight are going to be Lord and Lady Fordingley.'

Jem shuddered as the vehicle drew to a halt.

'Anthony,' Lady Ardenbrooke snapped, 'I suggest you look to improving your temper.'

★ ★ ★

The noise filling the theatre was unbearable. Hundreds of people and all talking in such loud voices. Jem kept her fan in front of her face, her eyes fixed mostly on the carpet and her body pressed close to Tony as he pushed through the mass of bodies and through the hot building, up some stairs and along a narrowed but pleasantly furnished corridor where they were shown into their box.

From dimness into light. The theatre was splendidly lit, spacious, airy, and yet still hot. The rustling of a hundred fans and squeaks from the orchestra tuning their instruments underlined the high volume of the chatter.

Tony pushed her forward to the welcoming embrace of Arabella who was arrayed splendidly in an apricot-coloured silk. Behind her stood a small portly man, no taller than Jem herself.

'Lady Fordingley, your servant,' he said, taking her hand. He pressed his lips on to her gloved fingers and she noticed the top of his hair had thinned to a bald patch. 'My lady wife has told me so much about you.'

This was Lord Houndsworth. No wonder Arabella had been piqued having to settle for him over Tony. There was no point in even making a comparison between the two men. Perhaps she was being unfair, Jem mused. Lord Houndsworth might be kind, and terribly in love with his wife.

Unlike . . . she swallowed a small lump that had risen in her throat.

'Come.' Arabella's hand gently pushed her arm.

She stepped forward with Arabella to the front of the box and looked out. They were high above the stage and on the side with a view over the stalls, indeed the whole theatre. Jem could not help casting her eye around the ornately decorated auditorium and then to the people, some seated, some still making their way to their seats.

And then it happened, a flicker in the corner of her eye and Jem saw a lady towards the back of the stalls was staring at her and pointing in her direction with her closed fan. Then her companion too looked at her unabashedly, and he turned to the lady sitting on his other side and she too stared up towards their box. Like a ripple starting slowly but then quickly gathering pace, Jem watched the news spread and more and more of the theatregoers stopped and stared. A hush started to fall over the theatre. She took an instinctive step back but Arabella's fingers closed on her arm not allowing her to retreat any further.

A pair of gleaming, malevolent eyes arrested hers.

In the fourth row from the front and dressed in immaculate black and white with his thin face and dead expression — had her imagination so run away with her? Jem took a deep breath and reminded herself of Tony's words in Portsmouth. Le Loup was dead. It was her mind, playing tricks, succumbing to the fear. The next thing she would see was her stepfather.

She stared again and the man nodded, the scar on his face showed white against the yellow cast of the candlelight.

Jem turned her head but Tony was at the back of the box in deep conversation with Lord Houndsworth. She tightened her grip on her fan. She had to say something but it needed to be done discreetly. She had no wish to bring any more attention to herself.

'Look, there are Lord and Lady Davenham,' Arabella said and waved. The couple raised their hands in return but Jem's gaze went back to the gentleman in the fourth row. He was still watching her. She raised her fan a little higher.

'Oh, how splendid! Everyone is here tonight. And the Comte de Guisement, down there look, Jemima, in the fourth row. He is seated next to Lady Herbert. How thrilling. The latest on dit is that she has caught Prinny's eye . . . '

Jem watched in horror as Arabella waved at the count and he nodded in return, his narrow-eyed gaze sweeping over again and making her shiver.

'It's . . . it's a little hot . . . I'd better sit down,' Jem stammered.

'Of course, my dear. The show is just about to start,' Arabella purred.

Jem's heart did not slow down until some of the lights had been extinguished and the play began. Jem kept her hands folded in her lap and tried to concentrate on watching the stage, rather than the fact that lots of the audience seemed to keep looking up in her direction. They were only looking at Arabella, Jem thought, trying not to panic. She seemed to know everyone and it was only natural . . .

One of the leading females in the cast came to the front of the stage, dressed as a man and held her finger to her lips. The ongoing murmurings of the audience quietened to a nearly complete hush.

'That is Miss Jane Scott, the author of the play. She also acts in her own plays,' Lady Ardenbrooke who was sitting at Jem's right, whispered.

'My lords, ladies and gentlemen,' the actress said. 'Tonight I play the part of Frederick but it is not only on the stage that a woman may play the part of a man. In

345

honour of our special guest, a slight amendment to the programme.' She motioned with her hand and every shoulder in the theatre turned, every eye looked up straight at Jem. 'Lady Fordingley, my lady.' Miss Scott curtsied. 'The Lady Soldier.'

18

A collective gasp rippled through the audience.

Jem sat rigid in her seat. She thought she might faint, gripped her fan in her hands as if somehow that could save her. This had to be a new twist to her nightmare but she knew she would awake. All of London knew!

'What the devil!' she heard Tony exclaim behind her.

'Anthony!' Lady Ardenbrooke rasped as a warning.

'Fearless and brave, she fought for England against the scourge of Europe — Bonaparte,' Miss Scott's voice continued relentlessly onwards. 'My lady, we at the *Sans Pareil* dedicate tonight's performance to you.'

The chatter in the audience rose.

'Stand up!' a gentleman shouted from the gallery.

Arabella nudged at her back. 'Go on, Jemima. Stand up.'

Jemima gave a brief glance, saw the self-satisfied smug smile on Arabella's face, and knew she had been set up.

'I'm not having a spectacle made of my

wife. We are leaving.'

'Anthony. Sit down and don't make things any worse,' Lady Ardenbrooke hissed.

'Worse?' Jem heard Tony's bitter laugh.

Lady Ardenbrooke leaned towards her and said, 'You had better stand up, my dear. And get it over with.'

Jem stood up and felt Arabella's hand on the small of her back, propelling her forward. She gripped the balustrade and looked out at the sea of faces.

Every person in the theatre rose from their seats and then from somewhere at the back came the sound of clapping. It ran like a wave around the theatre, growing in its intensity. They all clapped, even the players on the stage. She felt like an insect pinned to a card.

'A bloody standing ovation!' Tony snapped. 'I don't believe it. I knew coming to the theatre was a bad idea.'

Jem stumbled back into her seat, and wished Tony would fulfil his threat and take her home.

'And now,' Miss Scott's voice rose over the tail of the applause. 'May I present a special dance — the Lady Soldiers!'

It had very little to do with the play and Jem was forced to watch acted out on stage among a company of women, all dressed in military uniform, a country style dance.

'We're leaving,' Tony said, as the curtain fell for the interval. 'Jemima!'

He came to stand beside her and offered her his hand which she took thankfully as she rose to her feet. The familiar tingle rose up her arm and it felt so good to be on Tony's arm. Not that it mattered now, a little voice inside her said, the damage is done. Suddenly her heart was like lead.

'Is that wise, Anthony? People will talk.'

Tony barked with an uneasy laughter. 'The whole of London will be talking as it is. Remind me, Lady Houndsworth, to refrain from falling in with your plans again.'

'My lord.' Arabella cast her head to the ground but Jem could see a gleam and a satisfied smile. 'I only wanted to ensure that your bride, the woman you jilted me for, had the proper reception.'

'Anthony, do be reasonable — ' Lady Ardenbrooke began.

'No.' He tucked Jem's arm under his and made for the door. Behind it, the corridor was full. A wall of people. No escape.

'Fordingley, my compliments. When we heard the *on dit* that she had been a soldier, well . . . yet she's a beauty,' a tall, aristocratic looking man about Tony's age said. He pushed forward and lifted Jem's fingers to his lips. 'Lady Fordingley, the Earl of Chatterham presents his compliments.'

'Bloody hell,' Jem thought she heard Tony say under his breath, and then louder, 'Who's next?'

A pair of simpering ladies. Then another gentleman, and then another. Jem stood there as they all presented themselves to her and wondered if she was about to meet the entire *ton* this evening. She gave up trying to remember names as three ladies and another gentleman pushed their way through the crush. Tony tried to keep some order, fending off the crowd at the doorway.

'Jemima, you are such a success,' Lady Ardenbrooke observed, a beaming smile on her lips.

'Lady Fordingley, you are in looks tonight.'

'Lady Fordingley, I will send a card over for our ball next week.'

'Lady Fordingley, we shall come to call on you very shortly. On which mornings are you expected to be at home?'

Her head started to spin and she opened her fan.

'Lady Fordingley,' a familiar voice said, underlined with a trace of French. 'The Comte de Guisement presents his compliments.'

'Le Loup!' Jem exclaimed. She tried to signal to Tony. He had to believe her this time. And she had to prevent Le Loup from doing anything. But Tony's back was towards her. She started forwards. 'Tony!'

'That was unwise, my little one,' Le Loup said leaning into her ear and speaking in a voice so low only she could hear it. His hand dug into her arm. 'For the Comte de Guisement has never been in Spain. If I find anyone is talking of such a thing, I shall know where to find the Lady Soldier.'

Jem looked to Tony but he was still at the doorway, ushering in a trio of older ladies. The count pushed past them and disappeared.

'Ah?' Tony lifted his head and addressed the crowd outside. 'Ladies and gentlemen, the second half is about to begin. Please take your seats.' Sure enough the long squeak of violins could be heard as the orchestra began a tune. 'You may call on my wife tomorrow.'

To Jemima's relief, they seemed to listen.

'We're leaving,' Tony said, gripping Jem by the hand and pulling her out of the box. His face looked black as thunder. 'Well done, Arabella, you got the revenge you wanted. I hope you are now satisfied.'

★ ★ ★

351

'Now that is a sad face for a pretty girl,' Tony said as he stepped into the silent drawing-room the following morning.

'I thought you were out. You always seem to be out.' Jem looked up from the chaise and put down a large pile of what looked to be invitation cards.

Tony frowned at the accusation. 'Just arrived back from m'club.' He coughed. He had gone to White's to see how bad it was. Some of the right people had patted him on the back, and said that as soon as the *ton* had something new to talk about he would be in the clear. But it was not so much the men he was worried about. It was the wives. He would have to make plans to remove Jem to Warwickshire should the worst come to the worst and London turned against her.

'Excuse me, my lord.' Grieves coughed behind him and Tony moved out of the way of the doorway and watched as he and a footman carried in two extravagant flower arrangements. Then he noticed the bouquets of flowers that covered nearly every surface of the room. 'What's this? Are you planning on opening a flower shop?'

'They keep sending them,' she said and still she did not smile. 'They have been arriving all morning.'

'Oh.' They had swooped on his wife like

vultures last night, eager to snare a piece of scandal as their own, and now they fêted her with flowers as if she was some poxy actress, or worse! He could imagine the breakfast rooms of London now abuzz with it all. He cast his eyes about the room and they alighted on one arrangement that looked deuced odd.

'What the devil is that one all about? Lilies? It looks more suitable for a funeral than a lady.' Tony wandered over and fingered the card. 'The Comte de Guisement?'

Jem's countenance paled. 'Tony, he was the man I tried to tell you about last night, the man in the box.'

'For heaven's sake Jem, there were about a hundred men in the box fawning over you!' Which was another reason he wanted some of his wife back to himself.

'The Comte de Guisement is Le Loup, the French leader of the deserters, Tony. He is in London. And I saw him in Portsmouth. I didn't imagine it after all.'

'Jem!' Tony held out his arms and swept her up into his embrace. 'This has simply all been too much for you.'

'Don't you believe me? Tony, this is important — '

'Hush!' He kissed the top of her forehead.

'Tony, the man could be a danger to

353

England, if he is — '

'Jem, hush! If it will set your mind at rest I will make some enquiries about the count but I am sure we will find you are mistaken. I'm not surprised your mind is playing tricks on you after what you had to endure last night.'

She stilled in his arms and Tony hoped she realized he was right. He had brought her to London and now everybody wanted 'the lady soldier' to grace their ballrooms and drawing rooms.

'It actually appears my debut was somewhat successful,' Jem said her voice sounding curiously flat as she pulled away from him and motioned towards the piles of cards on the table. 'Flowers and invitations to dozens of balls, musicales, soirées . . . '

Tony gulped. He had sought her out this morning precisely because he wanted to cheer her up after last night's débâcle. She looked far too unhappy and wan. He cleared his throat. 'If, among all this you have a moment or two to spare your husband, I wondered if you would be willing to indulge in a spot of swordplay? There should be enough room in the library. I asked Grieves to move the chairs back a bit.'

Her eyes widened. 'What would your mother say if she walked in on us? Or the servants? Tony, you do make some outrageous suggestions!'

'She might be a bit upset,' Tony agreed. Jem had a point — what would the dear mama say to two swords flashing about the room? But making things up with Jem mattered more. He wanted to recapture some of the camaraderie they had enjoyed in Spain. He hurried on. 'But as long as we didn't damage anything, I don't think she will mind. She has seen this sort of thing before y'know.'

'Your mother has seen this sort of thing before?' Jem looked so deathly pale he thought she might faint. He circled his arm around her waist.

'Jem,' he said trying to sound as tender as possible, 'a bit of sport will enliven the old library.'

Jem looked up at him as two bright red patches flushed across her cheeks and said nothing. He thought she'd be overjoyed to fence, but she was looking as if he'd asked her to do something unthinkable. Perhaps it was, for a lady of the *ton*.

'Is that a new dress?' he said, suddenly noticing. 'It looks very nice, m'dear. If you really don't want to, we don't have to.' He brushed a quick kiss on her cheek and nipped outside to the hallway to get the foils.

'A pity, though,' he said, letting them

dangle from his hand. 'These cost a pretty penny. And I was looking forward to learning that little trick you did to disarm me.'

'Swords! You mean fence in the library.' Jem started to laugh. 'I thought . . . ' Jem blinked the wetness from her eyes and fumbled in her new tiny mother-of-pearl beaded reticule for a handkerchief. Tony had his own to offer her in less than a moment.

'Thank you,' Jem said and blew her nose liberally. 'I had thought you might have meant another kind of swordplay.'

Tony's eyes widened as his breeches tightened. 'You wanton creature! Still, it is an interesting suggestion.'

'Tony!' she chuckled and followed him through to the library.

Jem tried to think as Tony handed her the foil. She should be delighted Tony was being so considerate but the terror of what would happen once the true story about her stepfather was known kept circling through her mind. Last night, every time, she closed her eyes, the nightmare started to reappear growing in its intensity. She had been so scared that she had been tempted to go to Tony's room and tell him everything — but he wasn't even there. He had rushed straight off to his club after he had seen them home last night.

She lifted her chin and tried to smile. 'How clever of you to think of us having a fencing match.'

'You owe me a lesson. I want to know that cunning manoeuvre,' he said and grinned.

And it was all too much. Jem's face fell. 'Oh, Tony, I never thought the *ton* would behave like this.'

'No,' he said crisply. 'But I did. The *ton* thrives on scandal like leeches on a dying man's blood.' His tone sounded less than pleased. For a brief moment, she wondered if he, like Arabella, had wanted her to fail. Perhaps he wanted to send her away to the country, away from London — from him.

'Shall we start this fencing?' Jem said, twirling the foil and pushing her gloomy thoughts away. She would fight for their marriage before she gave up. She tried for a lunge, heard the slight rip of her gown's skirt and rapidly readjusted her stance. 'It would be easier in breeches, but I can make do in this dress if you wish to begin right away?'

'Perhaps a riding habit or something akin to it would be best?' Tony cleared his throat.

Jem thought guiltily of the breeches now residing under her bed with the rest of her uniform. It must have been Andrews who had saved it, and not Tony. Otherwise, he'd have mentioned it.

'I'll go and get changed now,' she said and tried for a smile.

She had only taken one step towards the door when it flew open.

'I had to see for myself.' Lady Ardenbrooke strode into the room. The burgundy ribbons of her cap quivered. 'The servants informed me you were fencing in the library but I couldn't believe it.'

'Mother, so good of you to join us.' Tony said, and moved away from Jem. Jem's hand dropped down to her side. 'And what precisely is wrong with fencing in the library?'

'It is unseemly. Anthony, we had this discussion before . . . '

'I could hardly take Jemima to Angelo and Jackson's Fencing Rooms. I thought this was the best place to fence.' He winked at Jem. 'And I do like to fence with m'wife.'

Jem's cheeks began to burn and Tony seemed to enjoy her discomfiture because his eyes twinkled and he winked at her.

'We have no time for such foolishness. The first of the afternoon callers, Lady Aske, has arrived and Jemima is needed in the drawing room.'

'Tell Lady Aske and the rest of them Jemima is not *at home* today!'

'You are impossible Anthony. The same as your father! Never a thought of what a

woman might want, only thinking of your-
self.' Lady Ardenbrooke looked stern.
'Besides Jemima was not *at home* this
morning and we had a number of cards;
Grieves has been informing callers Lady
Fordingley will be receiving after two o'clock.
It is now after two o'clock.'

'Oh dear,' Jem said. 'Is it really that late?
Lady Ardenbrooke and I talked about this at
breakfast, Tony, and decided my receiving this
afternoon would be best.'

'To the devil with society!' Tony said and
his brow creased.

Jem stilled. If only he knew how little
society meant to her too, but for the time
being, what else could she do but play along
and somehow hope for the best?

'I'm sorry, Tony, but I had better — '

'Yes, yes.' He raised his foil and made a
bow. 'It appears I must yield my wife to Lady
Aske and the other multitude of expected
callers.'

Jem felt his pique and tried to smile but it
only seemed to make him scowl further.

'I am holding a small dinner party here
tonight, Tony,' his mother said and peered at
him severely. 'Only sixteen guests. I thought it
wise to invite some old and trusted friends
and I expect you to be there. So far Jemima's
debut has been a little . . . unconventional . . . '

'Trying to shore up the defences, eh, Mother?'

'So you'll be there? No jaunting off to your club or wherever else you go. You are to be here to lead your wife into dinner?'

'Yes, Mother.' Tony clicked his heels and Jem thought for an awful moment he might even give his mother a salute. 'I will endeavour to be on my best behaviour.'

'See that you are.' Lady Ardenbrooke waved her fan towards the door. 'Come on, Jemima, Lady Aske is waiting.'

'I look forward to it. I shall look forward to leading my wife into dinner.' Tony nodded at Jem. 'Jemima, you would honour your husband greatly if you wore the little trinket I gave you on the road from Portsmouth tonight. I rather thought you might wear it last night to the theatre, but perhaps the sapphires did not suit with the lilac of your gown?'

'Sapphires? What trinket?' Lady Ardenbrooke snapped and Jem drew out a breath, relieved she had been saved from answering. 'Anthony, if this is another of your games . . . '

'It is a necklace, Mother. A present from a husband to his wife. And as I am to be deprived of m'wife's company until this evening I thought I was owed the pleasure of seeing her beautiful neck christened with my gift to her.'

Jem swallowed a tear.

'You bought a necklace? Anthony, you do know you are entitled to some of the family jewels.'

'Indeed, but I wanted to choose something m'self that suited.'

'Well, I expect Jemima will manage to wear the necklace for you.' Lady Ardenbrooke held out her hand and Jem took it thankfully. She had no idea what she was going to do, nor what she could say to Tony about the necklace that was not a downright lie. Enduring an hour or two of small talk with the curious *ton* suddenly seemed infinitely preferable than having to explain things to Tony. 'Come on Jemima.'

★   ★   ★

Jem stared at the note that had arrived with the late post addressed to Jem Riseley. Thank goodness, the footman had brought it to her along with the twenty other invitations and notes addressed to either Lady Fordingley or simply the Lady Soldier as she sat alone in the first floor drawing room, recovering from the thirty or so callers who had come this afternoon.

Her instincts had told her to distrust Levington and she had ignored them, so intent she was on her quest to find out about what had happened to her stepfather. And this was the upshot. Blackmail. She crumpled the piece of paper in her hand.

Levington was too clever to word his demands outright — who knew whose hands a letter might fall into — but his intention was clear. He had found the man she wanted, he said, and it seemed his expenses had risen and he required the sum of two hundred pounds to be paid to him tonight. He would be in Hyde Park, waiting and of the urgency of his obtaining the said monies she should be in no doubt.

Relief washed over her to read that her stepfather was not dead. The gallows no longer loomed. Tears gathered in her eyes, blinding her for a second. Perhaps there was a chance she could emerge from all this unscathed but she needed to be very careful . . .

'Is your head paining you again?' Lady Ardenbrooke asked entering the drawing room. 'It was quite a crush this afternoon. I've just had a short nap myself.'

'No, no. It was merely a note . . . from a well-wisher.' Jem said and toyed with the ball of paper.

She was sorely tempted to throw it away but it had very precise instructions. Why did the meeting have to be tonight? She could only pray the dinner party would be over by then. If not, she'd have to think of a way to escape early.

Jem stared at the clock as its hands moved steadily onwards.

★   ★   ★

The drawing room fire felt warm against her back as Jem sank down into a chair after withdrawing with the other ladies. She glanced at the clock above the fire. She had an hour at most. Jem tried to think how long it would take her to change and then climb out the window. She lifted her chin. She could do it.

The whole day had been awful, she considered, while pretending to remain interested in the details of Mrs Guernsey's health problems. And the dinner party was worse than she had imagined. Tony spent the entire evening glowering at her bare neck. Whenever the conversation had turned to Spain, he had intervened.

Tomorrow, no doubt, there would be more invitations to add to the pile she did not want, and slowly but surely she would be sucked into the round of dull dinner parties and soirées where people did nothing but drone on about the latest *on dits*.

'Forgive me,' Jem said, standing up after half an hour or so had passed. 'But I appear to have a frightful headache. If you would allow me to retire before the gentlemen join us?'

'Not sickening, are you?' Lady Arden-brooke boomed. 'But you do look pale. Run along up to your room and I shall make your excuses.'

'Thank you.' Jem headed out of the door.

'Is she always such a puny thing?' she heard Lady Box-Hedges exclaim. 'It is a wonder she was able to serve as a soldier for such a long time.'

'Dear Jemima was gravely injured, if you remember, saving my son . . . '

When Jem reached her room, she took a deep breath and started pulling off her dress and gloves. There was no time to lose. Leaving the clothes in a pile on the floor, she fastened her breeches and pulled her jacket on. She tore the money from under the handkerchiefs, threw open the window and started to climb out. She could do it, there was a tall cherry tree pressed up as high as the second floor and all she had to do was take care when she jumped . . .

The bedroom door crashed open. At the sound, Jem paused, with one leg thrown over the window ledge, her heart thumping in her ears. Tony strode in, face as black as the ace of spades.

'Why weren't you wearing the necklace at dinner?' His eyes narrowed, taking in the scene. All colour drained from his face. 'Jemima, what are you doing?'

19

Jem stared at him, her mind racing. How could she explain this? Dressed in breeches and ready to jump out of the window? His face seemed to grow darker by the second. Jem could feel the window ledge digging into her thighs.

'Tony . . . '

He crossed the floor in two steps and gathered her in his arms, pulling her from the window. His hands clutched her to his chest.

'Don't go, Jem,' he murmured against her hair. 'Please don't run away.'

'I have to go.'

'If it is about the bloody necklace . . . '

'It has nothing to do with the necklace . . . '

He held her away from him and searched her eyes. 'Jem, I am not an ogre. I can't believe I have driven to you this. I am not about to start beating you for disobeying me!'

Jem dropped her gaze. She found it impossible to look at Tony. He was making it so much more difficult for her to leave. In a moment, she'd be spilling out her whole story.

'I never thought you would beat me,' she whispered.

He clutched her to his chest again and the heat from him flooded into her. 'Please, Jem, tell me why you are not wearing the necklace. Please talk to me. I want to listen. I want to hear it. I know it is not of the first water, but it was the best Portsmouth had. I wanted to show you our marriage was a fresh start, a new life for you with me.'

A new life for her? Tears pricked. She had thought . . . No, she had not really thought. 'I had no idea.'

'We'll go to Bond Street tomorrow.' Tony said as if he had not heard her, 'and you can pick something that better takes your fancy. Will it suit?'

Jem wanted the floor to open and swallow her. An angry Tony she could deal with, but not a Tony like this. She had to tell him the truth. If she began with the necklace, perhaps it would give her courage to tell him everything. She hated to think of the expression his eyes would hold then, but she had to tell him. And she knew now her stepfather was not dead. What was the worst that could happen? The worst Tony could think of her?

'Yes, Tony, thank you. But there was nothing wrong with the necklace. It was a very pleasing necklace.'

'What do you mean, was a pleasing necklace? What has happened to it?'

Jem stared at Tony, trying to find the words to explain. She refused to lie. She was through with lies. 'I pawned the necklace.'

'Pawned the necklace? What the devil for?'

'I needed the money. I hated to do it, but it seemed to be the only way.'

'Needed the money? Why did you not simply ask me for it? We are not let in the pockets. Have you spent more than you meant to at the dressmakers? Did you not tell them to send the bill to me? I was joking before when — '

'It has nothing to with the dressmakers.'

'A gaming debt? Did you play cards with one of Mother's friends? I should have warned you, Jemima. They are sharks of the highest order. Tell me who and I shall settle it and next time be more careful.'

Tony brushed her hair from her forehead, his touch warming her painfully. She didn't deserve this kindness. She was in the wrong. His fingers tickled her chin as he slowly raised it upwards.

Jem gulped and looked into his eyes; she couldn't detect the slightest bit of anger, only concern.

'It is not a gaming debt. I needed to pay a

man.' She wrenched her chin away and shook her shoulders free of him. 'I had to try to find out what happened to my stepfather so that I wouldn't cause you further embarrassment.'

'Why didn't you come to me?' His gaze narrowed, his countenance looked twisted, confused. Jem sighed. That was the question he deserved some sort of answer to.

'I know you married me because you had to, because you felt a debt to my brother — and I refused to cause your family a greater scandal. I was afraid once you knew and fully comprehended the enormity of what I had done, you would banish me, send me away from you.'

There she had said it. She had said it before he had a chance to. Now, she waited for him to confirm it. She braced her shoulders and refused to cry as she waited for his confirmation.

'I'll leave in the morning,' she said in the silence. 'There must be somewhere quiet I can go in the country.'

'An excellent idea. Yes, I've already been thinking of it myself. I've had enough of m'wife being the *ton*'s latest sensation. And I have just the place in mind . . . '

A wave of nausea hit her. Tony was going to banish her to the country after all.

'Jemima? Jem?' she heard him call urgently

through the fog. Her knees must have given way because she was resting in Tony's firm embrace.

'In time you'll forget you did something as rash as to marry the sister of a long dead brother officer,' she murmured.

'Damn me that I will!' He invited her to nestle further against his solid form and Jem pressed herself into him, laid her head against his chest. He kissed the top of her head. 'You're going to the country and I'm coming with you. The *ton* is suffocating and horrid, place full of soirées, musicale evenings and people like Arabella Houndsworth. I want to rusticate with my wife . . . forever.'

Something sizzled through her head like a burning firebrand. She wasn't sure what he was saying, couldn't take it in, couldn't think.

'I didn't marry you because of Charlie,' he muttered and brushed his lips on her forehead. Then his voice changed and rang out more strongly. 'I married you because I was, because I am deeply and maddeningly in love with you. And I don't care whose sister you are, or what you might have done in the past. I only know you are the keeper of my heart and if you go, I will lose the reason for breathing.'

'You love me?' Jem could hardly believe what she was hearing.

'Every last infuriating inch of you.' He bent his head and captured her lips. 'And when I came in just now and saw you about to depart out of my life for good, I knew I had to fight for you, to make sure I kept you here by my side.'

Jem wanted to believe. She gave herself up to the kiss, luxuriating in its intensity.

'So why did you marry me?' he asked with a frown.

'Because I love you. I would like to say I have loved you since you kissed me that day at Cullen Park, but I know now that was only a school-girl's crush. I love you with the unswerving love of a woman.'

'You wore a rose pink gown and had flowers in your hair. And I knew I had to steal a kiss.'

'You remember the dress I was wearing!' Jem could scarce credit her ears. 'I thought . . . I thought you had done it as a joke, a way to be kind to Charles's little sister, that you were intent on marrying Arabella Triptree.'

'The kiss was no joking matter. Jemima, after I had tasted your lips, I knew I couldn't ask Arabella to marry me. She was nothing compared to the sweet kiss I'd stolen from Charlie's sister. It would have been wrong to marry her knowing that. But it wasn't until Spain if I am being honest that I knew you

371

were something to me.'

It seemed as if she had died and gone to heaven. She didn't deserve such happiness. And then she remembered and knew she didn't deserve it.

'But what about the things I have done? What about my stepfather, Alexander Cullen? He is alive, I know that, but I didn't tell you this before. I didn't tell you the whole story.' Jem had to swipe her sleeve at her eyes to wipe away the sudden wetness. 'I . . . I hit him with a candle-stick . . . There was blood all over the carpet. What if he should lay a charge against me?'

'I very much doubt that.'

'Why?'

Tony caught both her hands and held them to his chest. 'Because he is pushing up the daisies, and has been for some time.'

The world went dark at the edges.

Jem shook her head and forced her eyes open. She was lying on the bed, and Tony was pressing a glass of water into her hand.

'I killed him,' she murmured pulling herself up into a sitting position and pushing at the blackness that threatened to obliterate her mind. She should have died at Ciudad Rodrigo when she charged the cannon and then it would have never have come to all this. 'I hit him with the candlestick. It was the second blow that did it. No jury will ever believe me!'

Tony's hand came up and held hers. Its warmth seeped into her bones. She gripped it. Her body shuddered as he pressed his lips to her forehead. Her body turned to ice as the full horror of his words washed over her. She was a murderer.

'Oh, God, Tony, it will be the gallows,' she whispered.

'Jem, you are no murderer.' Tony gave her hand another squeeze before releasing it. 'He died in his bed alone and unloved on the nineteenth of January this year.'

'What?'

'Even you are not such a good shot, you can hit Cullen Park from Spain, my love. And not when you were leading the charge into a fortress.'

'Nineteenth of January, the day I was in the Hope. That same day he died?' Jem whispered.

'The very same. You had nothing to do with it.'

'How do you know all this?'

'Because after everything you told me that night at the cowshed and what you didn't tell me, we needed to know how things stood with your stepfather as soon as possible. So I asked my man of business to investigate.'

373

Tony smoothed back a curl from Jem's forehead. 'It was to get his report that I had to go out the other night, the night you asked me to stay. I wanted to desperately, Jem, please believe that, but I needed to hear the report. If the news was the worst, I was going to come back here and take you far away to the West Indies.'

'Why didn't you tell me?'

'I did not want to worry you until I knew. You seemed so out of sorts. I wanted to protect you. Then I thought you wouldn't believe me until I had the death certificate.' He reached into his jacket and withdrew a paper. 'This arrived this afternoon.'

Jem felt the heavy paper in her hands and the smooth wax of the seal. The words were there in stark black. 'He is truly dead. And I had nothing to do with his death.'

Tony leaned forward and his lips hit hers. A warm glow grew inside Jem. She pushed aside all the other thoughts that had been haunting her. Tomorrow would be time enough to convince Tony that Le Loup was in London . . .

'But what are we going to do about Alf Levington?' she asked, wriggling away.

'Alf who?' he asked, reaching for her again. 'Whoever he is, he can wait.'

'Alf Levington. The man I hired. The man

who wants to blackmail me. The man who said my stepfather was alive.'

'Leave him to me, I shall deal with him,' Tony said firmly. 'Have you given him the money he demanded?'

'No. And not without me, you are not. I want to be there.'

Tony ran a hand through his hair.

'Please Tony, I couldn't bear the thought of you being there without me. Go on, for the sake of old comrades in arms?' She raised her hand and caught his arm. 'Besides, you need me to show you who he is.'

Tony closed his eyes. When he opened them she knew she had won. 'Very well, Jem, but at the first sign of trouble . . . you are to leave.'

'I agree.' She paused and a small smile curved on her lips. 'But I have a better plan.'

'And what is that?'

'I'll tell you on the way there. Else you might change your mind and not let me come.'

Tony groaned and frowned. 'It had better not be dangerous.'

'Not dangerous, but more fun and it probably has a better chance of success.'

★ ★ ★

They stood in the shadows at the edge of the seemingly deserted park. The rustle of trees seemed to prick her with gooseflesh and Jem's heart thudded so loudly she thought people would be able to hear it in Kensington. Success depended on so many things. She swallowed hard, peered at Tony, his familiar profile and intent expression etched in the silver of the moonlight.

'Tony, you must let me go on alone,' she said.

'What are you talking about Jem? I thought we had agreed.'

'Neither Nye nor Levington knows I am Lady Fordingley. They only know me as Jem Riseley. I think it would be best if I reasoned with them first and found out what their blackmail plan is. We have no idea what they really want.'

'All the more reason for me to go with you.'

'Tony, I have my sword with me. I survived for over a year in Spain on my own. Two London ne'er-do-wells are hardly likely to be a challenge after the French.' She grasped his hand. 'You must see I have to do it on my own. Once we know what they are on about, then you can come and help.'

'You are quite determined about this.'

'I want to see the pleasure of their faces

when I inform them of my stepfather's death. Your immediate presence will only inflame the situation. Please, Tony for my sake.'

Tony cupped Jem's face between his hands and kissed her forehead.

'I allow you five minutes, then I am arriving with my sword drawn,' Tony said grimly. 'These are not men to be trifled with, but far be it from me to curtail your adventure. Had I told you more of what was happening this situation would never have happened.'

'Thank you,' Jem breathed.

'Five minutes and no more. The slightest hint of trouble and you must scream. Promise me.'

Tony slipped away, his form quickly disappearing into the darkness leaving her alone to approach the start of Rotten Row. She put one foot in front of the other, even, regular steps along the wide path and tried to ignore her pounding heart.

She tensed as she heard the snap of a twig beneath her foot. The park seemed deserted but her ears were sharp to every sound.

Then she saw them ahead, two dusky figures stepping out from behind the line of trees several yards in front of her. Jem tried to swallow but her throat had gone dry.

'Well, well, well, we should have had a

wager on it, Bill, after all. Your ol' sergeant has shown up. Didn't think he would.'

'The sarge's straight as an arrow, I told you.'

The voices of Levington and Nye carried through the night air and as she came nearer she saw their shapes better and recognized their faces. She stopped a few yards before them and gave Nye a quick glance but kept her gaze fixed on Levington.

'Ah, gentlemen, if I might use the phrase in its loosest meaning, I see you are on time. I trust our business can be concluded quickly.'

'Evening, Sergeant Riseley.'

'Would you be quiet, Bill, and let me do the talking?' Levington said. Jem watched as he cuffed Nye across the back of the head and a chill ran down her spine. 'Riseley, you have the money?'

'And you have the information?' Jem heard the small snigger from Bill. 'Or perhaps not . . . ?'

'Now why would you say that?' Levington said in a tone that made Jem think of a cat licking cream. 'And us having been all the way up to Warwickshire and all?'

Jem did not answer immediately. She listened a moment to the rustle of the trees and waited until she saw Nye shift uneasily where he stood.

'Alf . . . ?' he began to whisper.

'Shut up,' Levington spat.

Jem saw the unease flicker across Levington's face and knew it was time to speak. 'It reached my ears that Alexander Cullen is in no position to do anything about any information you might wish to impart. So I shall not be paying you the sum you were so kind to request.'

'Come now, Lady Fordingley! That is not very sporting of you,' a cultured voice said from the shadows. Jem froze, flickered her gaze about but only so far as she dared look away from Levington. She could see no movement, no shapes that could be a person, no one.

'After these men have gone to all this trouble,' the voice continued. A voice that was not very far away, and someone who knew her real identity.

'Yeah, after we've gone to all this trouble,' Nye echoed.

Jem turned her face to stare again into the shadows. Then she caught it in the corner of her eye, a movement betrayed by the piercing silver moonlight. A cloaked figure moved from behind one of the large trees and saw that she had seen him.

Less than a moment of hesitation and he came out on to Rotten Row in front of

Levington and into her full view. She watched and now wished she had kept Tony with her.

'So we meet again, Ensign, or is it Lady Fordingley I should be calling you now?' His familiar voice sent shivers down her spine. Cold sweat started to prick her neck. 'What name exactly are you going by these days?'

'Does it really matter to you, Le Loup?' Jem said, with more bravery in her voice than she felt. Her hand fingered the hilt of her sword. 'Or should I call you Comte de Guisement?'

'*Touché*. Le Loup will suffice. The Comte wishes to keep his reputation unsullied.' He snapped his fingers and Levington moved with more rapidity than Jem would have thought possible.

Before she even had a chance to draw her sword, her arms were pinned behind her in Levington's fast, painful grip and his hot, meaty breath panted on to the side of her face. Le Loup sauntered forward and pulled her sword from its sheath. He regarded the length of it and ran his finger down the side of the blade.

'Oh dear, clumsy me,' he said, showing Jem the glistening blood on his forefinger. Jem shuddered.

He stood in front of her, a strange smile

pulling at his lips and raised the point of her sword so it pricked her chin.

'My advantage, I believe,' he said, very slowly.

Jem squirmed against the arms holding her but Levington's grip was too strong. She swallowed hard as the point of the blade pushed into her throat, tried to block the searing pain from her mind and stopped struggling.

'You were supposed to be dead,' Jem croaked. She could hardly see anything now, tears she could not stop had so pooled in her eyes. 'I shot you. At the farmhouse. Tony saw the body.'

She did not need to see clearly to feel a chill at Le Loup's laugh. 'Reports of my demise were greatly exaggerated. No, my dear, I fear your aim was inaccurate. Twice you shot at me, and missed, and even with swords you were clumsy enough to let me escape, to live another day in the service of my emperor. Now, don't you think it's my turn?'

Jem blinked, willed the tears to hold back. The silver snake of his scar stood out on his face, and she saw the points of his ears. She remembered the señorita in the farmhouse and Le Loup's expression then. She closed her eyes, shutting out the images she did not want to think on. She refused to beg, to give into him.

'Why are you here in London, Le Loup?'

He smiled. 'As you ask . . . I have come for the killing season. My emperor wishes to ensure the English are weak and confused before he makes his move, and I am only to happy to oblige.'

'Whom are you planning to murder?'

Le Loup started to hum and Jem recognized the strains of 'God save the King'. She recalled he had been sitting next to the Prince Regent's latest mistress at the *Sans Pareil*. Her blood turned cold.

'So you are planning to kill the Prince Regent? And what are you going to do with me?' she asked, pleased to hear her voice did not waver. She stared at him directly. She would not flinch. If she had a chance, she would sprint, and alert the authorities.

'I am not a woman playing games with things she does not understand. You should have killed me when you had the chance, my dear. I never hesitate to kill.' The blade dug deeper into her throat, and then retreated.

Jem held fast and felt a thin, wet trickle course down her neck. The pain was nothing, she told herself. She would give him no advantage, show him no weakness.

'Then again,' Le Loup said. 'You may have

other uses. You may be worth more to me alive than as a corpse.'

Jem's blood ran cold. Le Loup was quite right. She didn't understand the whole of this. One thing she knew — Le Loup was a villain and a traitor. If only she'd kept Tony with her, she wouldn't be in this situation. What could she do when she could hardly move with the blade at her throat? She glanced about.

Her eyes rested on Bill Nye, standing there not looking quite comfortable with what was going on. Nye owed her something. She'd saved his neck. A bubble of hope rose inside her.

'Bill,' she called and caught his eye. 'Help me, get the Bow Street Runners, do something. This man is a traitor to the British Crown. He plans to murder the Prince Regent.'

Bill looked away. Frustration stabbed in her chest. 'Bill?' she called again.

'Don't you do anything Bill,' Levington warned. 'This here is our employer. He's paid us good money for finding this here lady.'

'This man is responsible for the murder of British soldiers. He is a French agent,' Jem pleaded. 'For the sake of the 95th, Bill.'

Bill hesitated and turned as if to run. A white flash and a loud explosion. Jem watched Bill crumple to the ground as the familiar smell of powder tickled her nose. Le Loup was still holding the blade of her sword absolutely still despite the recoil of the pistol he held in his other hand.

'Here, you had no cause,' protested Levington.

'I always have cause, Mr Levington,' Le Loup replied in a voice that was so cold and collected Jem thought her nerve might break. She bit her tongue between her teeth and willed herself to remain calm.

'Now, the woman if you please. Or perhaps you'd care to join your friend?'

'Sorry, luv.' Levington passed Jem to Le Loup.

The cold steel now passed straight across Jem's throat, holding her chin up. She heard Levington stumble, then run.

'Now, my dear,' Le Loup rasped in her ear, 'I have you all to myself.'

'This isn't Spain.' Jem said, dismayed to hear her voice quiver and sound so high pitched but she pressed on. 'You've just a shot a man in the middle of Hyde Park. People will have heard.' Tony would have heard, she knew. It gave her the strength not to crumple now.

'I fail to see anyone coming running,' Le Loup said. 'What were you hoping? That a

Bow Street Runner might just happen to be passing?'

'My husband will come and get me. He will have heard the shot,' Jem said with more conviction than she felt. Tony should have been here by now. He had to have heard the shot. Her stomach twisted, unless Le Loup had met him first. If she could only just keep Le Loup talking . . .

'Good, it will save me having to send for him.' He gripped her wrists tighter. He was a bony man, with an iron grip, different from Levington's solid bulk. Jem tried to twist, but his hands gripped more firmly.

'You don't think it was you I was after, do you?' he said. 'You are a bonus. When I spotted him in Portsmouth, I knew I had to end his meddlesome ways if I wanted to fulfil my emperor's orders.'

'You foul, disgusting pig.' Jem tried to struggle, to free herself. Le Loup held her tighter to him.

'Can you feel what you are doing to me?' Jem stilled. His breeches held a hard bulge. She wanted more than anything to get away from him. 'I like a woman with spirit,' his voice licked. 'It makes it so much more satisfying . . . in the end.'

Jem twisted her head as suddenly the threat of the blade became meaningless and spat in his eye. Le Loup's hand loosened in surprise and Jem tore herself free. She started to run but tripped. Pain shot through her left leg as she fell and then a boot pushed into her back, and her to the ground and a mouthful of damp grass. She couldn't move, the boot pinned her fast, pressing against her spine. She heard Le Loup laugh.

'Release the woman,' came Tony's voice, cold as ice. 'And fight a man for a change.'

Jem's heart leapt.

'He means to kill you, Tony,' she gasped, managing to lift her head a couple of inches and spitting the grass and earth out.

'Forgive me, Jem, but I thought you needed some assistance,' Tony's voice replied easily.

The boot left her back and Jem rolled over to see Tony's blade engaged with Le Loup's.

Round and round they circled, steel meeting steel. Jem knew she should run, get help but she found it impossible to rise, her left ankle shot through with pain and gave way under her every time she tried to push herself to her feet. She eventually managed to stand on her right foot only, using a tree for support.

Back and forth, Le Loup and Tony fought. Sometimes it appeared Tony had the upper hand, then Le Loup. Jem pressed her hand into the trunk of the tree as Le Loup beat

Tony to the ground, his blade flashed down but Tony rolled over at the last second, and stood up.

'Allow me to show you a little trick m'wife taught me,' Tony remarked.

'This isn't one of Mr Angelo's fencing classes.'

Tony crossed swords with Le Loup, forced his arm up and over and the sword went spinning out of Le Loup's hand. Jem willed all her strength to let go of the tree and hop over to retrieve it as Tony held the point of his sword to Le Loup's neck.

'You have no more courage than she,' Le Loup spat.

'As much as I would like to run you through, I have promised the Home Office to bring you in.' Tony pulled a pistol from his pocket and tossed it to Jem. 'I should refrain from making any sudden moves if I were you, Le Loup. M'wife's a crack shot y'know. Had the pleasure of teaching her m'self. I have never seen her miss the same target twice.'

'It's all right milady,' Jem heard Andrews' voice rumble behind her as she bent from her new tree to pick up the pistol. 'The Runners will take care of this. Sorry, my lord, for taking my time but I thought you wanted a bit of sport.'

'Just so, Andrews, just so.' Tony lowered his

sword as a pair of burly Bow Street Runners appeared as if out of nowhere and took Le Loup by the arms. 'If you would be so kind as to go with them, Sir John Featherstonehaugh among others wishes to have a word with the . . . uh . . . gentleman.'

'Of course, my lord.'

Jem watched Andrews depart with Le Loup and the two Runners. Then she looked back at Tony, suddenly shy. What would he say to her now?

'You're injured,' she cried, looking at a line of blood on his face.

'Only a scratch.' He wiped it away with a handkerchief as he strode towards her. 'Will you forgive me?'

'Forgive you for what?'

Jem felt as light as a feather as he gathered her into his arms. 'For not allowing you to finish him off, for stepping in to protect you. I know I promised, but I did feel I had to . . . in the end. I was waiting for Andrews at the gates when the shot rang out. You have never seen anyone cover ground as fast as I did, cursing my folly at letting you face down those two villains on your own. Then it took far too long before I was able to engage Le Loup.'

Jem leant her head against his chest, listening to the reassuring sound of his heart.

'Why was Andrews here?' she asked, perplexed.

Tony gave a sheepish grin. 'I informed him of the night's proceedings before we left. The name Levington rang a bell, you see. I went to see Featherstonehaugh about your sighting of Le Loup in Portsmouth. I wondered if perhaps I had been mistaken.'

'You never said anything?' Jem teased and was rewarded by a light kiss on the nose.

'I asked him to investigate,' Tony continued after a long moment, 'and he came back with the lead of Levington. Unfortunately I had not anticipated Le Loup would have been with Levington or I would have never let you come, but as it was, I sent Andrews for reinforcements, should they be needed. He was most put out at the thought of being left out of the fun.'

'Interesting notion you have of fun.'

'You have to admit — this was fun.' Tony's face wore a roguish grin, but he drew her tighter into his arms. 'A bit more fun than I had at first anticipated but thrilling nonetheless. Much better than musical evenings.'

'Anything is better than a musical evening,' Jem replied, before stiffening, as she remembered Alf Levington's words. 'I am sorry Tony, I have ruined everything. There will be no keeping this quiet now. Your family will be the laughing stock of the *ton*. Levington will make sure of that.'

'Alf Levington ran straight into the arms of a Runner and is now on his way to Bow Street. It appears he has a bit of explaining to do,' Tony remarked, carrying her along Rotten Row as if it was the most ordinary thing in the world. 'I dare say Mother can weather it and the rest don't care. As for the *ton*, they will find a new talking point within a day or two.'

A lump formed in Jem's throat. When should she tell Tony she hated the *ton*? Yet it seemed to matter so much to him. For his sake, she was willing to endure it. Somehow. She glanced at his face and saw it pale in the moonlight and she knew she didn't want any more secrets between them. Not then. Not ever.

'Tony, society holds no interest for me. I can't live my life on endless rounds of social calls and discussions about the latest fashions. If that is what you wish, I will try for your sake, but to me it is akin to a sentence of death. I have no desire to be a freak show rolled out for the amusement of others.'

She waited for his answer as the moon went behind a cloud shadowing his face. Had she ruined everything again?

'I was hoping you might say that, as it is my dearest desire not to spend a moment longer in London than we have to.' Tony said leaning his face towards her. He placed a kiss on the end of her nose before continuing. 'And it is on the basis of that hope that I have entered into negotiations for a house.'

Jem's heart soared. He wasn't angry with her. He wanted what she wanted.

'What house? Where?'

'In Warwickshire, but the owner is proving a bit of a problem.'

'What sort of a problem? Is there anything I can do to help?'

'You might be able to. The former owner recently died and left it to a soldier who has been on the Peninsula.'

'And so?'

'The new owner is proving to be a bit of a handful.' Tony slid his hand down Jem's bottom, cupping it masterfully. 'A bit more than a handful I'd say, definitely more than a handful.'

'Tony, do be serious.'

He pressed his cheek against hers and whispered against her lips 'I am being serious. I never joke about handfuls.'

'Tony! What is the name of this house?' Anything to distract her mind from the curling warmth building inside her.

'The name is,' he said, running a finger down the side of her face, 'Cullen Park, and you are the new owner.'

'Me?'

'Ye-es,' he said nibbling at her ear. 'You, m'dear, are definitely more than a handful. I can prove it if you wish.'

'But why didn't you tell me before?'

'I was about to, but events intervened. You are truly the new owner of Cullen Park. Now, does that meet your requirements?'

'Cullen Park would be wonderful, but Tony anywhere with you is where I want to be.' Jem decided she would ignore, for now, his coarse remark on the subject of breeding.

'My feelings exactly.' Tony captured her mouth for a long kiss. 'And now m'dear, I suggest we proceed with all speed to Audley Street.'

'Why?'

'Because I wish to demonstrate my love for you and although we most likely have the place to ourselves I very much doubt the open air of Hyde Park is the place to do that.'

'Yes, I agree, the ground might be a bit too hard. You have prodigiously proved to me a bed is quite the softest place to make love by far.'

'You are a minx,' he growled in her ear. 'But I can't live without you, my love, and I intend to spend the rest of my life proving that to you.'

'I look forward to it as I intend to do the same for you.'

Tony swung out of the park and on to Park Lane, and Jem heard a distant bell tolling the hour. How late it was. She had a feeling it would be a while before sleep claimed her.

Author's Note

A woman disguised as a man actually serving undetected in the military for any length of time is sometimes dismissed as a myth or a pleasant fiction of romantic writers. However, history is littered with examples of such women. Perhaps the most famous was Deborah Sampson who served for three years as Robert Shirtliffe during the American Revolution. Her sex was only discovered when she developed brain fever. The US Marine Corps recognizes Lucy Brewer as the first woman marine. She served on the USS *Constitution* as George Baker during the war of 1812. Nadezhda Durova served as an officer in the Russian cavalry during the Napoleonic Wars. On the battlefield of Waterloo during a lull in fighting, Captain Henry Ross-Lewin of the 32nd Regiment of Foot discovered two bodies of French women dressed in nankeen jackets and trousers and obviously involved in the thick of fighting.

It is tempting to think women were more easily discovered after the Napoleonic Wars, but records show some sixty women received battlefield wounds during the American Civil

War. Emma Edmonds recounted her exploits in her book *Nurse and Soldier* and later her time serving as Frank Turnball was confirmed through army records.

Most women such as Jenny Roth of the Royal Welch Fusiliers were only discovered when they fell ill or became injured. So it is impossible to determine the true number of women who served but remained undiscovered.

The reason for joining the military varied from a thirst for adventure, patriotism or simply a desire to escape an abusive situation. There is some evidence that a number of women may have had help from other soldiers or soldiers' wives. Unfortunately, for many of these women, they did not experience a happy ending and either died or had difficulties readjusting to life as a civilian woman again.

We do hope that you have enjoyed reading this large print book.

Did you know that all of our titles are available for purchase?

We publish a wide range of high quality large print books including:
Romances, Mysteries, Classics
General Fiction
Non Fiction and Westerns

Special interest titles available in large print are:
The Little Oxford Dictionary
Music Book
Song Book
Hymn Book
Service Book

Also available from us courtesy of Oxford University Press:
Young Readers' Dictionary
(large print edition)
Young Readers' Thesaurus
(large print edition)

For further information or a free brochure, please contact us at:
Ulverscroft Large Print Books Ltd.,
The Green, Bradgate Road, Anstey,
Leicester, LE7 7FU, England.
Tel: (00 44) **0116 236 4325**
Fax: (00 44) **0116 234 0205**

Other titles published by
The House of Ulverscroft:

THE DECENT THING

C. W. Reed

David Herbert lives a privileged life in Edwardian society but is dominated by his sisters, Gertrude and Clara. At public school he suffers bullying and at home his only friend is Nelly Tovey, a young maid . . . Living on a pittance in London after being disowned by his family, he becomes seriously ill and is nursed by the devoted Nelly. Although certain of their love, Nelly is aware of the gulf between them. David must find the courage to defy convention and breach the barriers to their happiness.

WINDS OF HONOUR

Ashleigh Bingham

The Honourable Phoebe Pemberton is beautiful and wealthy, but is the daughter of the late, disgraceful Lord Pemberton and Harriet Buckley . . . Phoebe escapes her mother's plans to teach her the family business of wringing profits from the mills. She dreams of running away, and, when she learns of her mother's schemes for Phoebe's marriage as part of a business transaction, she calls on her friend Toby Grantham for help . . . But Harriet's vengeful fury is aroused, leaving Phoebe tangled in a dark and desperate venture.

A LADY AT MIDNIGHT

Melinda Hammond

When Amelia Langridge accepts an invitation to stay in London as companion to Camilla Strickland, it is to enjoy herself before settling down as the wife of dependable Edmund Crannock. Camilla's intention is to capture a rich husband, and her mother is happy to allow Amelia to remain in the background. Camilla attracts the attention of Earl Rossleigh, but the earl is intent on a much more dangerous quarry, and it is Amelia who finds herself caught up in his tangled affairs . . . A merry dance through the Georgian world of duels, sparkling romance and adventure.

THE SQUIRE AND THE SCHOOLMISTRESS

Ann Barker

When Flavia Montague arrives to take up employment as a schoolmistress in the village of Brooks, she learns that the school has been closed for some months and that the previous teacher, Miss Price, has been involved in a scandal. Flavia is given welcome assistance in establishing the school by the handsome landowner Paul Wheaton, who seems attracted to her. It becomes clear that one of the pupils, Penelope, has been ill-treated by her guardian, Sir Lewis Glendenning — a name linked with the notorious Miss Price. But is Sir Lewis the brute that he appears to be? And what is the truth about Miss Price?

ROUGH HERITAGE

Janet Thomas

Rose Vidney and Joss Pencarrow form an unlikely childhood friendship. Rose is the daughter of a poor miner, whilst Joss is the local squire's son in the nineteenth-century mining heartland where they grow up. Meeting again as adults, their friendship is rekindled and it seems they are to be inextricably entwined forever. Destiny has marked Rose as Joss's nemesis, and he hers. Soon their stormy and forbidden love affair will tear both their lives apart. As tragic events are played out against the timeless Cornish coast, can Rose and Joss achieve true happiness against all the odds?